OUT
OF
SIGHT

BOOKS BY RUHI CHOUDHARY

OUT OF SIGHT

Ruhi Choudhary

bookouture

Published by Bookouture in 2023

An imprint of Storyfire Ltd.
Carmelite House
50 Victoria Embankment
London EC4Y 0DZ

www.bookouture.com

ISBN: 978-1-83790-879-0
eBook ISBN: 978-1-83790-878-3

To my readers for tagging along with Mack.

PROLOGUE

PRESENT DAY

Nick twisted Mackenzie around, securing her wrists in a harsh grip and restraining them in handcuffs. A high-pitched keening sound threatened to burst Mackenzie's eardrums as her thoughts drifted away from her like smoke. She stared at his face carved out of stone—chiseled and blank. Her partner at work since she'd joined the Lakemore PD.

Turned away from him, she faced the Detectives Unit. The floor that was always buzzing with activity—shuffling feet, rustling papers, ringing phones, and hushed conversations—was frozen in disbelief.

Nick nudged her to move. She walked in a daze, as her coworkers parted to make way for her, watching with a mix of confusion and shock. A hot flush burst under her skin, turning her face red. Words were stuck in her throat. Screams claiming her innocence were trapped in her chest. The truth was that deep down Mackenzie knew that she deserved this.

Time crept forward at an agonizingly slow pace as she passed the people she had disappointed the most. Her boss of a decade, Sergeant Jeff Sully, looked on with a furrowed thick unibrow, his hand immobile inside a bag of chips. Her coworker and foil-turned-friend, Austin's blue eyes were wide and thin lips parted. Lieutenant Atlee Rivera leaned against the door-frame, arms crossed and jaw clenched tight.

It was Mackenzie's worst fear come to life—her legacy of being a good, reliable officer of the law dismantled. Her reputation in shambles. Everyone she worked with watching her like they didn't know who she was anymore.

As Nick escorted her toward the staircase to take her to the holding cell, she noticed someone standing in the shadows.

Caleb's green eyes locked with hers. They spelled something ominous. His long, narrow face tilted down as a sly smile curled up his lips. She fisted her hands desperate to take a swing at him as Nick uttered the words that made her blood curdle.

"Detective Mackenzie Price, you are under arrest for murder."

ONE

"It's the fourth quarter. We got ten seconds left. They are down four." The light from the bright screen danced on Detective Nick Blackwood's face. His brown eyes watched the game with a thrill that Mackenzie noticed was reserved for only three things: his daughter, Luna, football, and those last tantalizing seconds before they found that final piece of the puzzle.

"They need a touchdown to win." Jenna, another junior detective in the division, handed him a beer.

The Oaktree Pub was a regular hangout spot for the Lakemore PD, being situated just across the street. Despite having a pool and foosball table and dartboard, the entire crowd was gathered at the front to watch the live match on TV. The pub was grungy with cheap cutlery and broken chairs, but they had invested in a new flat-screen TV that almost spanned the width of the bar. On the screen the Lakemore Sharks were up against Florida. The people of Lakemore might be withered and jaded, tired of the mediocrity and flatness of life, their brains dulled by the lack of challenge, but the Sharks represented the best parts of them. As their giant frames barreled across the field, chasing and crashing into each other, even the people of Lakemore remembered what life was really about—creating moments.

Mackenzie watched Nick and the rest idly. She didn't know how to have fun. Nor did she look like a particularly fun person. Her long, red hair was tied in a high ponytail. Loose strands fell to the sides like flames licking her face. She wasn't wearing any makeup to soften some of her harsh features. She wasn't pretty, but she had a striking face—like it had accumulated all the horrors she had encountered on this job.

She saw Nick laughing with the others without a care in the world. And then she caught her reflection in the mirror. She expected that same rigid woman to stare back at her. The one who moved with the strings of the past dug so deeply into her skin. But instead, she was smiling.

"I see you longingly staring at someone." Becky—Dr. Sullivan—slid next to Mackenzie and passed her a drink.

"It's only in your imagination."

"I think not." She waggled her eyebrows suggestively. "The energy between you two has been different for the past few months. Everyone can see that."

Mackenzie felt her cheeks heat. "It's nothing. Just something silly."

Becky gave her a deadpan look. "Girlfriends talk."

"I think we are too old to call ourselves that."

"Cougar babies talk."

She almost choked on her wine. "What's a cougar baby?"

"Google it. My twelve-year-old kid taught me that. But coming back to you." Her smile was conspiratorial. "Don't deflect."

Mackenzie's first instinct was to do just that. Her second instinct was to scrub away the water ring on the table that had been bothering her for the last hour. But she had decided to make some changes—the first was to learn to trust people, to shed some of her steeliness that hardened her skin into scales.

She eyed Becky from the corner of her eye, her heart thumping with discomfort at the thought of sharing a vulnerability with someone else—even a friend of almost a decade.

Mackenzie opened her mouth just as the bar erupted with a thunderous round of applause and cheers.

"The Sharks did it!" The voice of the commentator was just audible above the raucous crowd. "No one could have predicted this. With a mere ten seconds left on the clock, they were facing an insurmountable challenge but they rose to the occasion!"

With the embarrassing conversation forgotten, Mackenzie found herself swept up in the celebration. Strangers became friends. Glasses were raised. Toasts were made. Contagious smiles spread like wildfire.

"Did you see that?" Nick asked her, beaming.

"No," she admitted truthfully. But before she knew it, he was picking her up and swinging her around. He put her back down and turned around to clink bottles with Austin. Like this meant nothing. Except for the fact that Mackenzie's heart had galloped and she had turned as red as her hair.

She tried to compose herself when her eyes fell on a stranger in the pub.

Sitting in a corner and nursing his drink, an old man stared into empty space unfettered by the wave of pure elation. He was the only one who didn't care that the Sharks had beaten one of the giants in the realm of high school football.

As if sensing he was being watched, he stared back at Mackenzie. The noise and moving bodies around them dissolved into oblivion. Her vision tunneled. His ghostly eyes carried something heavy. It killed Mackenzie's joy, blossoming something revolting in her gut.

Like it was an omen.

Nick's voice called to her. When she turned around, his face was pale and he was clutching his phone. All that color from the excitement of the match had drained away. Behind him Becky's expression was pinched as she stared at her phone.

"What's happened now?" Mackenzie asked.

"Peterson just called. There's a body. A woman. He's sent us the location."

"Okay..." She dropped a bill on the table. "Let's go then." She didn't understand Nick's reaction. She glanced over her shoulder—the old man was gone.

When Nick spoke, a drizzle of goosebumps spread on her arms. "One of her eyes was gouged out."

TWO

A knot loosened inside Mackenzie as she gathered her jacket, badge, and Glock. A crackling humming pulsed under her skin. This was the part she was good at. The part where she solved a puzzle, where she righted a wrong, where she got the chance to pluck another evil out of her hometown of Lakemore, the part where she plucked some of the darkness from her.

One of her eyes was gouged out.

She tried to ignore Nick's words ringing in her ears. That image of the old man in the pub kept clouding her thoughts. Nothing was ever as it seemed in this town.

It was a silent drive to the woods behind the cemetery, which was on the opposite side of town. A fierce and unrelenting icy onslaught kept the speed of her car on a tight leash. A weather warning had been issued that morning—something about arctic winds ushering an ice storm in the Olympic Peninsula. Powdery snow blew onto her windshield. Hail showered the top of her car like bullets.

The car glided carefully through the empty winding roads of Lakemore. She passed a stadium under construction. Tucked between Olympia and Tacoma, Lakemore was a small town that found itself the epicenter of violence and scandals. Poverty birthed frustration and desperation which led to crime. Wealth bred greed and invincibility which also led to crime. And Lakemore had a blend of both.

When Mackenzie reached the edge of the woods, she brought the car to a halt. A throng of squad cars and vans were already there, and Nick's car was parked too. He had driven separately. Some uniforms were installing lights into the soil to illuminate the path leading to the body.

"Detective Price!" Officer Peterson, her frequent aide on cases since Justin Armstrong had made detective, approached her with an umbrella.

"What have we got?" she yelled over the showering hail.

"A jogger came across the body at approximately half past nine and called 911. We arrived twenty minutes ago and have started securing the body. Expecting Dr. Sullivan but in this weather..." Thunder clapped as if emphasizing his point.

"Yeah, she was at the bar with me but she was waiting for the CSU to pick her up. A jogger in this weather?"

"He claims that he did not check the weather and it started getting bad about ten minutes in when he decided to head back, and that's when he found her."

Mackenzie walked down the lit path, deeper into the woods. The soil sucked into the soles of her boot. The light's reach was limited to a few yards, leaving Mackenzie with a view mostly obscured by swirling and swooshing white hail.

They finally reached the spot bordered by the yellow crime scene tape. One officer was interviewing the jogger. Another uniform and Nick stood holding umbrellas, with their backs to Mackenzie. They had been quick on their feet to put a tarp over the body and the surrounding soil to conserve as much evidence as they could in the hailstorm.

"Why did we think we could have an uneventful Wednesday night?" Mackenzie attempted to crack a joke, drawing level with Nick. But when she saw the scene, her stomach turned.

The woman's body was lit up by the forensic markers. She was sitting on the ground, her legs sprawled at an awkward angle with her back propped against the rough bark of a tree. Surrounded by grass and weeds, lying on the soft ground, she had been hemmed in lovingly. Her tongue protruded from her half-open mouth. Traces of dried blood streaked her pallid face like brushstrokes. There was a horrifying void where her left eye should have been. It had been torn out, leaving threads of tissue crawling out of the exposed bone cavity of her eye socket.

"Oh, damn," Mackenzie whispered, suppressing the urge to retch.

"Yep," Nick agreed, towering over her. "The jogger takes this route twice a day, once in the afternoon and once at nine p.m. with his dog. He didn't see her in the morning, only this time."

"So she was killed here or moved here in the last few hours."

Mackenzie watched the jogger, a middle-aged man with a noticeable hunched back, finding refuge under a tarp as he gave his statement to the officer.

"Did you know that hailstones are not always white and clear? They can be green or black or other colors depending on what minerals are present in the atmosphere," Peterson chirped from behind them. It was his nervous tick, spewing random facts.

"Fascinating, Peterson." Nick bent on his haunches to level with the body, but maintained some distance. "No evidence of stabbing. But it's hard to see anything in this light and weather. Have her fingernails been ripped off?" He frowned at her bloodied, swollen fingertips. "Killer knows what he's doing."

"Her clothes are intact. No bruises on her face. No visible signs of assault." Mackenzie tried scanning the woods as ice pellets rained down from the sky, filling the air with a deafening roar. "I doubt there will be any witnesses in this weather. Any cameras nearby?"

"None," Peterson informed regretfully. "It's just a small patch of woods out of the way."

"Becky should be able to get something out of her for us to go on."

Peterson's radio crackled. "Dr. Sullivan is almost here."

"Check the area for... an eye," Nick instructed awkwardly.

"I'll head back to the station and check if there are any reports of a missing woman that matches her description." Mackenzie made a note of the victim's clothes and general physical appearance.

"It's almost midnight, Mack. Go in tomorrow. We can't do anything tonight anyway," Nick suggested. "We need the body to be moved and cleaned up for a clear description."

She nodded, still tasting bile in the base of her throat, so she changed the topic. "Are you going to see Luna?"

"Tomorrow morning," Nick replied. "I try to make the most of our time together. In three years, I'm going to be the last person she's going to want to hang out with."

They emerged from the woods, huddled under his umbrella. They stood by their cars, surrounded by squad cars and officers scrambling around in the hailstorm. She was suddenly aware of how loud it was and how close to each other they were standing under the umbrella.

She quickly took a step back. "See you tomorrow."

Nick stayed where he was, trying not to smile as Mackenzie jogged back to her car and quickly got in. The top of her head was throbbing from the battering of hail. She cautiously pulled back out onto the road, leaving the scene of the crime with an unsettling feeling that something darker was at play. Why would someone gouge out a woman's eye?

THREE

NOVEMBER 2

Mackenzie killed the engine of her car. She unbuckled her seatbelt, ready to start the day with a clear, fresh mind when she paused. Her brown eyes were reflected in the rearview mirror. She leaned closer to inspect the gray specks she'd inherited from her mother and the purple ring around her pupil.

Why would anyone want to rip out an eye? Was it because it was the most personal part of a person? Because eyes were the window to the soul? Or maybe it was because they saw secrets and absorbed memories before they made it to the brain. If Mackenzie wanted to keep a part of someone—what would she pick?

The hands that carried a dead body over twenty years ago or the toes that felt the soft mud where she sat witnessing a crime and did nothing to stop it. Or the eyes that couldn't see through her mother's lies or past the bleeding body on the kitchen floor.

She shook off her straying thoughts and climbed out of the car.

The storm had purged the morning air of whatever moisture and pollution had been hovering. Mackenzie's skin began to crack from the arid air as she crossed the parking lot to the box-like building surrounded by hedges. She resisted the urge to run back and paint her face so that she looked like a statue—unreadable and bulletproof.

It was how she always liked to be. It wasn't vanity; it was armor. It wasn't arrogance; it was cowardice. But in the past year, that armor was getting chipped away and the woman inside her was brave enough to face the world.

The Lakemore PD was as usual noisy and crowded. She weaved her way past moving bodies, nodding at faces until she reached the second floor with the Detectives Unit. There were eight desks, and seven out of eight were cluttered with takeout boxes, crumpled paper, and stacked cups. When Mackenzie reached her immaculate desk, she felt a burst of pride.

"Oh, your desk is so clean. Are you going to howl and beat your chest in joy, Mad Mack?" Detective Troy Clayton teased from the cubicle next to hers. His mop-like hair had been growing wildly, almost covering his entire forehead.

"Maybe Mad Mack wants a medal." His partner, Finn, said from Mackenzie's other side.

"I was thinking more along the lines of a parade in my honor, but a medal will do."

Troy's eyebrows bunched together. He and Finn exchanged brooding looks. "What happened to this one?"

Finn shrugged. "Alien possessed her body?"

"Do you even remember how to glare or have you become... *happy*?" Troy asked like the word was foul.

Mackenzie stared at them in anger. Her stare alone could wilt someone twice her size.

Finn pointed at her face with his pen. "She still got it. That's Mad Mack."

Mackenzie tuned out their mindless chatter and checked the database of Washington State Patrol's Missing and Unidentified Persons Unit (MUPU). There were a few Caucasian women in their twenties and thirties with dark hair roughly matching the victim. But their visual inspection of the victim was limited and not reliable given the hailstorm and poor lighting.

She drummed her fingers on the desk, her mind going back to that missing eye. A hollow feeling grew in the pit of her stomach. She hadn't come across this MO. She hadn't heard of any such case in Lakemore in her ten years here. It wasn't typical. Nobody removed the eye if the murder was a crime of passion... unless it was to throw them off. Her racing thoughts were silenced when Nick arrived and a chorus of birthday cheer and songs erupted.

It was the big forty.

Nick shook everyone's hands, a strained smile plastered on his face. Only Mackenzie recognized it. He never liked attention, and he got a lot of it especially being the son of a senator.

When he reached his cubicle, which was behind Mackenzie's, he sighed in exasperation. "Please don't."

"Wasn't going to." She whipped out an envelope and handed it to him.

He tore it open, curious. He pulled out the gift card and his eyes brightened. "Private flying lesson!"

"You've been wanting to go since when, a decade?"

"I have." He beamed. "But someone always ends up getting murdered in this town. Thanks."

"Yeah." She checked her watch.

"Looking at the crowd here, I don't think the details of our new case are still under wraps."

She swallowed hard and shook her head. It wouldn't be long before the mood at the station nosedived. Peterson was already walking around with dark circles under his eyes. Some of the officers were whispering among themselves.

"Time for briefing. What hobby do you think it is this week?"

Their quirky sergeant had a thick mustache, and his giant belly fostered a new hobby every week. It was the way he handled stress. Mackenzie had seen everything from knitting and archery to bottle ship modeling and origami.

They gathered in the glass-walled conference room. It was like being in a fishbowl. Nick immediately went to the coffee machine to pour himself his morning drug. Jenna, the only other female detective in the unit, was engaged in an animated conversation with Austin. Troy and Finn were watching the game on their phones.

Sully arrived looking grumpy, a stack of papers tucked under his arm. It wasn't until Mackenzie noticed that he was trailed by Lieutenant Atlee Rivera that she understood his irritation. Rivera was a sharp woman with dark hair and slanted eyes set slightly far apart. She had earned the nickname "The Surgeon" during her tenure in Ohio for her cutthroat and steely demeanor, a trait she shared with Mackenzie.

After several corruption scandals were unearthed in Lakemore with strong ties to the Lakemore PD, the force needed someone like Rivera to instill discipline and keep everyone on a tight leash.

"What do we have?" Sully grumbled, putting his papers on the table. Mackenzie leaned forward and noticed novice sketches of random things from a stapler and a vase to a car and a tree. She and Nick exchanged amused glances. So that was Sully's latest hobby.

"We have handed everything over to the prosecutor," Austin said. "I believe it should be enough for a conviction."

"I want to be in on that meeting with Brooks," Rivera said, referring to Sterling Brooks, Mackenzie's ex-husband.

"Mack and Nick, nothing on the bulletin?" Sully asked. "I can lend you to Special Investigations. They are always desperate."

"We got our plates full, Sarge," Nick informed him. "Homicide."

"When did this happen?" Sully asked.

"Last night."

His eyebrows shot up. "In that weather?"

"Yeah, it prevented us from doing a thorough visual inspection, but today we will head over to the morgue."

Sully nodded, but his eyes kept drifting to his sketches and his fingers fiddled with his pencil, like he couldn't wait to get back to drawing.

"Do we know who the victim is?" Rivera asked.

"Not yet. But one of her eyes was ripped out of its socket," Mackenzie said.

Sully's hand went slack. The pencil dropped from his grasp and fell to the ground. His head snapped up to look at Mackenzie, his absent-mindedness and indifference replaced with something that bordered on disbelief. "Sorry?"

Mackenzie repeated slowly, "Her eye was missing."

She had seen Sully's various moods over the years. Despite him always joking to dilute the seriousness of his job, there was a strict side to him that didn't tolerate carelessness, that even reprimanded Mackenzie if she made a mistake.

It was a look she hadn't seen on him before, but one she knew all too well, when the ghosts of the past had returned to haunt.

"Nick, what do you think about this?" Rivera said, frowning at Sully who had fallen silent.

"Too soon to tell. I know regular killers are not interested in their victim's eyeballs."

"Have we seen this MO before?" Mackenzie asked, but her eyes were pinned on Sully.

"Not to my knowledge." Nick looked at Dennis. "Dennis, you've been here the longest."

Dennis shrugged. "Nope. First time I've heard of such a thing."

While they pondered over the viciousness of the crime, Mackenzie couldn't tear her eyes away from Sully who had paled. Rivera took over leading the rest of the briefing while shooting Sully looks of disapproval. When they were all dismissed, Sully was the first one out the door, leaving his sketches behind.

"Did you notice that?" Mackenzie asked Nick as they left the conference room.

"Sully?" He loosened his tie. "He's probably feeling sick. Saw him finish two boxes of donuts yesterday."

Nick clearly didn't seem to think much of it. Maybe he was right. But the dreadful thought nagged at Mackenzie like a persistent woodpecker—Sully was hiding something.

Peterson came up to them in the hallway looking hopeful, so Mackenzie expected to hear some encouraging news.

"We caught a break on Jane Doe's identity."

"Who is she?"

Peterson brandished an evidence bag. Inside was a thin, faded black wallet, tearing at the seams, and covered in mud and twigs. "Uniform picked it up a few feet away from where we found her body. Either she dropped it while running away or it fell out of a pocket while her body was being moved."

"Whitney Smythe." Mackenzie squinted at the driver's license. "This is good. Let's run it in the DMV and get her add—"

Before she finished her sentence, Peterson presented him with piece of paper, a smile tugging at his lips. "Already done, ma'am."

"Jeez, Peterson, you keep this up and this department won't need us anymore," Nick joked.

"I can't imagine that day would ever come." He flushed and

left to catalog Whitney's wallet in the evidence room in the basement.

"She's got a little sister." Nick's eyebrows dipped. "Turned sixteen three months ago. Ready to tell her that her older sister was brutally murdered?"

Mackenzie pursed her lips. She was just about to leave when she saw Sully almost walk into the wall. When someone asked him if he was okay, he didn't seem to register. Instead, his eyes locked with Mackenzie. Shame burned in them before he marched away.

FOUR

The car jerked and came to a grinding halt at the red light, causing the contents in Mackenzie's stomach to swoop and rise to the base of her throat. Nick mumbled an apology but Mackenzie's mind was too preoccupied, thinking about how everything came down to moments. The moment she found her mother with a body in the kitchen. The moment she buried that body in the woods. The moment twenty years later that past returned quite literally to her doorstep.

"Earth to Mack." Nick snapped his fingers in her face.

She blinked, snapping out of her daze. "Sorry, I was just thinking about Whitney's sister."

"Yeah, only sixteen. That's rough." He tightened his grip on the wheel.

"Do you remember when your mom died?" she asked, before quickly backtracking. "You don't have to answer."

He blew out a breath. "No, it's fine. Yeah, I was sixteen. We were at the hospital. She didn't look like herself anymore. She was just skin on bones. No hair on her head. They had put her on morphine to ease the pain." His face became thoughtful. "I was holding her. She smiled, staring at me and then her eyes changed. She was gone."

"You never talk about it."

He cleared his throat. "But that doesn't mean I don't think about it every day. Moments like those stay embedded in your chest like a knife."

Mackenzie was hit by a wave of guilt. She had spent so long ruminating over her own past and memories that she didn't know much about the person she was closest to.

Nick hit the brakes when the trailer park came into view. On a sprawling field, there were rectangular trailers with tin roofs and faded white walls with dents and scratches. Some of the residents loitered outside, smoking, chatting, and reading newspapers, dressed in tattered clothes with heads that were either bald or full of stringy hair.

Mackenzie scrunched her nose, the smell of rotten food and grilled meat forming a potent mix. They asked around and were directed to Whitney's trailer.

"Ready?" Nick asked, stopping outside the door.

"Nope. You?"

"Never." He knocked a few times.

A young girl opened the door. She had a petite frame and long, wavy, blonde hair like Whitney. Her age was apparent—her skin was youthful and glowing. "What?"

"Are you Willow? Whitney Smythe's sister?" Nick asked.

She wiped her sweaty forehead with a cloth. "What did she do now?"

"Can we come inside?" Mackenzie said.

Willow's expression changed. "I see. Yeah."

The compact space was better maintained than Mackenzie had expected. The furniture was obviously old, but efforts had been made to improve things: a hand-knitted sofa cover to hide the tears in the upholstery; jars of potpourri to dilute the cigarette odor; indoor vines tracking over the windows; and artificial wisteria vines hanging on the windows for privacy.

What surprised Mackenzie most was a bookshelf stacked with books on medicine.

Willow sighed, resigned. "What did she do this time?"

"I'm really sorry, Willow, but your sister passed away," Nick said softly.

"Oh." Willow winced like someone had pinched her. A flash of annoyance crossed her face. "Okay... do I have to come with you to identify her body?"

Mackenzie and Nick exchanged a baffled look. Willow stared at them waiting for an answer. That's when it struck Mackenzie what was odd about this sixteen-year-old. She looked exhausted—lines of fatigue traced the contours of her face, her tired eyes revealed the lack of sleep, everything about her screamed signs of toil and carrying the weight of the world on her shoulders.

"Do you have any family?" Mackenzie asked.

"I have a grandmother. She's out somewhere." She gestured toward the door. "I know I'm only sixteen, but I'm the reason the three of us didn't end up being homeless. I am the one who runs this house and makes sure the bills are paid. I can handle it." She crossed her arms. "So what was it? Drugs? Alcohol?"

"She was murdered," Nick said.

She blanched, her eyebrows shooting up. "Oh... I... murdered?" She repeated the word and fell onto the sofa.

"I'm sorry for your loss," Mackenzie added softly.

Willow rubbed her temples, her mind visibly racing. "Do you know who did it?"

"Not yet. That's what we are trying to find out. Do you know anything?"

She gritted her teeth and stood up, going to the kitchen and turning on the faucet. Blinking away her tears, she began scrubbing the dirty dishes with excessive force. "God knows what she got herself into. She never knew how to be a grown-up. I get we had a messed-up childhood. I'm technically *still* in my childhood where I'm forced to live in this neighborhood surrounded by drug addicts and to take up a job after school. But the difference between us is that I don't use *childhood trauma* as an excuse to avoid responsibility," she asserted, but her voice cracked. "Yes, we went through shit. People go through shit. You learn to deal with it."

"Whitney didn't?" Nick guessed.

"I had *no* help from her. Ever since I can remember she would disappear for days or even months at a time. She went missing for a whole year until she turned up again two months ago. Who has to pick up the slack in the house? Me."

"Where did she go?" Mackenzie asked.

"I don't know!" she cried, and a plate fell from her hands. Pieces scattered into corners. She turned away from them and heaved. "Sorry."

"Maybe you should sit down," Nick offered.

But Willow ignored him and got a broomstick. Mackenzie watched Willow fight back tears as she cleaned the house, doing what life had conditioned her to do. Cling to anger to keep herself together.

"You didn't complain to the police when she was missing for a *year*?" Mackenzie asked.

Willow shrugged. "When I was ten, she ran away to Vegas for six months. So no. I didn't go to the police." She continued cleaning all the pieces of broken crockery as tears ran down her face. But defiance burned in her eyes.

Mackenzie and Nick gave her some time to process the news. When the water in the kettle in the little kitchenette started boiling, Willow turned her attention back to cooking. "I know I seem heartless to you."

She rambled on as she emptied a bag of pasta into a pot. "You just told me that my sister has been murdered and I'm making stupid pasta." She put a pan on the stove and turned on the gas. "But I don't know how to do anything else." She poured oil and garlic paste into the pan. "Whitney was a hot mess so I had to learn to always keep it together." She paused, hanging her head low. "At some point you have to make the hard decision to let go of people who bring you down. Even if they are your family. I'm going to get out of this dump, get into med school and make a life for myself. Just like our parents wanted."

"We're not here to judge you, Willow," Mackenzie assured her. "That wasn't our intention. We just were surprised. But we would like to know if your sister had any enemies?"

"I don't know."

"A boyfriend or a girlfriend?"

"I'm sorry but I have no idea."

"You guessed that it was a drug overdose. What was she using?" Nick asked.

"Few years ago, it was coke. She claimed that she was clean but then she started drinking... it was always something with her."

"Did she ever say anything unusual to you?" Mackenzie pressed. "Anything different from her strung-out monologues?"

Willow's eyes narrowed. "In the last month, she mentioned a few times that she thought someone was following and watching her."

"Did she describe the person?"

"Just that it was a man. I never saw anything. I just assumed that the drugs and alcohol had damaged her brain enough that she was now hallucinating."

"Had she shown signs of hallucinating or making up stories before?" Nick asked.

Willow took a shuddering breath and shook her head reluctantly. The horror on her face was palpable. Suddenly, her legs buckled and she broke down, like a pressurized cork shooting from a bottle. Tears spilled out and her body convulsed with uncontrollable tremors. "Oh my God. Oh my God! What happened to her? Who did this? Why?"

The chilling possibility hung in the air between them. What if Whitney had been telling the truth? What if the man who was stalking her killed her and then ripped out her eye?

FIVE

NOVEMBER 3

Mackenzie's feet thumped on the concrete sidewalk. A slow burn began slinking down her thighs as she pushed herself to the limit. Trees towered around her, Douglas fir and cedar, their branches reaching skyward and creating lush canopies that provide shelters from the frequent drizzle. She took deep breaths to pace herself, her nose filling with the scent of pine and damp earth. One of the many glistening lakes in town came into view, its mirror-like surface reflecting the swirling clouds in the grim sky.

Images of Sully's odd behavior kept flashing in front of her eyes. It all started the moment she mentioned that Whitney Smythe's eye had been plucked out. Could there be a connection to Sully? Did it remind Sully of something in his past? The sergeant was an uncomplicated man. He lived a simple life with his wife, Pam, complained that his daughters didn't call him enough, and took up different hobbies to have something outside of dealing with dead bodies and missing people.

But people thought that Mackenzie was also uncomplicated —that she was just a workaholic with a harsh demeanor, that she was too strong. They didn't know that when she was only sixteen that strength had faded.

Mackenzie dipped her elbow in the water, checking the temperature. It was perfect. She climbed into the bathtub and slowly immersed her body. It was hot enough to leave her skin pink but not red. Slinging her arms over the side, she rested her head back and took a deep breath.

This was good. Baths were relaxing. At least they should be. She focused on her breathing and every technique she had read up on. It had been weeks since she'd had a good night's sleep. Her eyes burned. During the day, she was a zombie. Numb. Robotic. Living the same life over and over again. Wake up, go to school, run track, come home, do homework, and help Grandmother with house chores. Then the nights came when she'd try to sleep with the memories from that night replaying in her mind.

Often, she would wake up and look at her skin. That night had been so deeply embedded in her that she thought her guilt would ooze out of her pores and scribble the words on her flesh.

Her chest swarmed with buzzing, accompanying a strange hollow ache. Her breathing turned erratic.

Mackenzie slipped under the water. Silence. She opened her eyes and saw bubbles swirling above her. It was peaceful. Her heart beat a steady rhythm. Her mind lulled into light-headedness. Ice daggers punctured her chest. Her body started wheezing, involuntarily. Bubbles escaped her mouth. She clutched the sides of the tub harder. Her lungs stretched and burned for air. A force tore her apart molecule by molecule. Her body writhed in the water, sending waves splashing all over the floor.

Few more seconds.

She was close. She knew her grip on the bathtub's edges was weakening. Her thrashing legs weighed heavier. The light from above flickered and dimmed. Streams of bubbles took the shape of a flower with four petals.

How strange.

A hand thrust inside the water and pulled her up.

"Ah!" Mackenzie was lifted up from the water. Her throat throbbed and sputtered out the water. She held her pounding head as the image of her grandmother sharpened.

Eleanor's eyes pooled with tears. "Mack!"

She pressed a hand into her chest where a dull ache bloomed behind her ribs. "Grandma…"

"What were you doing, child?"

When Mackenzie found her voice, it was scratchy. "I don't know."

When her phone started ringing, the old memory disappeared from her mind. It was Nick. "Peterson and some other officers talked to Whitney's friends." He sounded tense. The sound of traffic grazed the background. "None of them know where she was during that one year."

"That's strange."

"Well, her friends are strange. Doesn't sound like they cared and only hung out together to drink or get high on something. They did mention that she thought someone was following her though."

"Did anyone see anything?" she asked, turning around and walking back home.

"One of her friends mentioned that she had seen a black Honda CR-V on more than one occasion. But she didn't get a plate number."

"That doesn't help. What about her cellphone? We pinged the carrier, right?"

He clicked his tongue and honked. "We should have the records in a few hours. But Becky is done with the post. I'm on my way to you."

"Already? That was fast."

"Yeah, Sully requested to rush this one."

Her heart sank. "I see."

Mackenzie and Nick entered the brightly lit examination room. Mackenzie's eyes almost hurt from the bright light reflecting off the white and metal surfaces that populated this massive rectangular room. Despite the building being old with limestone floors and stained yellow tiled walls, the rooms had been modernized. A newly renovated sanitization station with lockers on their left and wall-mounted dissection bench running along the right wall. Four draft-ventilated post-mortem tables situated in the center with pull-through fridges on the back wall.

Becky stood next to the body on the table, wearing her lab coat, hand on hip. "You know the drill."

"What's your body count, Becks?" Nick asked, grabbing them fresh gloves.

"Excuse me?" Becky raised a sharp eyebrow.

"Yeah, how many bodies have you cut open? Do you keep count?"

She chuckled. "Oh *that's* what you mean."

"What else could it be?" he quizzed, looking at her and Mackenzie.

"Let's just say when Luna grows up, she'll expand your vocabulary." Becky peeled back the white cloth to reveal Whitney's naked body. A trunk incision that had been closed with a classic baseball stitch ran the length of her chest. Her face had been cleaned—the dried blood and dirt removed. Her right eye was closed. The left eye socket was like a black hole. It had lost some of its grotesqueness without the blood, but now it was a different kind of disturbing—very clinical and aseptic.

"Becky, have you seen anything like this before? This MO of a missing eye?" Mackenzie asked.

"Nope." Becky checked the clock on the wall. "I'm just waiting—"

Sully barged into the room, swinging the door shut with a loud thud.

"Sully?" Nick's forehead crumpled.

Sully didn't acknowledge Nick or Mackenzie. He was panting and drenched from the rain. Becky opened her mouth to protest Sully creating a mess but at the sight of him even she sealed her lips. He was blinking hard, staring at the corpse like he was one nudge away from blowing up. A storm inside a bottle.

The air turned brittle.

Becky cleared her throat. "The cause of death is head trauma. There's evidence of blood pooling in the cranium." She pointed at the X-rays pinned to a board. "There was extensive damage to C_1 and C_2 vertebrae in the neck region. The sinuous and transverse processes have been fractured near the foramen magnum, which is the large opening at the base of the skull. The force of the trauma was strong enough to drive the cervical column into the victim's skull, penetrating the base of the brain. This caused tearing of the major blood vessels inside the brain. Death was instantaneous."

"What kind of weapon was used?" Nick asked.

"I don't know yet. I'll examine the bones more thoroughly."

"Any signs of sexual or physical assault?" Mackenzie asked.

"There are no signs of sexual assault. No injuries to the breasts, thighs, or pubic region. No saliva or bite marks or semen. Her clothes were also intact. I have sent them to the crime lab to lift anything useful from them." She directed their attention to Whitney's neck and arms, marred with bruises. "She was physically assaulted though. The killer tried to strangle her but it wasn't enough to break the hyoid bone.

There are some defensive marks on her arms, indicative of a struggle."

"DNA under her fingernails?" Sully inquired.

Becky's mouth flattened as she raised Whitney's hand. "Her fingernails were ripped off."

Mackenzie noticed Sully frown. He wasn't expecting that.

"The eye... was it post-mortem?" Nick asked.

Becky nodded. "Thank God, it was. The fingernails too. They were all removed after she was dead."

Nick rubbed the back of his neck. "I get removing the fingernails. She might have scratched the killer when she was getting strangled. But why remove an eye?"

Mackenzie kept glancing at Sully. He flinched at Nick's question. His face puffed like he was going to throw up.

"There's something else." Becky crossed her arms. "She gave birth approximately two months ago."

"How do you know?" Mackenzie asked.

"There are sutures applied to her perineum. I ran her blood and there are elevated levels of progesterone. Also her breasts show signs of lactation; they are engorged."

"Where the hell is her baby? Her sister didn't say anything about that." Nick turned to Mackenzie.

"She was away somewhere for a year. She had a baby and came back home without it? Left the baby with the father maybe?"

"We should check all the hospitals," Nick said. "That should give us an idea about what happened in that year."

"I wouldn't get my hopes up," Becky warned. "Whoever applied these sutures did a shoddy job. The technique isn't professional. I wouldn't be surprised if it was a homebirth."

"Who should we reach out to?" Mackenzie turned to Nick, hands on her waist.

"Dylan Matthews from Special Investigations. He's the best, and he owes me one."

Mackenzie had heard about him. "All right, maybe he can start with the midwives in town."

"What was used to take out her eye?" Sully asked suddenly, an edge to his voice.

"I-I don't know that yet. We are still running tissue samples to analyze—"

"Prioritize it."

Becky blinked, baffled, as did Mackenzie and Nick. "Of course." A door to the transit area swung open. A technician called for Becky. She excused herself, leaving the three alone with the body.

Sully kept his eyes on Whitney as he spoke. "I'll call Anthony and push for the lab to get something from her clothes."

"Shouldn't we prioritize looking for her infant?" Mackenzie challenged, stepping forward. She caught a whiff of something pungent radiating from him.

Nick came up next to Mackenzie. His nostrils flared. He smelled it too.

But Sully didn't meet their eyes. His clothes clung to him and water trickled down, pooling into a puddle around where he stood. "Find out how her eye was pulled out." With that he walked away, his boots making a squelching sound. "There's no evidence of the infant being in danger. Give that to Special Investigations."

Mackenzie took a shuddering breath. That smell was engrained in her memory. Growing up she rarely breathed any air without it.

"You smell that?" she asked.

He ground his jaw. "He's drunk."

Mackenzie fiddled with the vintage watch on her wrist. The faded brown leather was weathered, but its worn texture had entrapped the countless times her father had touched this watch. It was the only tangible connection she had to him.

Nick played mindlessly with his lighter. "I suppose you're right. Something's off."

"Finally." She leaned against her desk. "He's *never* been drunk on the job before."

Nick looked at the closed door to Sully's office. "Maybe there's something going on at home. We all go through shit in our lives which we end up bringing to work."

"This isn't that," Mackenzie argued, whispering as they weren't alone. Austin toiled at his desk, flipping through a thick stack of reports. Justin was on the phone. Finn was eating his sandwich and watching highlights from last night's game. "I'm telling you it has to do with this case. When was the last time Sully showed up for an autopsy?"

Nick looked conflicted when Lieutenant Rivera interrupted them.

"Do you know what's going on with Sully?" she asked, distracted with the open file in her hands. Her glasses rested on the bridge of her nose.

"Nope," Nick answered quickly. "Why?"

"He missed an important meeting with the captain. Now I know he'd rather spend time scrapbooking but he doesn't drop the ball."

"He was with us getting the autopsy rundown."

Rivera paused and looked up at them, her eyes bouncing between them. "Sully was there?"

"Yep," Nick replied.

"He misses being on the field." Mackenzie shrugged.

"He likes to change it up from time to time," Nick added.

Rivera's lips twitched. "You two are telepathically linked. No wonder you work so well together." She walked away, smiling.

They looked at each other. A reluctant understanding

passed between them. This was Sully. As messed up as it was to show up to work drunk, there was too much history and friendship between them to tattle to Rivera without even talking to him.

Mackenzie knocked on Sully's door gingerly.

"What?" Sully growled.

Mackenzie pushed the door open. Sully's office was typically cozy and personal. The little room with wood-paneled walls and map of Washington State spanning one of the walls was always littered with Sully's latest hobby. Or huge boxes that he would tear open gleefully to catch a break from the latest budget crisis in the Lakemore PD.

But Sully's office was squeaky clean. His thick stacks of papers were neatly placed on an uncluttered desk. The air was cinched with the stink of whiskey.

"You might want to open the window, Sully. To keep the smell out in case Rivera comes in." Mackenzie couldn't hide the accusation in her voice.

She felt Nick stiffen next to her. His approach was always gentle. "Sully, we need to talk."

Sully didn't meet their eyes. Gruffly, he opened the window behind him. There were bags under his eyes. "What do you want?"

"We need to discuss something," Nick said softly.

His head jerked up. "Becky found out the weapon to remove the eye?"

"*No.*" Mackenzie scowled. "We need to talk about why you're reporting for duty drunk."

"It's none of your business, Mack," Sully replied, staring at some page open in a file. But his hand kept twitching. Nick and Mackenzie exchanged a tepid glance. Nick dragged a chair back and sat across from Sully. But Mackenzie remained standing, her back plastered to the door. She didn't recognize *this* Sully.

"We know you know something about this Whitney Smythe homicide." Nick placed his elbows on his knees and dropped his voice. "We have known each other for years, Sully. You know you can trust us." Sully's eyes snapped to Mackenzie. She narrowed her eyes but Nick looked over his shoulder and glared at her. She gave Sully a curt nod. "Mack, too."

"Is this a threat?" Sully asked.

Nick sighed. "No, it's a request. Help us. I can tell you care about this case more than any of us."

Thunder clapped. The sound itself could cut the tension in the room. Sully spun round on his chair to look outside. A jagged streak of lightning lit up the sky, reflecting in Sully's eyes when he started talking. "There was a storm just like this thirty years ago…"

SIX

Sully

The rain pelted the windshield of the police cruiser as Officer Jeff Sully and his partner, Officer Mike Ortiz, sped through the darkened streets of Lakemore. The storm had left the streets deserted. It was Sully's third week on the job, straight out of the academy. He was brimming with ambition, an unquenchable eagerness to prove himself, to live the dream he had had since he was a little boy—wear a uniform, carry a gun, and bust bad men.

"How are you liking Lakemore?" Ortiz asked. He had been with the Lakemore PD for almost three years now.

"It's always green and wet." Sully switched gears. "How's your wife doing?"

Pain clouded Ortiz's face. "Not well." He tightened his grip on the wheel, carefully navigating the slippery roads, the headlights of the car piercing through the sheets of rain. "Third miscarriage."

Sully swallowed hard. "I'm sorry."

"I wonder if it's in the cards for us. The IVF is taking its toll on her. The mood swings, the fatigue, nausea... sometimes I don't even think it's worth it, watching my wife's body break down like that."

"If you don't mind my asking, have you considered adopting?"

Ortiz nodded. "I would love to. Being a parent is about raising a child. But my wife always wanted to experience pregnancy. Now I think she's beginning to accept that adoption might be the only way."

Sully didn't know what to say. He was so new, so unsure of who he was and what he wanted. But Mike had been a good friend to him. He had gone out of his way to make Sully feel at home. "I hope it works out for you, man."

Ortiz gave him a wan smile. "Thanks."

The crackling radio burst to life, the dispatcher's voice cut through the storm's symphony. "Unit 23, come in. We have a 10-16 at 56 Elm Street. Possible homicide. Proceed with caution."

A chill climbed up Sully's spine. His pulse thrummed. This was it. This was the moment he had been waiting for. Until now he had only worked on domestic disturbances or catching dealers. This was the meat every officer wanted to sink their teeth into.

His first homicide case.

They reached the address. A row of dimly lit old houses with towering trees in the backdrop, giving way to a moss-covered forest. They were the first officers on the scene. Climbing out of the cruiser, Sully's discerning gaze scanned the area. The door to the house was open. A young woman stood on the porch with a boy. Sully's senses were on high alert as he and Ortiz approached the woman.

The woman grabbed Sully's arm, her eyes wild and unhinged. "Inside! Inside! I came to babysit and found her like *t-that*!"

Sully's eyes fell on the boy. Unlike the woman, the boy was calm but sad. Sully and Ortiz entered the house. A sense of dread hung heavy in the air. The metallic tang of blood mingled with the musty scent of wood. The booming sound of thunder echoed. It only took a few seconds for Sully to spot the body.

She was sprawled on the kitchen floor. Her dark hair fanned around her head. Her eyes vacant, staring into the void. Her pale skin contrasted starkly against the crimson pool of blood in which she lay. Blood spilled out of her torso, staining the tiles and tracing paths between the crevices. The macabre trail slithered toward Sully, seeping into his boot. But he didn't notice that. His gaze was fixed on one thing—the victim's empty eye socket.

"That's a first." Ortiz cursed under his breath.

A gut-wrenching cry pierced the air. "Not my wife! Grace! Grace!"

Sully's training kicked in. He pulled himself out of his daze and headed back to the front of the house. A burly man with a receding hairline burst inside, tears streaming down his face. "What happened to Grace?"

Ortiz and Sully had to physically block him from seeing the body, both to protect the crime scene and the man's sanity.

"I'm sorry, sir. But you need to wait outside," Sully said.

"Where's Rose?" the man begged. When Sully and Ortiz drew a blank, the man turned to the young woman and his son. "Did you get Rose?"

"She wasn't there," the babysitter sobbed.

He looked at his little boy who hung his head low, the corners of his mouth turned downward.

"Who is Rose?" Ortiz asked.

The man's eyes were filled with terror. "My baby Rose. She's only two months old. Where is she?"

SEVEN

"Baby Rose," Sully whispered, his eyes welling up. "Baby Rose..."

"You never found her," Mackenzie guessed correctly.

Sully shook his head, wiping his mouth with a shaking hand.

"Who killed her mother? Who killed Grace?" Nick pressed.

"We arrested a Jake Lawson. He was a plumber who had done a job for them a week before the murder."

"What was the evidence?" Mackenzie asked.

"A shirt with Grace's blood on it." Sully's features tightened. "He didn't have an alibi. Died in a prison fight sometime later."

A flicker of doubt crossed Mackenzie's mind. She probed Sully's expressions—the subtle change in the way he held his composure, the tilt in his tone, the deepening of his voice. She couldn't put her finger on it, like shadows dancing just out of reach. But a voice kept nagging her that Sully was lying.

It was the same voice that had persisted over the years coaxing her to dig deeper into the truth of that night when she helped her mother bury a body. A voice she had mistaken for the enemy. But it was a constant companion that guided her through the labyrinth of the human psyche to uncover the painful truths lurking within.

"Were there any traces of Rose?" Nick asked.

"Baby Rose," Sully corrected. "A few months later, we found tiny bones in the woods behind their house. The bones were contaminated with significant environmental DNA or eDNA." He explained how the DNA from animals, plants, and soil can be absorbed by the bones and co-mingle with human DNA, rendering ambiguity in results. "We could only do a physical inspection of the bones but they were human. She was perhaps... eaten by bears or coyotes."

Mackenzie noticed Nick's shoulders tense, but she had more questions to throw at Sully. "What was she doing in those woods? What did Jake Lawson say?"

"He never confessed."

"Why did he snatch the baby? Why did he remove Grace's eye?"

"I don't know!" Sully shouted, fury etched on his face.

"Sully, she's just collecting intel," Nick warned darkly, the first time he wasn't gentle since he'd walked into the office. "We have to do our job."

Sully shot up from his seat, agitated and began gathering his things. "If you want to do your job then find out what that murder weapon is made of." He stormed out of the office, bumping into Mackenzie's shoulder.

As soon as he left, Mackenzie and Nick shared a grave look. "Tell me that I'm not the only one who doesn't believe that story with all those loose ends."

Nick looked thoughtful. "It *has* been thirty years. His memory must have gotten hazy over time."

"There's something about his reaction that tells me that *this* is the case that he'll remember even on his deathbed. He's still hiding something from us."

"Let's just focus on what we have," he decided. "A new lead. We have another victim who had recently given birth and was found dead with her eye removed. That MO is too specific for it to be a coincidence. There has to be some connection."

An unsettling thought made Mackenzie's insides squeeze. It might have taken thirty years for there to be a second victim. But what if the third victim was just around the corner?

EIGHT

"Today I bring you the story of Tobias Mathis, the visionary man behind Lakemore's thriving crafts business—CraftMaster." Laura beamed at the cameras dressed in a silk blue shirt. The visuals switched to a collection of several items in a store as Laura continued with her narration. "From stunning pottery and intricate textiles to exquisite woodwork and dazzling jewelry, CraftMaster showcases the remarkable talent of local artisans. Under the visionary leadership of Tobias Mathis, CraftMaster has not only helped revitalize Lakemore's economy but also expanded its reach, becoming a trusted supplier of exceptional handmade products throughout Washington State." The camera panned to an attractive, slender man with Italian features and the thickest mane of black hair Mackenzie had ever seen on any man. Despite obviously being in his late fifties, Tobias was fit as he waved at the viewers with a gleaming smile. "Join me in anticipation of the upcoming Lakemore Artistry Festival—"

Mackenzie turned off the television. It was all she'd been hearing about for the last few weeks on the news. Either the Sharks' winning performance or Lakemore bringing back the

Artistry Festival after more than thirty years. She chewed the insides of her cheeks and stared out the window into her front yard. The weeping willow stood sturdy in a mournful grace. Its long sweeping branches swayed in the frigid morning breeze. In front of her was a file containing Whitney's phone records.

She had spent all night combing through them. There were no text messages or suspicious phone calls. Whitney's sister was right—her "friendships" were all about partying. She barely texted or called her sister. There was a big question mark hanging over the year she went missing.

Mackenzie was startled by the sound of her doorbell ringing. Without thinking, she opened the door and found Nick. He was frowning at his phone but when he looked up at her, he did a double take before his eyes widened. "Nice."

"What?" She looked down and realized she was only wrapped in a towel. "Oh!" she squeaked and hid behind the door. "What are you doing here?"

He waved a blue file in the air, his lips twitching in amusement. "Baby Rose case file from HITS." He was referring to the Homicide, Investigation, and Tracking System.

"Right." It had slipped her mind that Nick had texted her that morning.

"It's chilly outside." Nick pushed his way in. "Besides, it's nothing I haven't seen before."

Her jaw dropped. "*Excuse me?*"

"Come on, Mack." He shrugged off his jacket. "We've been partners at work for almost ten years. We're basically a married couple." He rolled up the sleeves of his shirt over his sculpted arms with a splatter of just the right amount of hair.

"Yeah, except for the fun part." She exhaled, staring at his arms.

"What?" Nick spluttered, trying to control his laugher. But Mackenzie was already sprinting up the stairs to get dressed.

"God, stupid, stupid," Mackenzie muttered, biting her

tongue as she put on her pantsuit. She scrutinized her reflection. To her horror, her cheeks were pink and she wasn't even wearing any makeup. The thought of Nick—or anyone— reading her face and knowing how she felt made her nerves prickle her stomach. She furiously applied a tinted moisturizer and tied her long hair in a tight, high ponytail. Once she had restored that reliable air of harshness, she went downstairs, fierceness back on her face.

"I went through her phone records from when she returned from wherever she'd been," Mackenzie said, joining him at the kitchen island. "But she doesn't mention anything about having a baby or a stalker or where she was."

"What about that year when she was *missing*?"

"She wasn't using this number. That's for sure."

Nick spoke while scrolling through his phone. "Dylan from Special Investigations was asking if we have any information on the infant. The sex, a description, anything belonging to it."

Mackenzie clicked her tongue. "Well, we're at a loss. None of the hospitals recognize Whitney."

"Yup. Makes his job harder. He's looking into shelters around the area. Not every woman can afford to give birth in a hospital in this country."

"Whitney's life might have some answers, like the identity of the father of her child."

Nick nodded. "We need to extract her socials. Maybe there's something there." He dialed Peterson who answered immediately. "We need access to Whitney's computer—her email, Facebook, Instagram... everything. Get the laptop from the sister and give it to IT."

"Yes, sir." Peterson's voice filtered through the line. "Did you know that Facebook was originally called "TheFacebook" and then they dropped the 'The'?"

"Do you have anything for us?" Mackenzie asked impatiently.

"Y-yes, sorry," he mumbled. "I spoke to the people at the party she was on her way back from. One of them said that she saw something on her phone and was *elated*."

Mackenzie's eyebrows knotted. "Did she tell them what it was?"

"No, but she left in a hurry. In a good mood."

"All right, thanks. Let us know about the laptop." Nick disconnected the call and turned to her. "Nothing in her phone records?"

"She didn't receive any text messages or phone calls in that window," Mackenzie confirmed. "The last message was in some group chat giving directions to this party."

"It must be a third-party app then." Nick scratched his chin. "That can be a pain in the ass."

"We still haven't found her phone in those woods so we don't know what apps she had installed. It could be a dating app." A spark lit up her eyes. "Maybe that's why she was so happy? She was on her way to meet some guy."

Nick agreed. "That could definitely be a possibility. Luna is staying away from the Internet."

"Good luck with that. Did you get anything from that murder thirty-one years ago?" She tipped her chin at the file he was holding.

"I got that we should be grateful for the technology we have today. Everything here corroborates Sully's story. Jake Lawson was a convicted sex offender." Nick showed her the mugshot of Jake—a shaved head, serpent tattoos crawling up his neck and a sneer. Mackenzie tried not to let any bias seep in. But even she winced at his picture. "He raped two women in Olympia when he was only seventeen. And then there is Baby Rose." He turned the page to a picture of bone fragments.

Mackenzie's heart sunk to her stomach. "Oh my God."

"Yeah." Nick's expression was grim. Several beats passed before he closed the file.

"Do you think Jake Lawson actually did it?" Mackenzie wondered aloud. "They found her blood on him, but... removing the eye after killing a woman and stealing the baby doesn't sound like the MO of someone like him."

"Which is why I tracked down Rose's father, Barry Fontaine. Maybe he can answer some questions for us."

NINE

Barry Fontaine used to have it all. Back in the late 1970s, he opened the first store in Lakemore that rented equipment for recreational activities. At first he only sold simple outdoor apparel like hiking boots, camping equipment, and backpacks, but soon he began expanding to include fishing rods, tackle boxes, harnesses, and carabiners. As Barry's business blossomed, so did his local popularity—he appeared on television ads and newspaper articles alike. A tall, rugged, charismatic man, he was on the verge of becoming a legacy in Lakemore, of amassing replenishable generational wealth. It wouldn't be fair to attribute it all to his grit. Barry possessed something that was a necessary prerequisite to all successful men—the perfect American family. A slender wife who never missed church and welcomed new neighbors by sending them casseroles. A shy son who excelled in academics and sports. And finally, a beautiful baby girl to complete the family.

And then one day, he returned home to find half of his family violently ripped away from him.

Overnight his business plummeted. His previously unsinkable life was now shredded beyond repair. Barry Fontaine went from being in the news for his booming business to being in the news for his murdered wife and missing infant.

That's how it always was. Happiness was gradual—it came in fragments that had to be put together with time and effort. Grief arrived with the swiftness and suddenness of a jackhammer.

The tires scrunched against the gravel as the car jostled over the ruddy path through the dense woods. The secluded cabin came into view, almost blending into its surroundings. There was a rocking chair on the porch. A truck in the driveway. The snow-capped summits of the Cascade Range contrasted against the lush greenery of the forest.

As Mackenzie climbed out of the car, she was overwhelmed by the scent of pine and cedar. Moss-covered branches reached out like delicate fingers and brushed against her. The air had a bite to it. A sharpness that numbed Mackenzie's skin. She and Nick knocked on the cabin door and heard shuffling footsteps. With a creak, the door opened.

A man's face was in the doorway. Wispy strands of gray hair covered his head and lines marred around his nose and mouth. "Who are you?" When Nick flashed his badge, he frowned. "What do you want now?"

"I'm sorry, sir. Are you Barry Fontaine?"

"Yes."

"We wanted to discuss something. Can we come inside?" Nick asked.

Barry stepped aside to let them in. The cabin wore a cloak of neglect. Dust clung to every surface and danced in the air. The furniture was worn and threadbare. Dirty dishes were piled in the sink still bearing crusts. Mackenzie resisted the urge to clean everything in sight. This home was supporting a life that was about surviving, not living. The only care was given to a wall of pictures. Not a speck of dust on the frames. Pictures of his family.

When Mackenzie saw the picture of Barry holding Baby Rose in his arms at the hospital, she was transported to the time when Luna was born.

Mackenzie didn't like hospitals. She had seen too much death and too much blood. But as she walked the halls with her husband, inhaling the air tinged with the smell of antiseptic and latex, her heart drummed erratically.

For the first time, she was at the hospital for a good reason. Nick had texted to say that his ex-girlfriend Shelly had given birth to a healthy baby girl a few hours ago.

"What are you supposed to do with babies?" Mackenzie asked Sterling, her husband at the time. "Like, does it even understand anything?"

Sterling chuckled, draping an arm around her. "You might want to start by using the pronoun 'she' instead of 'it'."

Mackenzie's ears turned hot in embarrassment. "Oh my God."

"You'll be fine, babe. They are very good judges of character, you know. Got lots of intuition, which we lose with age."

"Really? A blob of flesh has all that intuition?" Mackenzie quipped.

They reached the room and knocked on it tentatively. When they got the green light to enter, Mackenzie spotted Nick sitting on an armchair holding a baby wrapped in a white blanket. There was an exchange of polite interactions. Shelly was in the washroom.

"Ready to hold her?" Nick asked Mackenzie. She swallowed hard. She had seen her first dead body when she was twelve. But the thought of holding a newborn was more terrifying. The fragility of something this innocent and pure. "You'll

be fine. I'm right here," Nick added with sincerity and handed her his baby.

When Mackenzie saw her twinkling black eyes, just like her father's, she felt her heart expand and swallow all her other organs. When the baby opened her tiny mouth to yawn, Mackenzie almost melted. She had spent so long being hard that she didn't know what to do with this fuzziness in her chest that made her all gooey.

She handed her back. "Do you have a name?"

"Luna." Nick smiled.

After spending a few minutes with them and congratulating Shelly, Mackenzie and Sterling decided to leave. Mackenzie threw one last glance over her shoulder. Seeing Nick with Luna stirred something inside her. A longing that perplexed her.

When Sterling laced his fingers with hers, the only feeling she was left with was guilt.

"What is this about?" Barry fell on a chair, rubbing his knee. "There was a time I used to talk to cops every day. But that was years ago."

"Well, yes," Nick said. "We don't mean to rehash painful memories, but we have a case that might be related to what happened to your wife."

Barry's eyes narrowed. "What do you mean?"

"Another woman who had recently given birth was murdered and her eye was removed," Mackenzie said. She bit her tongue. Perhaps, she should have been softer. But Barry wasn't offended. Instead, he was suspicious.

"Are you sure?"

"Er, yes," Nick replied, baffled. "Why are you skeptical?"

He shrugged. "It's been thirty years. The killer is dead."

"Jake Lawson. What did you think about that? About him being the killer?" Nick asked.

"I didn't think anything. He had a history of violence. They found... Grace's blood on him." His lips quivered.

"What exactly happened that night?" Mackenzie inquired, taking out her little notebook. "We just want to confirm the details since sometimes old cases are missing documentation."

Barry wiped his glasses and took a few moments to gather his thoughts. In those moments, Mackenzie could feel the silence of the cabin, the silence in his life. "I was supposed to take Grace out for dinner that night. That's why we had called our babysitter. She was a good girl. Had babysat my boy, Garrett, a few times. God bless her soul; she died a long time ago from some illness. Grace was apprehensive as it would have been the first time we were leaving Baby Rose behind." His eyes misted as he recalled what happened. "But I convinced her. I told her she deserved a night out. But when I arrived home that evening, I saw a cop car parked in front of the house. And I knew something terrible had happened."

"The babysitter gave a statement that she discovered the body when she arrived," Nick recited from memory of the notes. "She had an extra key to the place?"

"We kept one under a flowerpot for emergencies. She must have used it when no one opened the door."

"What about your son Garrett?" Mackenzie asked. "He was asleep throughout the ordeal?"

"Yes." He looked down and shifted uneasily. "He would sometimes take a nap. He was a deep sleeper. He woke up when the babysitter started screaming."

"And there was no sign of Rose?" Mackenzie confirmed.

Barry shook his head. "The police were confused. They thought it was an abduction. But then why would her... eye be gouged like that?"

"I'm really sorry, Barry." Nick rubbed the back of his neck. "But her... remains were found a few weeks later in the woods."

"Her finger bones," Barry confirmed, too weathered by tragedy to form tears. "Phalanges, they are called."

"The police say in their report that Jake snatched her to confuse the police and then left her in the woods. Did you believe this version of events?" Nick asked.

"I have no reason not to believe it. You said there is another victim? With the same MO?"

Nick nodded.

"Well, then you have a copycat. This case was big thirty years ago."

Mackenzie had considered the possibility, but it was uncommon to have a copycat emerge three decades later. "Did you have any suspects at the time? Had you noticed anything suspicious? Perhaps someone lurking around the house?"

"Nothing like that."

"Has anyone come around asking questions about this other than us?"

Barry looked away again and waved his hand dismissively. "Nobody."

Mackenzie and Nick shared a glance. They were thinking the same thing. He was hiding something.

"Can we talk to your son Garrett? Perhaps he remembers something you don't?" Nick asked.

A forlorn smile curled up Barry's lips. He pointed at the window facing the backyard. "You'll find him there where I can see them every single day. With everyone I have ever loved."

Mackenzie frowned. She and Nick made their way to the backyard. Barry remained where he was. She pushed the door open, stepped outside and froze. The backyard ringed with pine trees had three tombstones. One for Grace. One for Rose. And one for Garrett. Garrett died ten years ago.

A gust of wind blew, making the hair on Mackenzie's arms stand.

"Poor guy," Nick whispered. "Born with the worst luck or what."

"It's like he's punishing himself."

Mackenzie's throat was dry. She had lost everyone she had ever loved too. Either to death or betrayal. The only person she loved was standing next to her.

Nick's phone rang. He answered without checking, and Mackenzie watched the color drain from his face.

TEN

Nick emanated a chaotic fury as he tore through the station at Lakemore PD. Mackenzie struggled to keep up with his long, purposeful strides. He had been quiet the entire ride back to the station. She had known him for ten years. She knew when to probe and when to give him space. His eyes were blazing. His jaw tight. Everyone who saw him took a step back. He headed straight for the holding cell.

Dennis, another detective from their unit, was there. "Nick, he asked for you."

Mackenzie maintained a distance, watching the scene unfurl. Inside the cell was a man—tall, lanky with blond hair. His arms dangled through the bars, his face pressed against them. A toothpick between his lips. His green eyes glazed over.

As soon as Nick laid eyes on him, he blanched. "Caleb."

"Hello, partner," he cooed.

"What happened?" Nick asked Dennis.

"Special Investigations busted him dealing ketamine."

Caleb let out a laugh. "Come on, man. We used to work together!"

Mackenzie gasped. The realization hit her like a bolt of

lightning. Caleb Mercer. He was Nick's partner before Mackenzie. He was paired up with Nick for two years before he was suspended for good. She didn't know what exactly went down, but to be honest, she wasn't bothered enough to ask. But she couldn't help but stare at Caleb and dissect his bony face and paper-thin skin with her eyes.

Caleb's cackling stopped when Nick faced him. A flash of something sorrowful crossed his face before he was grinning again. "Long time no see, buddy."

Mackenzie could only see Nick's back, but she had gotten pretty good at reading him from all angles. She felt the air puff with tension. "I didn't know you were in town."

"I was in Riverview." He was referring to Lakemore's doomed neighboring town. "I hear you have been closing some high-profile cases. All those dreams we had together, fulfilling them with someone else." Caleb tilted his head to the side to look at Mackenzie. "Hello, there. I'm the first one."

Mackenzie squared her shoulders and gave him a curt nod.

"So you called me to what? Bail you out?" Nick scoffed.

"I thought after everything we've been through you could do me a solid."

"You've exhausted your favor bank with me," Nick replied in a low voice.

Caleb swallowed hard. "You've really become a cold son of a bitch." He regarded Mackenzie. "Is he like that with you too?"

"Don't talk to her." Nick gritted his teeth and stepped forward.

Caleb made a clicking sound with his tongue, his eyes twinkling like he had just connected two dots. "I see what's happening here. Let me guess. I'm that part of your life you don't tell her about because you're ashamed of me."

"The only reason people see you that way is because you see yourself like that." Nick turned to Dennis. "Do what you want with this one."

Nick whooshed past Mackenzie so quickly before she could fully fathom their dynamic. She followed him out into the hallway, feeling Caleb's curious gaze burning a hole into her back.

In the deserted hallway, Nick's outline was a jarring contrast against the white walls and light gray floor. The dangling light bulbs above cast shadows on the walls, their bright white light piercing Mackenzie's eyes when she looked up at them.

"Nick... what was that?"

He leaned against the wall and played with his lighter. Turning it on and off repeatedly. "I wish you hadn't seen that."

"You never mention Caleb. Truth to be told, I didn't ask enough about him." She shoved her hands in her pockets and rocked on her heels. "But I heard he was suspended."

Nick frowned, remembering an unpleasant memory. "He was my first partner when I made detective. We worked together for a good two years but in the last few months... he started behaving erratically. Mood swings, mistakes at work... Turns out he was using."

"Using what?"

"Vicodin and oxytocin from what I saw."

"And you didn't say anything?"

He hesitated. "He had a really tough childhood. Eventually, it came out and he was thrown off the force."

Mackenzie pressed her back to the wall next to him. It had been her sole badge of pride, that despite having all the excuses in the world, she hadn't succumbed to any addiction. It was a common fallacy in her line of work, when that constant exposure to violence and the worst side of human nature wore one down that they needed something to stay afloat. "Did you know? Before others did?"

He scoffed but looked like he was in pain. "I did. Though I denied it at the time. He made so many false promises that he would quit and I believed him because I wanted to."

"How did you know he moved to Riverview?"

"I checked in on him every now and then. But I never reached out to him. Can't fault me for being curious."

"I don't," she said. "When did he start selling?"

"Guess that was the next step after using."

"And in *Lakemore*?"

"What do you mean, Mack?"

Mackenzie licked her lips. "He was part of the force here. One of us. And then he was suspended. Why would he come back here?"

"I don't know." He sighed defeated.

She searched his stormy eyes. "Why does it hurt you this much? Seeing him?"

"It's just sad." He loosened his tie. "You know how close partners can get. All that wasted potential and what-ifs."

A lump hardened in her throat as she locked gazes with Nick. He was lying. He knew she knew it. The knowledge was suspended between them, burning hot, and threatening to infect their relationship.

Nick was the first one to break eye contact. "Running late. Have to pick up Luna from her piano lessons. See you tomorrow."

She didn't get a chance to press him further as he was already walking away from her. She went back to the holding cell and found Caleb leaning against the bars, the collar of his jacket raised all the way to his chin. When his glazed eyes fell on Mackenzie, he snickered.

Mackenzie gestured the officer on duty to take a walk. When the sound of his footsteps had faded, Caleb's lips spread into a coy smile. "I was hoping we would get to know each other."

"Why are you here?" she asked.

He narrowed his eyes. "Why am I here?"

"You were a police officer." His mouth tightened at her

words and his nostrils flared. "You went through the academy. You served here for two years, formed relationships, closed cases, earned a reputation. No matter what wrong path you went down later doesn't change the fact that you have a conscience." Her voice dripped with a sincerity that surprised her. "So why would you return to the scene of the crime?"

Caleb pretended to think about it. "That's a good question. I'll get back to you on that."

"Ah, so a bad attitude is also on the list of what's wrong with you." Her eyes swept over him in distaste.

"Does Nick know that his partner is an overthinker?"

Mackenzie stepped forward, her face inches away from him. She relished the fact that he was slightly taken aback. "What Nick doesn't know is that you're back in town for a reason that has nothing to do with you selling ketamine. The shame of facing everyone again would have kept you away."

"And why do you say that?"

Mackenzie opened her mouth but then shut it. She knew the shame only too well. It was that cold, sharp edge of the blade that exerted just enough pressure against her throat. Except she hadn't run away from Lakemore. She had returned and lived here, under the constant threat of exposure.

Caleb's lips parted. "I get it. I'm not the only one. Does Nick know?"

"Nick and I don't have secrets."

He stood up, walked toward her and pressed his face against the bars, looking around animatedly. "What about everyone else? Do all your colleagues and your fans know the shame of the town's darling detective?"

Mackenzie waited in the parking lot with bated breath. Her palms were sweaty against the leather wheel. The conversation with Caleb had left her with flutters in her veins. He was shrewd—he had to be. He was an officer like she was, used to reading between the lines, trained to examine every passing emotion under the microscope. But Mackenzie couldn't shake off the feeling that Caleb was going to be a thorn in her side.

Everyone was hiding something. Sully, Caleb, and even Barry. Barry had exhibited classic signs of deception when asked if anyone had ever come asking questions. He had broken eye contact and made exaggerated body movements.

She punched a message to Peterson.

M: Keep tabs on Barry Fontaine—specifically if he's meeting someone.

P: On it.

When Sully finally emerged from the building, she straightened, alert. He was busy thumbing his phone, his raincoat draped over one arm. Usually, Sully looked the happiest to leave the building. He would walk out, a beaming smile on his face, but this time he didn't even look up.

When he kickstarted his car and pulled out on the street he failed to notice Mackenzie tailing him. Rain fell sparsely. She turned off the radio and the sound of drops bopping the top of the car filled the itching silence. She was following her sergeant, her boss, one of the few good role models she had in her life.

Guilt reared its ugly head. Maybe this was paranoia. What was she expecting to find? She had been trying hard these past few years to overcome her mistrust of people. A whisper of a lie and she was back to her old habits that had left her isolated, bordering on contemplating what she lived for in the first place. But Sully's behavior kept stinging her.

She was about to force herself to turn back home when Sully's car took an unexpected right turn—not in the direction of his house. Mackenzie's curiosity spiked. She took a right turn too, ensuring that there were always at least two cars between them. The lights from the lampposts and stores danced on her face. Her heart careened from beat to beat as she followed Sully through the zigzagging, blackening roads of Lakemore.

After around twenty minutes, Sully's car began to slow down. Mackenzie glided the car along a curve leading to a row of houses. She parked at a distance and watched Sully plod out of his car, toward a house. He rang the bell. The house was a cookie-cutter, semi-detached townhouse with an orchard tree in the front yard. A light turned on, illuminating what looked like a living room. The front door opened.

Mackenzie squinted to see clearly. It was a young woman, perhaps in her thirties. They exchanged words. The woman went back inside and a few seconds later a man came to the door. His hairline was receding, his frail figure dwarfed by Sully's bulbous frame. The man let Sully in. When the door shut, an idea unfurled in Mackenzie's mind. She unlocked her phone and began searching for Sully's old partner, Mike Ortiz.

She found a picture of him and his daughter—Violet—on social media. Their address was listed in Lakemore. Sully was visiting Ortiz at this late hour. Questions clamored in the back of her skull.

Through the open curtain, she saw the scene unfolding inside. Sully and Ortiz were engaged in an animated conversation. Sully paced back and forth, his hands waving in the air. They were arguing. Their necks turning red. Their mouth moving like they were yelling. Their chests heaving.

Had this case perturbed Sully enough for him to reach out to someone who would understand? An old friend who was haunted by the same gruesome crime scene and forced to live with the flimsy explanation of what happened to Baby Rose.

Then why were they fighting? Why would they argue this vehemently if Sully was looking for comfort?

She was jolted out of her thoughts when her phone rang. It was Austin Kennedy.

"Hey, what's going on?"

"Mack." He sounded uncertain. "A body washed ashore on the riverbank. I read on the bulletin about the case you and Nick are working on. Pretty sure this is related."

The contents inside Mackenzie's gut shifted uneasily. "What happened?"

"Female victim. Her left eye has been removed."

ELEVEN

Mackenzie arrived at the scene with jangled nerves. The riverbank was already swarming with officials—squad cars and white vans parked haphazardly, the muggy air tingling with activity, bodies moving, whispering, and taking notes. The rain had stopped, leaving the sweet scent of wet soil in the air. To her right, the dark waters of the Nisqually River drifted. The vapid currents churning around a sharp bend. In the dark, the waters looked deep—fathoms and fathoms of swirling blackness.

"Mack!" Austin ducked under the crime scene tape and came up to her. His blond hair danced in the gentle breeze. "I couldn't reach Nick."

"He's with Luna." She shouldered past him. "What do we know?"

"Some nighttime construction workers found her about an hour ago and called it in."

The body was surrounded by technicians taking photographs and bagging evidence. When they parted to allow Mackenzie access, her throat constricted.

The woman lay on her stomach—her dark hair was soaking wet and tangled with seaweed, her bluish skin wrinkled and clammy starting to slough off the bones in patches. Her left socket was missing an eye. The remaining frosty blue eye was open, like a ball of glass, reflecting the horrified faces staring at it. Her beige dress had been shredded by the rocks and sharp-toothed fish.

Mackenzie bent on her haunches and put on her gloves. "No ID on her?"

"None." Austin sighed. "We will get some divers in the water first thing in the morning to find any evidence but..." He hitched his thumb over his shoulder at the flowing currents. "I don't have a lot of hope."

"It's hard to tell what she looks like." Mackenzie winced as more skin cascaded down the victim's slowly vanishing face. "Peterson, check missing persons records when you get back to the office."

"Yes, ma'am." He was standing further away, maintaining a safe distance from the corpse.

"Becks, what can you tell me?"

Becky was on her knees, supervising her technicians. "Based on early-stage skin slippage and the blowfly eggs deposited in the socket, I would put time of death at twenty-four to forty-eight hours. It doesn't look like she was underwater for more than a few hours based on bloating and discoloration. I will have to do a more thorough examination."

"The construction workers said that she wasn't here last night when they came into work," Austin said. "She must have washed ashore in the last twenty-four hours."

"Her clothes are intact. The damage seems to be mostly from being in the river. Less chance of sexual assault," Mackenzie said. "No wounds on her arms or legs."

"I'll have to cut her open to find cause of death. But there is no injury to the back of the head." Becky pointed out.

"Unlike Whitney Smythe." Mackenzie finished for her. But there was a common thread between the two victims—the missing eye. Disgust thickened in her throat watching her fear manifest in this grotesque scene.

"Can we find out where the body was dumped?" Austin asked Becky. "This river cuts through the entire town. Can we narrow down the search space?"

"Possibly. Stomach contents and particulates could give us drift patterns where she was left before she was washed ashore."

"Did you know that the stomach can expand to hold up to around four liters of food and liquids?" Peterson called out from afar.

Under typical circumstances, it would have dispelled some of the tension, but the grisliness of the scene was overpowering. The violence of the act had turned the air brittle, biting into Mackenzie's skin with its sharp teeth.

"Can I say something we are all fearing?" Austin looked around. "Two victims within a week with a missing eye. Are we looking at a serial killer?"

Mackenzie felt a sense of unease creep in. "I fear so."

NOVEMBER 5

There was something different about that morning at Lakemore PD. Mackenzie sat at her desk, staring at a picture of her mother, Melody, she had found in her old things a few weeks ago. Deciding to take her first step toward moving on, she had brought the picture to work. Her mother with her curly, black hair and gray, saucer eyes were a stark contrast to Mackenzie's straight, flaming red hair and brown eyes. Her mother had been a complicated woman. It took years for Mackenzie to untangle her web of lies and then even longer to resolve her feelings toward her, which always felt like a giant knot in her chest.

But work had always been different. Even though she kept everyone at arm's length, there was a solidity and comfort this place offered. That lopsided grin Sully had when she knocked on his door. That crooked smile Nick gave her when he found her—and his—desk scrubbed clean first thing in the morning. But today Sully marched to his office without raising his head to greet anyone. And Nick's face was impassive.

The subtle changes left her cold. Her eyes darted to her mother's picture again. Perhaps her mother wasn't the only one she never truly knew.

Sully emerged from his office and barked orders about a briefing in the conference room.

Mackenzie gathered her files and glanced at Nick, hoping he would also note Sully's attitude. But he didn't look at her, lost in his own thoughts.

"What's up with Sully?" Austin appeared at her side, smoothening his tie. "Never seen him like this."

Mackenzie observed Nick's tense shoulders. "Me neither."

"Did you know that he ordered a rush on the autopsy of our Jane Doe?"

"Really?"

"Dr. Sullivan probably pulled an all-nighter."

They settled around the table. Mackenzie gingerly took a seat next to Nick who was scratching his chin, his vacant eyes boring into a page. He seemed so disconnected from her. It almost felt like she was missing an organ. She touched his arm lightly. It snapped him out of his trance. Their eyes locked. Palpable fear swam in his black eyes.

"Have we IDed our Jane Doe?" Sully grumbled.

"I ran her description through the MUPU database and the DMV," Peterson said. "But there wasn't a match on either. She definitely hasn't been reported missing."

"Just like Whitney Smythe," Sully noted. "Do we have an update on her stalker?"

"Clint has been working on her laptop. It's all password-protected," Nick said. "It looks like she had enabled iCloud backup for all her apps. Clint has to use some specialized software to extract and analyze data from it. It will take a few days."

"What the hell are all of you doing?" Sully slammed his fist on the table. Mackenzie flinched at his outburst. "We have a serial killer on our hands."

"I think we should look into Jake Lawson again," Mackenzie said. Sully's expression fell, but he tried to hold his composure. "Maybe someone in his orbit knows something."

"It was a famous case back in the day. Do you think it's related?" Austin wondered out loud.

"It is a very specific MO for it not to be. But I haven't been able to find a connection between the Fontaine family and Whitney Smythe." She looked at Nick. "What do you think, Nick?"

He cleared his throat. "I... sorry, what? We should look into Jake Lawson."

Sully punched some numbers on the keypad and set the phone on speaker. "Maybe Becky will have something new since my detectives are busy sitting on their asses."

Mackenzie grinded her jaw. Becky's tired voice cut through the undercurrent of disquiet that had taken hold of the room. "We have been up all night, Sergeant."

"I appreciate it, Dr. Sullivan. Were you able to ID the victim?"

"No. I ran her prints through CODIS and didn't find a match. *But* I did find a locket that was melted into her lungs during putrefaction. We have cleaned it as best as we could and are sending you a picture. I believe you can track the buyer of this locket."

Sully clicked his fingers at Jenna. She stood up and nodded. "On it." Her heels clacked as she waltzed out of the room.

"Do we have cause of death?" Sully leaned on the table.

"I have definitely ruled out any head trauma or strangulation as all the injuries in that region are post-mortem from being in the river. The preliminary cause of death is a high-velocity injury based on the fractures in the neural arches."

"English please." Nick groaned.

"Injury to the spinal cord killed her."

"She was shot. Can we get the model of the gun?" Mackenzie made a note in her diary.

"Not yet. I'll have to clean off all her bones. There was no bullet embedded in her and also no exit wound. But there is pitting, which is consistent with a bullet, including some additional pitting and microfractures to the posterior of the ribs and sternum."

Nick's eyebrows dipped. "No exit wound, but there is bone evidence of a bullet but you can't find it?"

Becky sighed, frustration seeping into her voice. "I know. I'm working on it. Have been all night. Regarding your request, Sergeant, about if we could identify what was used to remove Whitney's eye?" Becky reminded him.

"I'm listening." Sully's face was stony.

"We swabbed the tissue in that area and ran a mass spec. It picked up camphor oil in large quantities."

"Camphor oil?" Austin repeated, puzzled. "What is that used for?"

"Insect repellent and aromatherapy, mostly," Mackenzie replied.

"Whatever instrument it was, was dipped in camphor oil?" Sully confirmed.

"That's my conclusion. I'm running the same test for our Jane Doe's tissues too and will let you know what comes up for our second vic."

Sully released a long-drawn breath and fell back on his chair. His thick mustache wiggled as a hysterical sound came from the back of his throat. "Okay... okay..." He squeezed his eyes shut and when he opened them, they were bloodshot. "We have two dead women and no clue why. Has the media picked up on this yet?"

The media in Lakemore fanned the flames of growing disdain among the residents. Despite football being a common thread, the sole symbol of unity, this depraved town existed with a constant anger simmering beneath the surface. Anger that there was a widening gap between the rich and the poor. Anger that the people here were just puppets with their strings attached to a select few who had far more power than they should have had. Anger that while the rest of the world invited ideas that led to growth and transformations, Lakemore was somehow planted in the past—a slow, simple, and unimaginative way of living.

"Why does the media hate us so much?" Austin asked. "I've worked in other towns too, but in this town it feels personal."

"Because everyone understands the concept of a villain," Sully said. "And when you have dead women with their eyes scooped out and no solid leads, it's easy for us to be the villain."

"Any signs of sexual assault?" Mackenzie asked.

"None. But this victim also recently gave birth just like the other victim Whitney. Around six months ago by my estimate."

TWELVE

"The Lakemore PD is investigating two separate cases involving the brutal murders of two women, both found with a missing eye. Both victims were murdered within the span of a week. As per our sources, the police have been unable to establish a connection between the two victims," Laura reported, a concerned furrow between her brows. "However, due to the distinctive nature of the crimes, the police are assuming they are connected. The identities of the victims remain unknown at this point, and there are no solid leads. Our request for a statement from the Lakemore PD went unanswered. While it is hard to ask for any help from the public regarding the crimes without knowing any of the details, we do urge everyone to exercise caution." She inserted a rehearsed pause before signing off with a chilling message. "We *might* have a new serial killer in town."

Unease slithered down Mackenzie's spine. She was watching the television in the common area outside the conference room, stuffed with couches and vending machines. Someone switched the channel to the highlights of last night's football game and only then Mackenzie felt something loosen around her neck.

"I'm actually impressed." Nick joined her, ripping open a packet of Sour Patch Kids. "She was very professional. Not trying to rile people up."

"It's a refreshing change when reporters remember their job is to report and not use this platform to share their unsolicited views." The previous reporter of Lakemore, Debbie Arnold, lacked natural charisma, but she made up for it by being a loud mouthpiece and using provocative language to cause trouble. Mackenzie's chest squeezed as she remembered Debbie's fate and her role in it. "We need at least three bodies to use the term serial killer."

"I would have liked a stronger link than just the MO. But without even knowing the identity of the second victim yet, we are in the dark." There were black rings around his eyes. But Mackenzie knew that had more to do with Caleb.

"Did Special Investigations have any updates?" she asked. "Why aren't they sharing that information with the public?"

"They know what they're doing, Mack." He sighed. "They specialize in this. They don't want to spook out the guy that's behind this into leaving town or the state."

"We don't even know the sex of the infants, their names, identification markers or any details that could help us in the search."

"Exactly. I talked to Dylan this morning. He alerted his network of criminal informants in the state for illegal adoption or... trafficking." He couldn't keep the horror out of his voice. "But Dylan also told me that our best bet is to find out who the father is."

"Jenna might find something from that locket," she said, trying to reassure him. "What concerns me is that it looks like neither of the victims were held captive."

He nodded. "Whitney was killed on the same night she left the party, and Jane Doe wasn't reported missing, so I'm assuming there wasn't a lot of time between her being taken and killed. And there are no signs of ligature marks."

"I don't want this guy to leave a trail of bodies in his wake by the time we catch him." Resolve pulsed through her, hot and heady as Laura's words *we might have a new serial killer in town* played over and over in her mind. This town had been through the ringer—it had been stretched and twisted and poked and ripped; it had been bent out of shape and smashed; and every time it was built up again. Unfortunately for Mackenzie, she found herself at the center of it.

"Detective Price, Detective Blackwood." Peterson approached them, his thumbs hooked into his belt. "I might have something on Mr. Barry Fontaine."

"What is it?" Mackenzie asked.

"I followed Mr. Fontaine early this morning. He met with another man in a café just off exit 32A on the highway. They seemed to engage in a charged conversation. Turns out the man is a regular at that café so I was able to get his name and run a quick background check. His name is Russell Grant. No priors. But he used to be a private detective around thirty years ago in Lakemore."

The wheels in Mackenzie's head spun. "Maybe Barry had hired him all those years ago to look into his wife's murder. It makes sense. His wife was killed and his daughter was missing. He had money. Maybe he wanted more than just the police looking into this."

"And now he reached out again after hearing about the new murders with the same MO. This Russell guy must have done some digging."

"Maybe he knows something the police missed that could help us now," she added.

Momentum had been injected back into the case even if it reinforced the dreadful possibility that had been looming over them since the beginning. Did Sully and his partner, Ortiz, make a mistake thirty-one years ago? Could that be the key to solving the current murders?

THIRTEEN

The gym was bustling with moving bodies grunting and breathing deeply. The swishes of spinning kicks and thuds of fists hitting pads filled the sweat-infused air. The walls were adorned with mirrors and motivational quotes. In the middle of the gym was a boxing ring where a group of people were sparring—throwing and blocking punches, their gloves slapping against each other, and the occasional cry of pain echoing. A tall, muscled, bald man wearing a whistle around his neck walked among them with a rigid posture and hands behind his back, his presence commanding as he observed and corrected their form.

"That's him." Mackenzie tipped her chin. "He looks good for his age."

Nick frowned and shrugged. "Looks all right to me."

Her lips turned up in a smile. "Are you jealous?"

He scoffed and then looked at her seriously. "Maybe. Mr. Grant!" he called out to the coach, holding his badge out.

Russell scowled at the interruption but when he saw it was the police, he excused himself. "Is it about that kid? He signed a waiver that I'm not responsible for any injuries around here. Not my fault he's a pansy."

"This isn't about that," Mackenzie said. "Do you know a Mr. Barry Fontaine?"

A fleeting moment of surprise and then understanding dawned in his eyes. "Oh. Yes."

"How?"

"He hired me when his wife was killed and Baby Rose went missing." Russell tore off the wrestling tapes from his hands. "I was a private detective back then."

"Did he hire you after the investigation was over or during?" Nick asked.

"During. He wanted more resources on it. Mad times back then." He shook his head. "Biggest news of the year."

"And did you discover anything noteworthy in your investigations?"

Russell's eyes bounced between them, like he was trying to work out if they could be trusted. Mackenzie could sense he was a man who had served in the military or the police at some point. There was an old scar in his shin from a bullet wound. His eyes didn't just see, they recorded. The tips he was giving his students proved that he had combat experience.

"You must have seen the news. We have two bodies with the same MO as Grace Fontaine," Nick said, imploring him to cooperate. "Luckily, the news outlets haven't picked up on that old connection yet. But if you know anything about Grace Fontaine's murder that could help us..."

He sighed and swallowed hard. "I can tell you one thing. Jake Lawson was innocent. He did not kill Grace."

Mackenzie's insides tightened into a knot. "What makes you so confident?"

"Lawson was undergoing therapy at the time. There was an exercise in which they would record videos of themselves, talking to the camera like a self-reflection thing or some shit. His alibi was that he was making that video during the hours Grace was killed and Baby Rose was snatched. But he couldn't produce that video... until I found it. It had been accidentally discarded," he explained, crossing his arms over his bulging chest. "I watched it and the timestamp confirmed his alibi. It was not the outcome I was hoping for, to be honest. This guy was scum and it would have been so simple. But it wouldn't have been ethical for me to sit on that evidence. So I went to the police station with the evidence. I left it at the front desk with some cop who said they would give it to the officer in charge... when Lawson was charged, I went back to the Lakemore PD station. The front desk denied receiving any video."

Mackenzie turned to Nick, who was trying hard to hide his disappointment. But the corners of his eyes were crinkled. A vein in his temple was throbbing. "Do you know who you gave the evidence to? Can you describe that person?"

He shrugged. "Just a regular white man. But he was just some uniform busy on the phone. It was ringing off the hook with tips about Baby Rose from all over the state. The station was plunged into chaos. I couldn't find anyone to talk to. In hindsight, I doubt that guy even really paid attention to me. I should have been more careful with that evidence."

Mackenzie knew how things could get at the station especially when there was a missing baby the entire state was looking for. There was no time to breathe or contemplate. Everyone operated like machines fueled by the fear of the worst-case scenario.

"Did you try reaching out to any of the investigating officers or anyone from the force? The DA's office?" Nick pressed.

"I went to the DA's office but no one was willing to listen." A shadow crossed his face. "Lawson was a self-confessed serial rapist. He had served time in prison and was out on parole. They were relieved that this case was solved quickly and the bad guy was someone easy to convict. But to be fair, Lawson could never explain how the police found Grace's blood on him."

"Did you talk to him? Did he have any theories?" Mackenzie asked.

"He thought someone was framing him. By the time he was imprisoned, he had become too paranoid." Someone called him over. "Do you guys have more questions?"

"Not for now, but if you remember something then let us know," Nick said.

Russell nodded and gave them both a firm handshake before he left.

"Are we looking at a cover-up or an honest mistake?" Nick muttered under his breath. "Knowing this town, I'm inclined to believe the former." His phone buzzed with a notification, and bewilderment marred his face before his eyebrows shot up. "Jenna tracked down the place the locket was purchased. Luckily, it wasn't some generic, mass-produced design. But we'll have to go there to get the buyer's information."

"Where is it?"

"CraftMaster store. The one owned by Tobias Mathis."

FOURTEEN

Tobias Mathis knew how to weave magic with his words. At fifty-six years of age, he had a lithe but muscled body, a head full of black, tousled hair and a string of pearly white teeth thanks to veneers. His eyes were like narrow slits, bordered by thick lashes. As Mackenzie skimmed through his pictures online, she could tell he had had work done to look younger. His strong, angular face lacked any lines or signs of aging, but at the same time, he didn't look artificial. His dark features were underlined with a sense of mischief and hedonism.

Wearing sunglasses and dressed in loose-fitting natural fabrics of earthy tones, he posed for the cameras as they wrote about his burgeoning empire of crafts. He talked about how much he loved Mother Nature and earth, how his purpose in life was to uplift others and create more life, and how his home-town of Lakemore had hidden gems beyond the realm of football.

Mackenzie watched a short clip of him, trying to get a read on him. The interviewer trailed alongside him as Tobias showed the garden he had crafted himself. His eyes twinkled, his lips twisted when he spoke, and his body moved through the oasis, exuding both grace and power. His charisma didn't charm; it captivated. It didn't stir any feelings of attraction, but that of belief.

But despite his popularity, Tobias Mathis was also an enigma. He was famous for being private. He would give interviews but spin his words in such a way that would focus more on his ideologies and business rather than his lifestyle. There were all kinds of rumors circulating about him on the Internet. Some wrote he was a hippie growing drugs and others called him a sex addict.

When a sharp wave of nausea hit Mackenzie, she opened the glovebox, rifling for Gravol. Nick always stocked it in his car. But her hand found an empty pill bottle. She glanced at Nick behind the wheel. His eyes were fixed on the road, but his mind was far away.

She lowered the window to let in some fresh air. "So, did Caleb make bail?"

He stiffened. "He was let off with a warning for now as it was a small quantity of weed and his first offense."

"Did you help him get off?"

His smile was bitter and didn't reach his eyes. "Never again."

She was onto something. "You have helped him out before?" He didn't answer. She felt him clamping up again. That wall materializing between them. "He was your partner, Nick. I'm sure you thought you were doing the right thing."

"I don't want to talk about it." There was a finality to his tone.

"Yeah, I've only been your partner for what, ten years?" she snapped.

"This was before your time, Mack. It has nothing to do with you. No need to beat a dead horse."

"Because this is upsetting you. You are distracted and stressed. If getting it off your chest will help, then do it."

"It won't affect my work," he promised. "This is just a temporary reaction."

Mackenzie's ears burned. "Do you think that's why I'm worried? How this will get in the way of our case? Because why would I care about your personal wellbeing."

His lips pressed into a thin line. "I'll talk about it when I'm ready. Can we drop this?"

Mackenzie whirled her head away to look out the window. Angry tears pricked her eyes. She had laid herself bare for him when she'd told him her darkest secret—she had buried a body with her mother. There wasn't a single part of her life that Nick wasn't familiar with. Their clash had left her feeling raw like she would bruise easily. Before Nick, there was only one person who had that power over her—and it wasn't her ex-husband.

"Mel, it's her sixteenth birthday," Eleanor whispered harshly into the phone. Her fingers curled around the squiggly telephone line.

Mackenzie peeped through the inch-wide space between her door and the frame. The cancer had eaten away parts of her grandmother. She looked bony, her back hunched over. But she was recovering. Mackenzie knew her grandmother to be steadfast. If there was anyone who could overcome anything, it was her.

"You missed Easter! You show up once a year."

Mackenzie gripped the edge of the wooden door. It was jaded with splinters poking out.

"It's bad enough that her father went missing. Now, you're distancing yourself from her... no, no, I know that's not your intention, but it sure looks like it."

She pressed harder. The splinters cut through her skin. She wasn't alone in thinking her mother was ignoring her. Eleanor thought so too.

"She's at an impressionable age, Mel," she scolded. "I

know you're busy there, helping with the search, but it's been four years! Let him go. He was deadbeat anyway. Don't ruin your relationship with your child."

It was too late. Melody's betrayal felt like burning embers inside her. It made her spiritless. It made her bleed. She could almost hear her father's mocking words. "You buried me to protect someone who doesn't even want you, Micky. What a waste."

When Mackenzie hopped out of the car, a harsh chill enveloped her body. She snuggled deeper into her leather jacket and scowled at the clear sky. The blazing sun was a lie. The air was still and frigid, sticking to her skin and slithering down her collar and up her sleeves. It was a rare dry kind of cold. The moisture had been sucked out of the air after heavy rainfall in the early hours that left puddles and a few fallen cable lines in its wake.

Mackenzie's phone trilled. There was an email from Becky, which Mackenzie read out. "She's finished running mass spec on the tissues around Jane Doe's removed eye."

"And?"

Mackenzie didn't have time to study the attached chromatograms like she generally would, to double-check everything with her own eyes. Instead she continued to read out Becky's email. "Camphor oil."

"Just like Whitney Smythe."

"At least we have another solid link between them." Anticipation tingled her palms.

"Here it is." Nick pointed ahead.

Mackenzie's eyes fell on the sprawling grounds. Expansive fields stretched with hues of leafy greens, golden grains, and ripening fruits. Rustic huts with weathered wood and moss-covered roofs were sprinkled throughout. The main hut was at the center, soaring above the landscape, its thatched roof alive with wildflowers and vines, its frame sturdy, made from hand-hewn timber. A wooden sign at the edge said *The Farm*.

They ventured in and Mackenzie thought she had stepped into another world. The fragrant smell of herbs mixed with the earthy scent of oil overwhelmed her senses. In a stark contrast to the rest of Lakemore bathed in dull hues of greens and blues, The Farm was a tapestry of vibrant colors. A carved-out path weaved through The Farm, leading them to different huts and areas.

The next thing that Mackenzie noticed was that there were only women and children in The Farm. Some of the younger children waddled around, playing, and squeaking in delight, while the older ones either carried supplies, cut grass, or assisted the women. All the women were dressed in long beige dresses. Their wrists and necks adorned with beaded jewelry with local designs steeped in Lakemore's history.

They came to a stop between two huts. One functioned as a station where the women molded clay into lamps, bowls, and other pieces, and the other hut was where they threaded jewelry.

"Can I help you?" A woman with dark skin and curly black hair dressed like the others came up to them. "I'm Zoe." There was a trace of a British accent in her voice.

"We are from the Lakemore PD." Mackenzie showed her their credentials but the woman wasn't concerned. "We are looking for the owner of this locket." She pulled up the picture of the locket on her phone.

Zoe took the phone and blinked. "That is one of our designs. It has a blue gemstone so she was probably working over there with perfumes." She gestured over to a hut next to the main one.

Mackenzie noticed the red gemstone in Zoe's locket. "Your locket has a red gemstone... what does that mean?"

"That means I'm kind of the manager around here." She

pinched the locket and winked at them. "You look familiar...
oh!" Her eyes widened. "Weren't you in that documentary
about a year or so ago?"

"Yes, sorry just getting back to your locket here. The colors
on the gemstones correspond to different activities?" Nick interjected, sensing Mackenzie's discomfort.

"We have so many things to do." Zoe shrugged. "The
company is getting bigger so we have to be more organized. Yes,
the blue corresponds to our aromatherapy branch. We have
about ten women working there. Though..." her eyebrows
furrowed, "no one reported a missing locket to me. The women
come to me with such things, so I assume this belonged to
someone who used to work here."

Two pieces of a puzzle slotted together. Whitney's sister
had told them that Whitney was missing for almost a year. Was
she at The Farm? Could that be the connection between their
two victims?

"Do you know a woman by the name of Whitney Smythe?"
Nick had read her mind.

"Yes." Zoe's eyes shimmered. "She was with us for almost a
year until she left about two months ago."

Mackenzie noted the change in Zoe's demeanor. Her tone
was no longer serene but cagey and curt, the emphasis on each
syllable shortened. "Was Whitney also working in
aromatherapy?"

"No, I believe she was assigned to pottery. She didn't have a
very sensitive nose."

"Is there anyone who recently left your Farm who worked
in the aromatherapy hut?"

Zoe bit back a smile. "Jennifer Peyton. She left seven
months ago."

"Why?"

A gentle breeze blew a lock of hair onto Zoe's face. She
tucked it behind her ear with a pinched smile. "I think it would

be better if Tobias answered these questions. Would you like to follow me to the main house?"

"Lead the way." Nick made a sweeping gesture. As soon as Zoe had her back to them, he whispered into Mackenzie's ear, "Did you catch that? Jennifer Peyton worked in aromatherapy."

"Camphor oil is popular in aromatherapy. We found trace evidence of that in the eye sockets of both Whitney and the second body. Jennifer might be our other victim. And our killer might be on this Farm."

FIFTEEN

Before they entered the main hut, Mackenzie felt vibrations in the ground reverberate up her legs. There was the sound of a drum beat coming from inside. The seconds between the beats stretching longer, pregnant with anticipation and dread.

Thump.

Thump.

Thump.

It wasn't the kind of beat that instilled any joy. It filled Mackenzie with unease, like needles swarming inside her chest. Suddenly, the sky above darkened into a steely gray, eclipsing the sun. Wind blew against her face, trying to keep her away from the ominous structure that lay ahead. There was a glimmer of resistance to the tug she felt. But the pull was too tempting and that glimmer died.

Thump.

Thump.

Thump.

Mackenzie inhaled deeply, her insides loosening, her lungs expanding, her bones liquefying. Everything merged into one—until she was just one soft muscle.

She surrendered to the beat of the drum. It carried her inside the hut with a towering roof. Timber beams weathered by time stretched overhead, forming an intricate lattice. Torch-lights danced on the rough-hewn walls, casting flickering shadows. The walls and pillars were engraved with ancient symbols and drawings. The smoldering scent of incense lingered in the air.

A small group of women stood in a circle, their lips moving in unison as they chanted something in a foreign language. Their timbre low, their voices ebbing and flowing.

Mackenzie and Nick followed Zoe who made a space for them in the circle so that they could also witness like the other women.

In the center of the circle was a bed. A man and a young woman were on the bed, naked and sweaty and making love. The man was Tobias Mathis. The women were watching him and the woman in what could only be described as a mating ritual.

Mackenzie was dumbfounded, unable to tear her gaze away from the scene before her. Her mouth was dry. Nick was standing right next to her. When his arm brushed against her, pleasure pulsed through her veins like quicksilver. She looked up at him and met his eyes.

Heat flooded her and she leaned closer. As did he.

The chanting stopped. The music stopped.

The invisible trance between them shattered, throwing them back to reality. They pulled apart, blinking and baffled.

Tobias Mathis was now on his feet, securing a robe around himself. The woman was being ushered away by the group of women. The only people left were Mackenzie, Nick, Tobias, and Zoe.

"Ah! We have guests." Tobias beamed at them without an ounce of awkwardness.

"These are detectives from the Lakemore PD." Zoe made the introductions. "I brought them straight here."

It took Mackenzie several seconds to regain her senses and collect her thoughts. There was still a lingering haze, similar to the feeling of waking up from a deep slumber. "Yes, Mr. Mathis. We have some questions. First of all, what was *that*?"

Tobias grinned. "That was our little community celebrating life... by creating one."

"What?" Nick blurted.

"Yes, hopefully she will be pregnant." He crossed his fingers and fetched himself a glass of water, which he poured from a clay jug. "Fresh from the river. Do you want some?"

"No, thanks." Nick looked at Mackenzie and mouthed *what*.

"We are a family here," Zoe explained, seeing their confusion. "We are not just a business. We are connected by deep bonds of sisterhood and motherhood. All the children in this Farm have been fathered by Tobias."

"That's..." Mackenzie started.

"Unusual?" Tobias raised an eyebrow.

"Creepy."

Tobias smirked haughtily. "It's not something everyone will understand, Detective Price. I don't blame you; in fact I pity you. You encounter the worst side of human beings and I focus on and hone their potential. You are surrounded by death and violence and betrayal. I am surrounded by life. Bountiful harvest in the fields. Art and creativity overflowing. But at the center of it is not me." He pressed his hand to his chest, shaking his head. "It's the female spirit."

"Only the females in your community," Nick pointed out.

"Inherent power and wisdom resides in the female spirit. We are creators and women are the most important creators to exist." He smiled dotingly at Zoe. "We celebrate the divine feminine energy that flows through every aspect of creation.

The best way to give back to Mother Nature is to give it more life."

"And you think that you are the chosen man to father all these kids?" Mackenzie challenged, glancing at some of them running around outside. "Why not let the women choose their own partners?"

"We view this process as an exchange of energies. This is no place for dominance or control." He made a sour face. "These women consent to procreating with me. They are free to leave if our beliefs don't align."

A part of Mackenzie was curious. But the dominant part of her knew she shouldn't engage with a madman. But was he as crazy as he seemed? She scanned Zoe—she had a sharp gaze, an intelligence in her face. Why was she mesmerized by this man's absurd ideologies?

"Wait a minute, you have children with all the women in this community?" Mackenzie repeated, a dreadful realization dawning on her.

"Yes, except for Zoe. She is our doula and my right hand. It would be inappropriate."

"Whitney Smythe and Jennifer Peyton. Both of them gave birth recently, this year."

Tobias pursed his lips and clicked his tongue. "Yes, they left us. One two months ago, and the other, I think, seven or eight months ago?"

"They gave birth here?" Nick looked around.

"Yes. Surrounded by their sisters," Zoe said. "One of them went to medical school but didn't practice medicine. She helps with the deliveries."

"Where are their babies?" Nick asked.

"Here and well taken care of," Zoe assured them.

"We'd like to take a look for ourselves," Nick said.

Tobias made a face but Zoe beamed, throwing Tobias a reassuring look. She led the way outside the hut to another one right behind it. Mackenzie didn't know what to expect. She trailed behind Nick, whose hands were balled up inside his pockets. Being a father himself, he was more tuned to these matters.

As soon as Mackenzie stepped through the threshold, currents swept across her skin. The chamber was like a nursery from a horror movie. Wooden cradles lined the walls. Flickering candlelight cast strange shadows across the room. The faint scent of baby powder intermingled with earthy scents infused the warm air. Three women clad in simple dresses moved among the cradles, rocking them, their fingers brushing the edges of the blankets with tenderness.

"It's naptime," Zoe whispered. Mackenzie and Nick padded their way through the hut, looking at the babies. "We have only five currently. Another one on the way. The youngest is three months old. Whitney's son." She stopped next to a cradle.

Mackenzie peered in and found a baby gurgling. His eyes enlarged when he saw her and he began to coo. Before she could react, one of the women swooped in with a formula bottle to feed him.

In the corner was a section with toys and books. The only colorful spot in this otherwise dreary hut. Mackenzie and Nick inspected the babies and found them healthy, well-fed, with no signs of neglect or abuse. The cradles were hand-carved but sturdy. Even the baby monitors were in order. But the nursery still made Mackenzie's skin crawl. Nick's body was wound tight. He felt it too.

"Jennifer's daughter is now over a year old." Zoe pointed at a baby waddling outside with the help of a woman.

"We'll need to get their DNA samples for verification," Mackenzie croaked as they left the hut. "We'll send a team later."

"Certainly." Tobias smiled with pride. "They are my blood, Detectives. I take very good care of them."

"It's like he's raising them to sacrifice them," Nick muttered low enough only for Mackenzie to hear.

Mackenzie turned to Tobias and Zoe. "Whitney was murdered. And we believe Jennifer Peyton was also murdered, but we will have to do a DNA test first."

"*Murdered?*" Tobias gagged and shivered. "That's an abomination. Taking away a life."

"Why did they leave your community?" Mackenzie asked. It was evident to her that Tobias was only capable of expressing two emotions: pity and arrogance. He pitied those who chose to live differently and exhibited an inflated sense of self. Like he viewed himself as a messiah.

"They didn't want to continue living this simple life. They missed their phones and laptops, parties, cigarettes, and alcohol." Tobias shrugged like he didn't understand the appeal. "So they left. Our harmonious community isn't about ownership. People are free to leave whenever they want."

"And they just left their babies here?" Nick couldn't hide the disbelief in his voice.

"Detective Blackwood, the women who seek refuge and comfort here are often troubled," Tobias explained. "They struggle with addictions. In their original state, they wouldn't be suitable mothers. Here we condition them to embrace their femininity, we nurture their souls and make sure they live a healthy lifestyle. Those babies are safer here than they would be in the outside world with their mothers."

"We haven't heard or had any contact with Whitney and Jennifer since they left us. I can confirm they didn't return to The Farm to see their babies," Zoe informed them. She began to neatly fold the bedsheets and comforter. Tobias watched her with a puffy chest and a half-smile.

"Can you think of anyone who would want to hurt them?

Did they argue with anyone here?" Mackenzie asked, controlling her grimace.

"No. We live together in love and service to each other and Mother Nature."

Mackenzie wanted to throw up. She wanted to go home and shower for hours and forget about this pocket of Lakemore run by a delusional charlatan.

Zoe began lighting some candles to dilute the musky odor. "Tobias, I think we need more sheets. Should I send Caleb?"

Nick's eyes narrowed into slits. Mackenzie registered the name. Her first instinct was to dismiss the possibility. But she couldn't help voicing the question—"Caleb who?"

"Caleb Mercer. He doesn't live with us but helps out," Tobias replied.

It was the same name. It had to be the same person. Zoe's next words confirmed it. "He's an ex-cop. We are a community of so many women and children. He kind of acts as our bodyguard."

Mackenzie's stomach did somersaults. Caleb Mercer barreling his way back into Nick's life at the same time that two women from The Farm he worked at had been murdered didn't feel like a coincidence anymore.

SIXTEEN

Later that night, Mackenzie got home, her head crowded with many thoughts.

Caleb Mercer worked at The Farm.

Whitney and Jennifer both lived at The Farm where they gave birth and then left.

The MO was the same as Grace Fontaine's murder thirty-one years ago.

Jake Lawson had an alibi for the night of Grace's murder but it had got lost at the station.

She floated through the foyer, dropping her keys in the drawer and shrugging off her coat and jacket. Her mind trying to disentangle the overlapping facts of this case. But they were too tightly wound into a knot. Whenever Mackenzie tried to focus on one thread, she found herself thinking about another one.

Ignoring the constant buzzing ringing in her ears from the stress, she poured herself a glass of red wine. She leaned against the counter and took a leisurely sip, the velvety texture coating her tongue. Through the window, she observed her front yard. The grass needed to be mowed. The flowerbeds were infested with weeds. The weeping willow was arched, mourning in grace. Her house was clean but cluttered. A few dirty dishes lay in the sink, fresh laundry sitting on the couch still not put away. She could spot some dust on the coffee table.

Mackenzie's nerves felt raw and scratchy under her skin. Jitteriness bubbled inside her. Stillness was a new emotion to her. If she wasn't thinking hard then she was moving fast. There was always some muscle that was working. Because stillness paved the way for old memories and regrets. But tonight, Mackenzie spent a few minutes trying to stay still.

She planted herself next to the window and stared outside as the weeping willow got battered by the rain. Wind whooshed, shaking the window in the frame. But soon the storm began to retreat. In a few short minutes, her front yard was sitting still again and not on the verge of getting destroyed. All she needed was some patience.

Her phone rang. It was Nick.

"I can't sleep."

She chewed her lip. This was uncharacteristic of him. "Do you want to come over?"

"Can't. Luna is sleeping here tonight." He sighed. "I contacted child protective services. They said they'd pay a visit to The Farm first thing tomorrow and check on our victims' babies as well. I told Dylan to call off looking into any missing infants."

She curled her legs under her, embracing the cozy night. "Good. It's worrying to think those kids will be raised in isolation by a creepy man who thinks he's doing a service to the world by spreading his seed and having weird sex rituals."

He chuckled but then it faded. "We also have to talk to Caleb. Ask him if he knows anything about Whitney and Jennifer."

"Hmm." She ignored the queasiness in her gut. "So, our

victims knew each other from The Farm. That's one connection solidified. But how are they related to Grace Fontaine?"

"The Farm didn't exist thirty-one years ago. I ran Jennifer Peyton through the DMV and found her next of kin. There was a fiancé she was living with but they broke up when she left for The Farm."

"Oh, wow."

"Yeah. Hopefully, he might know something." He stifled a yawn. "What do you think we should do about Jake Lawson?"

Her chest rattled with a shaky breath. "I can't think of a reason why Russell would lie to us about Jake's alibi. He must have shared this information with Barry too back in the day."

"But Barry believed the police after Grace's blood was found on Lawson. And now with similar murders happening again, Barry reached out to Russell wondering the same thing we are."

"Sully and Ortiz made a mistake," Mackenzie finished the grim thought.

"Sully is already not himself. He'll be devastated when we tell him what Russell told us."

Or he might lie, she thought. Nick wouldn't understand. Her partner always saw the best in everyone. He was kind—*too* kind. But in their line of work, kindness could cloud judgment. She had seen how her own mother, despite her good intentions, was driven to commit heinous acts.

"We should also call Mike Ortiz when we tell Sully," Mackenzie decided. "Ortiz was the detective on the case."

Nick hesitated. "I think we should give Sully a heads-up at least. He'd appreciate it."

She rubbed her fingertips together. "I'm sure he would. But we should go by the book. You know how Rivera can get."

Nick conceded, although he didn't sound too happy with the plan. But Mackenzie could sniff out lies when she was surrounded by them. She had grown up being more intimate with dishonesty and hidden motives. Her senses were the most heightened when secrets loomed like shadows.

Sully was hiding something. She was going to use Ortiz to throw him off and hopefully get him to reveal the truth. Because something more must have happened thirty-one years ago which was why everything was happening again.

Her grandmother, Eleanor, used to always say, "History will keep repeating itself until the lesson it's trying to teach is learned."

NOVEMBER 6

Mackenzie stared at the grainy video playing on Clint's laptop. "What am I looking at?"

"I'm not sure. It's a strange one," Clint said. "I pulled up what I could from the camera on that street around where Whitney was found."

The footage was dark with occasional illumination from the taillights of cars speeding by. Static kept cutting across the footage. The timestamp showed the night of the murder—approximately the time Whitney left the party in a good mood, presumably to meet someone.

Clint, the spectacled IT guy with a long neck, cracked his eyelids open and squirted drops on them. "I can't clean it up more than this."

"Long night?" Mackenzie eyed his dark circles.

"Sully's been on my case," He complained gruffly. "Do you know how difficult it is to extract usable data from the cloud? We need special software."

"Do you have it?"

Clint laughed and pointed at his surroundings. "I work in a basement. We need to ask the FBI."

Mackenzie sighed in frustration and continued staring at the screen, eagerly waiting for Whitney to show up. Her eyes darted all over the screen trying to catch even a suspicious shadow. After about ten minutes, a woman appeared on screen —running down the road.

Mackenzie's pulse ticked faster. "That must be her!"

Clint paused the video and played it frame by frame. It was hard to make out her face but she was wearing the same clothes and boots that Mackenzie recognized.

"She is running from someone," she whispered.

But in the next five seconds, a strong gust of wind blew, making the pole bend at an angle. It came crashing down and the video abruptly ended.

"What happened?"

"Lakemore's weather happened."

Mackenzie slumped on the chair, deflated. "Is this all we got?"

"This was the only camera in the vicinity. The storm knocked out a bunch of poles in the area."

She rubbed her temples. "We were *so* close. She was literally getting chased by someone and the damn storm ruined our shot!"

Clint looked uncomfortable, peering at her over his glasses. "Can I do anything else?"

Mackenzie immediately clammed up. Her frustration locked the muscles in her face. No one at work was used to seeing any display of emotion from her except for determination. She looked and functioned like a robot. She didn't laugh, she didn't cry, she didn't slouch, she didn't tire, she didn't get frustrated, she didn't lose patience. She was Mad Mack.

"Thanks, Clint." She stood up and straightened her blazer. "Hopefully, you can get something from her phone."

On her way back to her cubicle, her mind wandered to Nick —it was routine for him to call or message her first thing in the morning while she was out on her run. He would always suggest traveling to work together and she would always say no.

But today she didn't hear from him. It was a small deviation but that's how things always began to unravel—slowly and inconspicuously.

"Detective Price." Lieutenant Rivera was at her cubicle dressed in red button-down, her hand resting on her hip. "I was just looking for you."

"I was with Clint. What's up?"

Rivera offered her a cup of coffee. "Want some?"

"I don't drink coffee."

She smirked. "You really are mad. What updates do you have for me? Sully canceled our briefing yesterday, and today he's too busy getting some approvals."

"We identified the other victim, Jennifer Peyton. We just have to get the DNA sample from her kid to confirm—"

"Ah, yes, Nick is there at The Farm with CPS and Becky."

That was news to Mackenzie. She had messaged Nick but he hadn't replied. "Right." She wavered, not knowing what to do with her hands.

Rivera's sharp eyes made quick work of her response. "You didn't know?"

"I must have missed his message. Busy morning." She schooled her face to show indifference.

But Rivera was a calculating woman. She didn't tolerate nonsense and had the nose of a hound when it came to sniffing out a lie. "You and Nick have been partners for almost a decade. You are bound to hit rough patches. Detectives partnered together—it's a lot like a marriage."

"Well, I've already been through one divorce," she muttered without thinking and instantly bit her tongue. "Sorry, that was inappropriate—"

"Are you that worried about your partnership with Nick? Do you think it's on the verge of breaking?"

She and Nick hadn't even quarreled. Perhaps that was the problem. The problem was that they weren't fighting, They weren't talking, and Nick was withdrawing. Something Mackenzie had done a long time ago when she mistakenly believed he had betrayed her. But she remembered how he had persisted. How he would try to talk to her despite her being short. How he would watch her when he thought she wasn't looking.

"No," she asserted. "We are fine."

Rivera narrowed her eyes but nodded. "An observation that sometimes helps me manage. Men don't handle emotional friction as well as women do."

Mackenzie cracked a smile. "Maybe not."

"They'll find corners to hide in but women will encourage dialogue and cooperation."

Mackenzie wasn't sure how much she agreed. She spent her entire life hiding behind a fortress because she was afraid of the world. "I suppose."

"Coming back to Jennifer Peyton. What do we have?"

"I contacted her ex-fiancé. Sean. He's on his way to the station."

"Did you run a background check on her?"

"I did. The sheriff's department had a file on her." Mackenzie showed her the monitor. "She was busted for possession when she was a teenager a couple times. No arrests after that."

"Her profile is similar to Whitney Smythe then. Both have a troubled history and potentially unstable childhoods."

"That's why they were drawn to The Farm. Tobias's promise of a community and familial bonds compensates for everything they lacked growing up."

"Keep me apprised." Rivera started to turn but paused. "Do you know what's going on with Sully?"

"Sorry?"

"I'm not a fool, Detective Price, and neither are you. Do I need to be worried that my sergeant isn't doing his job?"

Mackenzie's breath hitched like a shard of glass had lodged in her throat. She shook her head; it felt heavy. "You can trust Sully."

An hour later, a short, beefy man with muscles bulging under his polka-dotted shirt arrived at the station, his expression wary. His hands were inside his pockets, his shoulders too stiff like he was contemplating rushing out the door at any moment.

"Are you Sean?" Mackenzie asked. "Jennifer Peyton's ex-fiancé?"

Sean blinked repeatedly. His eyes beady through the glasses. "Y-yes. You are Detective Price?"

"Yes, please follow me." She escorted him to the conference room, noting his skittish mannerisms and incessant swallowing. She directed him to a seat. "I'm very sorry, Sean. But we found Jennifer. She was murdered."

The tip of his nose turned red. "I-I see... what happened to her?"

"We are working on that. What I'd like to know is when was the last time you saw or spoke with her?"

He leaned back, his fingers drumming on the table. "Two years ago."

"What was your last conversation about?"

"We were fighting." His lips quivered; tears welled in his eyes. "She was always unhappy. Everything would be fine between us but she would self-sabotage. That one time we went to the cottage with my family for a weekend. Everything was going great but then she decided to show up drunk at breakfast in front of my whole family."

"Was she an alcoholic?"

"Yes. On and off over the years. Toward the end of our relationship, it was becoming a problem."

"Did you ever try contacting her after she ended things with you?"

"Of course I did." He sniffled. "I called but her phone was unreachable. I talked to her friends but they said she'd probably ditched town."

"She went to The Farm."

"What's 'The Farm'?"

"Do you know Tobias Mathis?" Mackenzie said, avoiding the question.

"Yes. The one who sells all that jewelry and honey. Jennifer used to buy candles from his store."

"I see. Did she ever mention him?"

He looked puzzled. "No. Should she have?"

Mackenzie braced herself for the uncomfortable conversation they were about to have. "That's where she went. She was living with him as part of his community... she gave birth approximately nine months ago."

Sean's eyes bulged. "*What?*"

"She left The Farm seven months ago."

He scrambled for words, his mouth opening and closing like a fish. "That's *bizarre*. No, she didn't. Where's her child?"

"At The Farm. CPS is over there right now investigating."

"She left her child there?"

"That's what it seems like."

He guffawed. "No, no, that's not possible. She wouldn't do that. I *knew* her. She wouldn't abandon her baby like that at some *Farm*." He scrunched his face in disgust.

Mackenzie took a deep breath. "Sometimes we think we know someone but... she did join a cult. Perhaps—"

He removed his glasses in frustration. "No, no, you don't understand. Jennifer was adopted. Her birth parents abandoned her outside some church! That's one of the reasons why being around my family upset her. It triggered unresolved abandonment issues. Trust me. She wouldn't have left her child by choice."

Mackenzie nodded. She didn't doubt he believed what he said. But there was also the possibility that he was wrong about Jennifer. Why would she abandon her child just like Whitney did? Did they sign something that took away their legal rights? They knew each other from their time at The Farm—did they stay in touch once they'd left?

SEVENTEEN

Mackenzie brought the car to a screeching halt. The modest white house before her was made of weathered planks, fractured windows lousily taped with tattered curtains behind them, an uneven porch with a weathered welcome mat. Overhead electric wires were tangled and clustered. Weeds and unkempt grass encroached upon the house, brushing against the peeling paint. Like nature was reclaiming its territory, trying to get rid of the ugly sight.

When Mackenzie climbed out the car, she was greeted by flurries dancing in the air. The glum weather of Lakemore was grating her nerves. It rained occasionally as it always did but the storms lacked their usual ferocity. Even the wind came and went in squally dusts. Then they would stop suddenly as if they were being reprimanded. Mackenzie looked up at the soot-like clouds suspended in the sky. Even the weather was on edge. Waiting for the right time to lose control.

She jumped when her phone rang. It was Nick.

"Where are you?" he asked brusquely.

"I just got to Jennifer Peyton's address. Peterson got the judge to sign a warrant."

"Why didn't you tell me you were going there? I've been looking for you."

"I would have but everyone knew you went to The Farm, apart from me. What about that?" she challenged.

Silence.

"It must have slipped my mind."

"I'm sure it did. I'll see you at the station later." Before he could reply, she hung up. All the different ways she could have responded pinballed around in her head. She slid her focus back to Jennifer's house as she put on gloves and fiddled with the lock.

The house was in such a poor condition that the door unlocked easily without Mackenzie having to use one of her bobby pins. She twisted the knob and pushed it hard enough. It opened with a rattle. A puff of dust blasted in her face and she coughed.

It was a one-story house on a small piece of land. She flipped a switch and light flooded the room. Jennifer's place had been turned over.

Mackenzie's instincts took hold. Her focus sharpened. Her hand went to her gun as she entered the house. The couch had been shifted. The carpet upturned revealing the underside. A single chair knocked over. All the drawers in the kitchen cabinet were open.

She made her way to the single bedroom. It was in the same chaotic state. Someone had turned over every piece of furniture and items looking for something. Jennifer's green sheets lay rumpled on the floor. Her toiletries splayed on the tiled floor. All the clothing from her dresser sprawled in a chaotic display.

Mackenzie tucked her Glock back into the waistband of her trousers and called Dispatch to send over CSU for forensic support. Her gaze drifted around the house. What was the perpetrator looking for? And did they find it?

As Mackenzie waited for CSU to show up, she wandered

around the house, hoping to find something the perpetrator might have missed, or anything interesting in this bland life that Jennifer had returned to after spending more than a year at The Farm.

But nothing stood out. Jennifer Peyton lived the same life as most of the residents of Lakemore. Stagnant and constantly struggling to stay afloat. The lack of motivation or creativity was evident in the dullness of the house.

Sweat matted Mackenzie's back and plopped in beads on her hairline. She shrugged off her blue blazer, wondering why it was so hot, when it struck her. Where was the HVAC unit?

She searched for any doors in the house that might lead to the basement but found none. She stepped outside, relieved by the chill air cooling her skin. She circled the house looking for an external access point.

Behind the house, shielded by overgrown vegetation and layer of dirt, was a small hatchway. Gripping firmly, she pulled at the rusted handle. It gave way easily to reveal a dark staircase that led to the basement.

Mackenzie ventured down the steps, using the flashlight on her phone to guide the way. The scent of damp earth assaulted her senses. The deeper she went, the more the sounds magnified—dripping water, mice rustling, pipes murmuring.

The last time she was in a basement she was being held against her will. She had almost died. Her muscles coiled like springs ready to release. The memory kept pressing into her—heavy and brutal. It was clamoring to be acknowledged. She felt like she was being crushed. She closed her eyes. Instead of ignoring it like habit dictated, she let the memory ripple through her.

Then she was able to breathe more easily and bring her focus back to Jennifer. The earth was soft underneath her shoes. There wasn't enough light in the basement and she could only make out the shadows of the water pumps. She groped blindly in the dark for a light and felt a string. She pulled on it.

Mackenzie staggered back. The wall opposite was completely covered in pictures and news article clippings. Jennifer had been investigating something. And it all boiled down to one person—Rose.

EIGHTEEN

Mackenzie stirred her hot chocolate. The sound of the stirrer clinked against her mug. It was a Christmas gift Sully had given her last year. It said Mad Mack. While she had given him an instruction manual on how to build his own telescope—which he did, following which he spent an entire week first getting acquainted with astronomy and then astrology. And then even the stars couldn't hold his attention.

Now Sully's demons kept him preoccupied. Through the glass walls of the conference room, she watched Sully engage in an animated conversation with Captain Murphy before the latter slammed the door shut in his face.

"What are you planning?" Nick leaned against the door; his arms crossed.

"What?"

"You have that look on your face."

"What look?" She looked away, hating how he could read like her a book.

"The look you have when we play chess and you make a move thinking I'll fall for it. And then I pretend to."

She rolled her eyes. "Please. Tell yourself that."

He smiled and tucked a file under his arm. "The CSU is dusting Jennifer's house for prints and DNA. Jenna and Peterson are working on whatever information Jennifer had collected on Baby Rose."

"What happened with the CPS at The Farm?"

"Whitney's daughter and Jennifer's son are both in good health, and so are all the other kids. CPS is still looking into the legality surrounding custody but none of the children showed any signs of abuse. No one is malnourished. They are all vaccinated."

"Well, that's good."

"Yeah. At least there's that."

"Jennifer lived alone. There was no evidence of anyone else living in that house. So why would she keep her investigation in that smelly basement with mice?"

"Rats," he corrected.

"I don't know the difference."

"You know how mass spectrometry works and yet you can't tell the difference between mice and rats?" He restrained a smile.

"I don't find animals interesting," she deadpanned. "Anyway, do you see my point?"

He pocketed his hands. "I do. She wanted to keep the investigation hidden."

"From whom?"

"The person who ransacked her house maybe?" he ventured.

"Could this be the same person who was following Whitney?"

They continued to bounce ideas off each other before Mackenzie noticed something from the corner of her eye.

Mike Ortiz had arrived at the station accompanied by a young woman—his daughter Violet. He was shorter than she had expected but had a solid build. His eyes were dark and intense. A straight nose. Features rough around the edges but the posture and presence of someone in command and disciplined. Dyed black hair sleeked back. His smile was warm as he greeted some passing officers.

Violet was tall and slender. Her hair fell to her waist in loose curls with the tips dyed pink. She was dressed in a flowery, cotton dress, and she kept grasping at a straw bag hung over her shoulder. While her father chatted with a detective from Special Investigations, Violet's blue eyes flitted around the station in quick movements, trying to latch onto something but at the same time avoiding contact with the world. The minute she looked at Mackenzie, her gaze dropped despite the timid smile that curled up her lips.

Nick stiffened. "You called Ortiz!"

"It's time, Nick. We need to get to the bottom of this."

"Yeah," he admitted reluctantly. "I'll get Sully."

Mackenzie put on her rehearsed bright smile and proceeded to greet Mike. "Mr. Ortiz, I'm Detective Mackenzie Price."

He shook her hand. "This is my daughter Violet. She gave me a ride so I thought I'd show her around my old place of work. It's changed quite a bit."

"Nice to meet you, Violet," Mackenzie said but Violet's eyes were downcast. She stepped back and tugged at the hem of her sleeve and adjusted her glasses.

Ortiz was apologetic. "Violet is shy. She takes time to open up."

"All good. Let's go to the conference room. No one will disturb us there. Can I get you guys anything? Coffee? Water?"

"I'm okay, thanks. Violet?"

Violet shook her head.

"It's confidential information so, Violet, would you mind waiting here?"

Violet nodded meekly, still not making eye contact with

Mackenzie. Mike patted Violet's arm before following Mackenzie.

"How can I help you, Detective Price? You weren't very clear on the phone." Ortiz took a seat at the table.

"You must have seen the news. We have two bodies on our hands, each missing an eye."

"Yes." Ortiz grimaced. "It's bloodcurdling."

"I believe you had a similar case some thirty years ago. Grace Fontaine." She watched Ortiz like a hawk. He was a detective too. He would have excellent control over his reactions.

His forehead crumpled. "Yes. But her murderer was imprisoned. I believe he died."

On cue, Nick entered followed by Sully. When Sully's and Ortiz's eyes collided, alarm mounted behind their eyes. They weren't expecting that. Mackenzie exhaled sharply. This is what she wanted. That first dent in that wall that Sully had resurrected around him. Now she had to strike while the iron was still hot.

She interlaced her fingers and gave them both her most fierce expression. "We have reason to believe that Jake Lawson, the man who was convicted of Grace's murder, might have been innocent."

Sully couldn't contain his devastation. He fell onto a chair, his mind racing. His face contorted. Panic began spreading across Ortiz's features as he raced to control it. He shifted, he blinked furiously, he fumbled for words.

"Why would you say that?" Ortiz finally found his voice.

"Barry Fontaine hired a private detective, Russell Grant, thirty-one years ago," Nick explained. "He discovered proof of Jake Lawson's alibi. In fact he dropped off the video with the evidence at the station but it was misplaced."

"Video?" Sully was horrified. "What video?"

Was Sully truly in the dark?

A tense silence followed. Ortiz looked over his shoulder at Violet, worry written all over on his face. She stood against a wall, trying to blend into her surroundings. When one of the officers walking by stopped and said something to her, she turned away, an unexplainable twitch possessing her fingers and face.

"Violet was bullied when she was young." Ortiz noticed Mackenzie watching her. "She was always... socially challenged and those mean kids at school didn't help." He released a long-drawn breath. "Please. Just keep my daughter out of this."

"Did you know about the existence of such a video?" Mackenzie asked.

"Yes," he confessed in a small voice. "I did."

Sully glared at him. "What the hell are you talking about, Mike?"

But Ortiz ignored Sully. His shameful gaze focused only on Mackenzie and Nick. "I never saw the video or got my hands on it. Russell Grant had approached me about it back then. We were getting a lot of tips about Baby Rose. Finding her was top priority. You know how it is with a missing baby. I told him I'd get to it when I could. By the time there was room to breathe... I didn't know where the video was. It was lost."

"How does a piece of evidence get lost at the station?" Mackenzie was appalled. "We have due processes to—"

"We were understaffed," Ortiz shot back. "*Severely*. There was a missing baby whose mother had been murdered. Come on, Sully, tell them! How many times was I, a detective, on patrol because of staff shortages? The chaos the station was in those days?"

But Sully wasn't listening. He was getting riled up. Mackenzie could feel the charge building inside him.

Now was the time.

Mackenzie presented three pictures. Whitney. Jennifer.

Grace. All of them dead and missing an eye. "This isn't a coincidence."

Ortiz recoiled. Being retired for some time now, he wasn't so used to the violence anymore.

"And don't tell me that there's a copycat thirty-one years later." She directed her burning gaze at Sully. "Also, did I mention that one of our victims—Jennifer Peyton—was looking into Baby Rose?"

Ortiz whispered aghast, "*What?*"

"None of this is coincidence. Something went wrong thirty-one years ago. What was it?" Mackenzie asked, raising her voice.

Sully burst. He'd finally had enough. It poured out—all that bottled guilt. "We framed Jake Lawson for Grace's murder by planting her blood on him. Now you are saying that Jake had an alibi that was missed. So who killed Grace and took Baby Rose?"

NINETEEN

THIRTY-ONE YEARS AGO

Sully

Ortiz paced back and forth. The tension in the room was palpable. Sully swallowed hard, standing his ground.

"This is our only way out, Sully." Ortiz was desperate. "We frame this guy and make it stick. It's our ticket out of this."

Sully shook his head. They had been arguing about this for days. But something about this argument felt different. It was the exhaustion in Sully's bones from working day and night to catch Grace Fontaine's killer. It was that constant pressure behind his eyes whenever he closed them. It was that impending sense of doom as the clock kept ticking and they were no closer to getting any answers.

"Look at this town!" Ortiz dragged Sully to the window. There was a vigil outside the station. The entire town had gathered outside the Lakemore PD holding signs and pictures of Grace and Baby Rose. Some of them jeered and protested loudly—denouncing the police for doing nothing, for being useless, for not doing their jobs. But most of them sat on the ground silently, just looking ahead with hope in their eyes that was slowly starting to dim.

It was the quiet ones that felt like a punch to the gut to Sully.

"Every husband is worried for his wife. Every parent is worried for their child. This is the first time a baby has gone missing in our town! Baby Rose isn't just Barry and Grace's. She's *ours* now." Tears gathered in Ortiz's eyes.

"I get it!" Sully clenched his fists. "I do. But we can't *frame* someone."

"Not someone. Jake Lawson. He's a serial rapist. He was a plumber at the Fontaines *and* he doesn't have an alibi. It's perfect!"

"We are *police officers*," Sully yelled, trying to ignore his weakening resolve. "We follow the law. This is fucked up, Mike." He was panting now, vaguely registering that he had just sworn at his superior.

But Ortiz didn't mind. "I've been at this for years, Sully. You are new. Hell, this is your first case. What we do is not always black and white. I know you joined the force thinking you'll be a hero. I thought that too. But then I learned the hard way that in this job sometimes you have to make the difficult decision—"

"There's nothing difficult about this." Sully's voice was unwavering. "This is just wrong."

"I know it's wrong!" Ortiz cried. "You know what is *more* wrong? Us not giving Barry a chance to move on with his life. Us not giving this town *hope*. Baby Rose is already missing. The least we can do is give them Grace's killer. And the killer is a serial rapist who, should I repeat for the millionth time, doesn't have an alibi."

"We'll find another way! We'll work together, dig deeper."

"That's exactly what we have been doing! This is the real

world, Sully. You are new. You are naïve. Sometimes... we never find the truth. This will haunt us forever. Unsolved cases follow us like shadows. But does this really need to haunt Barry and this town? Can't this just be *our* burden?"

Sully ran his hand through his hair. He was being pulled in all directions. Fatigue clung to his eyes like heavy curtains. Ortiz kept filling his ears, telling him how Sully was new and too idealistic, how this was the only way out.

How sometimes hope must triumph justice.

To his horror, he felt his strength fading. Their voices clashed repeatedly until Sully became hoarse.

This was Mike Ortiz. The lead detective on this case. His mentor. His first friend in Lakemore. A police officer everyone admired. Was Sully being unreasonable? The long hours, the sleepless nights, the pressure from the brass, the slander by the media, the public outcry—it all weighed heavy on him. He wasn't prepared for this.

It was only his first case.

Eventually, Ortiz fell onto a chair, shoulders slumped. "My wife's pregnant."

"Mike! That's... congrats." He smiled despite their fight.

"We might just make it this time." A hopeful smile pulled on his lips. "The doctors are optimistic. After three miscarriages, this is a blessing. We'll relocate to the east coast temporarily so that her sister can help out."

"I'm happy for you." Sully clasped his shoulders.

"I'll retire."

He gasped. "What?"

But there was peace on Ortiz's face. "I know it's too early for retirement. I'll find something else to do. But I want to focus on my family, man, and not do anything dangerous. Once this is over, I'll hand in my resignation and just be with my baby... I just can't do this without you, Sully."

Something broke inside Sully. He knew this was going to haunt him. That a part of his soul would be blackened forever. "Okay, Mike. I'm with you. Whatever you decide to do."

TWENTY

Like the snap of a rubber band, there was a thunderous downpour over Lakemore when Sully finished telling his side of the story. Rain fell in torrents. Lightning streaked the darkened sky in jagged flashes of brilliance. Thunder rumbled in the distance.

Mackenzie felt the harsh truth deep in her bones. Something shattered inside her as she stared passively at Sully. The sergeant she had always trusted and looked up to, the one who often corrected her when she made a mistake, that solid, dependable figure in her life—he was corrupt.

"Don't look at me like that, Mack," Sully whispered, looking down. "Please don't."

Ortiz jumped in, still trying to justify their actions. "It's not like we framed an innocent man. He had raped more than four women!"

"That's what we should do. Pin crimes on criminals. Take the easy way out." Mackenzie slammed the file shut.

"You don't know what it was like back then." Ortiz's eyes bulged. "We weren't used to handling cases that big—"

"I don't want to hear it." She raised her hand. "I'm sure you think you did the right thing, and now we have two women who are dead."

What irked Mackenzie was the blaring silence from Nick who was standing next to her. He rubbed his fingertips together, a contemplative look taking hold of his angular face. Why wasn't he as angry as she was?

"Sometimes hope must come before justice," Ortiz said. "And... I take full responsibility for this." Sully opened his mouth but Ortiz cut him off. "No. I was the detective on the case. You were just out of the academy. This is on me."

Anger bubbled inside Mackenzie. "Well, you can play the blame game later. But we have a case to solve thanks to your massive fuckup."

"Were there any other suspects?" Nick asked.

"None." Sully sighed. "Neighbors saw nothing. Grace got along with everyone. Barry didn't notice any suspicious activity leading up to the day of the murder. Everyone in Grace's life was shocked by this."

"Why did you zero in on Jake?"

"There were no signs of a break-in," Ortiz recalled. "We concluded that Grace must have known her killer and let him in. We began looking at friends and acquaintances when we found out that Jake had fixed a pipe for them a week earlier. Turned out not only did he have a damning criminal record, but he also didn't have an alibi."

"For years, I told myself that maybe it really was Lawson." Sully spoke in a thick voice, his face twisted in pain. "Even though the MO was so different and with Baby Rose missing... I knew it didn't make much sense, but I told myself it must be him. That we'd ended up framing the real killer."

"And when Whitney's body showed up with the same MO, that rattled you." Nick nodded solemnly. "It made you revisit the worst decision of your life."

"An MO like that is more typical of a serial killer. When

there were no more killings like that after Grace, it reinforced my belief that we did catch the right guy."

"That's why you were so keen on finding out what was used to remove the eye? You were hoping that if it didn't match the evidence found on Grace then maybe this was someone else."

"Yes." Sully's eyes kept flitting back to Mackenzie, waiting for her to say something.

But Mackenzie didn't know what she felt. Numbness had spread across her synapses while her blood sizzled hot. Her body and her mind stood at odds. Icy detachment and pulsating fury.

"We'll need to open the files and go through everything again." Nick muttered to Mackenzie.

"B-but what does that mean for us?" Ortiz asked helplessly, gesturing at himself and Sully. "Please don't tell anyone about this."

"The statute of limitations for tampering with physical evidence is three years for felonies," Mackenzie replied, her jaw tight. "You don't have to worry about going to jail."

"That's not what this is about. My daughter..." Ortiz jutted his thumb to the common area where Violet stood awkwardly. "She's all I have. My wife died many years ago." Tears collected in the corners of his eyes. "Do you know what she and I say to each other every day? It's you and me against the world." A wan smile crossed his face, his hands fidgeted. "I don't want our lives to be disrupted. Even if I don't go to jail... I just want peace."

Mackenzie observed Ortiz. His aging face contrasting against a strong physique—he looked like someone who survived on scraps after life had snatched away almost everything from him. He and his wife had tried for a child for years and now all he had left was Violet, standing on the ruins of all they had lost.

This would destroy Sully's career. But he didn't need to remind them. His beseeching eyes sent the message loud and clear. For thirty years, Sully had carried this secret. So much time had passed and there were no more murders of that kind that the memory of what he did must have lodged itself deep in those dark recesses of his mind.

Until Whitney showed up dead and then Jennifer.

Mackenzie pushed back her chair and shot out of it. She marched out of the conference room, pushing past Austin who called after her, but she didn't stop. She flung open the door to the bathroom and ordered the deputy inside to leave.

Once she was alone, she paced the room, trying to burn the charge building in her. Her vision swam. She leaned against the sink and stared at her reflection in the mirror. Her face was gaunt, her skin pallid. Her red hair pulled tightly into a high ponytail. Her makeup minimal. But something had shifted. Something monumental. Her place of work, her sanctuary desecrated.

Seconds later, Nick barged in. "What happened to you?"

"I don't know." She dragged her hands down her face. "I... I just can't look at him."

He winced. "Mack... he was manipulated by his handler—"

"You're going to make excuses for him?" She was appalled. "Seriously?"

"I'm not making excuses for him. What he did was deplorable. But you of all people should understand that people make mistakes."

Words died in her throat. Nick had brought it up for the first time since she confided in him about burying her father in the woods with her mother when she was only twelve years old.

Seeing her face, he backpedaled. "I didn't mean it like—"

"It's fine." It was too late. She had hardened to a stone. "We're going to have to look at all the Fontaine case files again. Maybe recruit Austin to help out since we have a lot on our plate already."

"Mack, please." He stepped forward as if to touch her. She

flinched and left the restroom. As the door closed behind her, she heard Nick curse under his breath.

The clock struck 10 p.m. It had been hours since Mackenzie and Nick dismissed Ortiz and his daughter. Sully had retreated into his office. Despite the late hour, the office was still bustling. Rain battered on the windows. The radio crackled with news that there were several road closures in town. To everyone's dismay, the game between the Sharks and Riverview's Ravines was canceled.

"Damn it!" Troy threw down his pen dramatically. "We had bets on this!"

"Yeah, you should be grateful. Now you won't owe me a hundred," Finn quipped.

Mackenzie was engrossed in reading the case files from Grace Fontaine's homicide. She had pulled the files from the database and spent the last three hours reading every single statement from everyone who had been questioned thirty-years ago. One of them could be the murderer. The files could contain some information that Ortiz and Sully had missed.

Her computer chimed with a notification. It was an email from the crime lab in Seattle.

"Anthony is also burning the midnight oil?" Nick said from behind her. He'd received the same email. He was trying to break the ice with her. But she needed some time away to reassess and collect her thoughts.

She clicked open the email with all the attachments. "They finished analyzing the particulates from Whitney's clothes."

Nick wheeled into her cubicle to read from the same monitor. Her skin flushed from the closeness. "Pseudotsuga menziessi?" He struggled to pronounce the words.

"Douglas fir," she replied automatically.

"*Acer circinatum.*"

"Vine maple."

"We should change her nickname from Mad Mack to Google." Troy teased from Mackenzie's side.

"Ha. Ha." She rolled her eyes.

"This is vegetation common to Washington State. Matches the woods where she was found."

She stifled the butterflies in her stomach from Nick being so close. Did he always smell like this?

"Wait." His thick eyebrows knitted. "That doesn't make sense."

She focused again. "What?"

"Pinecae pollen. That comes from pine trees. But there are no pine trees where she was found."

"Hmm. But pine trees are the most common kind in the state."

Nick's skin grew ashen. "Yucca brevifolia."

She had to look that up. "That's pollen from Joshua tree. Not native to the state. What about it?"

He took a shaky breath, placing his elbows on his knees. "It was this case before you joined. That's where I saw that word."

"What case?"

His sharp Adam's apple bobbed. Mindlessly, he took out a cigarette from the packet and began rolling it between his fingers. It was his tick. He was a smoker before Mackenzie nagged him until he finally quit. "Cecily Rodriguez. She went to these woods with her friend, Tracy. But she disappeared."

The name didn't ring a bell. "I haven't heard of this. Only Cecily disappeared?"

"Yeah. Tracy said Cecily wandered away, that she couldn't find her. There was a search, but with no leads the case was inactive."

"Where did this pollen show up there?"

"The woods that they went to had Joshua trees planted." He perched the cigarette between his lips. "It's south of the national park where some non-native vegetation has been planted."

Mackenzie rummaged for a map in a drawer and unrolled it on her desk. She uncapped a red marker and drew an X where Whitney's body was found. "She was at a party before that which was two miles away over here." She drew another X. "It would take her thirty to forty minutes to walk that distance."

"Which it did. From that CCTV footage, where we saw her running."

"The Joshua trees are... here." She circled the spot, realization dawning on her. "It's not that far from The Farm, Nick."

He frowned at the map. "You're right. That's less than a mile away."

"So she must have visited this area earlier in the day for it to be still on her clothes." She chewed the insides of her cheeks. "Was there anything else about that case that you remember?"

"It wasn't mine. It was Stephen's." He was referring to a long-retired detective. "I just... happened to be curious." He avoided eye contact.

"Was Caleb your partner back then?"

"Yes." He waved a hand dismissively. "Anyway, it's just a coincidence. We need to figure out why she was in that patch of the woods."

"Maybe she was at The Farm." Unease danced along her nerves at the memory of the initiation ritual with Tobias Mathis and the woman. "She was with them for a long time. She must have tried to get back to her baby?"

"But didn't Zoe say that they hadn't heard from Whitney since she left."

"Yeah, but what if Zoe was lying to protect Tobias?" Mackenzie challenged. "She's his right hand. Her loyalty is to him."

"Or maybe Whitney snuck in? What if she wanted to see

her kid? It's not easy to walk away especially that soon after giving birth."

Grim possibilities hung between them. They hadn't realized that the rain had softened to a pitter-patter. Some people began filtering out of the office. Sully still hadn't left. Nick said something about checking up on him. He was concerned about him. But Mackenzie decided to focus on what needed to be done—someone had to. She was making a list when her phone rang.

It was an unknown number.

"Detective Price," she answered.

"This is Zoe," the familiar voice said from the other side.

Mackenzie froze. "Hi, Zoe. What can I do for you?"

Zoe whispered, "I'm not supposed to be calling you. He told me not to do anything yet until we get more information..."

"What are you talking about?"

"Hazel Martin. Another sister on The Farm. She's missing. I think she was abducted. Please don't tell anyone I talked to you."

TWENTY-ONE

In an instant, the weight of sleep dissipated. Mackenzie was fully alert, driving to The Farm with a purpose through water-clogged roads. The car sliced through the pooled remnants of the rain. The headlights revealed the veil of mist hovering above the glistening road. The lingering scent of the downpour perfumed the air. It was Mackenzie's favorite weather—the hours post-heavy rain. It cleaned the air and left everything looking brighter.

"Why does everything get traced back to The Farm?" Nick said, chugging coffee in the passenger seat.

"Of course it does," she said dryly. "What happens at that Farm is abnormal. Abnormality breeds complications. Complications trigger crime."

"What else did Zoe say?"

"Nothing. She hung up immediately because she heard someone come into the room."

"Maybe Zoe's loyalties aren't entirely to Tobias."

Mackenzie recalled the sharpness in Zoe's eyes. She didn't look or sound like a troubled woman who had been lured by Tobias into this cult-like lifestyle. She exuded a quiet strength, and there were no signs of crushed self-esteem or vulnerability like Whitney and Jennifer.

Several lights had been knocked out by the storm. She had to squint to see the sign of "The Farm" to confirm they had arrived at the right destination. They exited the car and walked down the path to The Farm in total darkness. No lights were on in any of the huts dispersed throughout. Mackenzie could only decipher silhouettes.

It was like The Farm had vanished into the abyss.

Then a figure came into focus—a man standing at the edge of The Farm in a raincoat.

"Caleb," Nick said in a tight voice when they reached him.

"Nick, Mackenzie." Caleb nodded at them. A toothpick between his lips like always. "Tobias sent me."

"We received an anonymous tip that one of the women here, Hazel Martin, has gone missing. We are here to investigate."

"It's midnight. Come back tomorrow."

"Did you not hear us?" Nick retorted.

"I did but everyone's asleep so I don't know who called you about this." Caleb shrugged casually.

"Step aside and let us do our job." Nick tried brushing past him but Caleb blocked his path.

For a second, they stood toe to toe, glaring at each other.

Caleb spoke first. "This is private property and Tobias Mathis doesn't consent to you trespassing. If this is an emergency, get a warrant. Otherwise come back tomorrow."

"Time is of the essence in an abduction," Mackenzie pushed back.

"I agree. And what evidence do you have of an abduction?" Caleb cocked an eyebrow. "Other than some anonymous tip? That's not enough to have reasonable concern for someone's safety. Maybe it was a prank call."

Nick scoffed. "Look at you. From cop to a madman's lapdog."

Caleb blanched. The hurt on his face was evident but he managed a forced smile. "See you tomorrow. Please leave now."

Mackenzie had to pull Nick away by the elbow. "Nick, he has a point. Zoe's call isn't enough to get a warrant."

"You do know what's happening right?"

"Yes. By tomorrow morning, they might have tampered with evidence of an abduction."

NOVEMBER 7

Lakemore emerged from darkness, submersed in the gentle glow of the early light of dawn. The first thing Mackenzie heard was the chirping of a bird. Her eyelids felt heavy as she opened them. She had fallen asleep at her desk. Again.

"Morning," a deep voice said from above. She twisted her head to find Austin hovering over her holding a cup of coffee. The steam made his face all swirly.

"Oh God." She wiped the drool on her chin. This wasn't the side of her anyone was supposed to see. "What time is it?"

"Eight thirty. How long were you working for?"

"I was just doing a background check on a potential victim." She took a few moments to allow the haze of slumber to clear. "We got a tip that someone from The Farm had been abducted. But we weren't allowed on the premises to investigate or talk to anyone so we can't verify the information."

He swayed on his heels. "The same Farm that Jennifer Peyton came from?"

"Yes. And Whitney Smythe. Did CSU find anything at Jennifer's place?"

"No prints or hair. Or shoe prints."

"Interesting." She tapped a pen against her temple. "Usually, you'd find shoe prints. People tend to be more careful about wearing gloves than covering their shoes."

"Especially in Lakemore with the weather." He scowled. "You'd think you'd find something. Unless it was somebody who is very familiar with protocols." He gave her a knowing look.

She caught on to his meaning. "Like an ex-cop."

"Don't get me wrong. A very shrewd criminal could plan for everything. But in my experience, that panic and adrenaline leads to mistakes. It's usually someone whose instincts are wired to think of everything at a crime scene…"

"Caleb Mercer." She leaned back on her chair. Nick's cubicle was empty. He was probably dropping off Luna to school. Even though Luna lived with her mother, Shelly, Nick spent as much time as possible with her.

"I would question him," Austin proposed, gauging Mackenzie's reaction. "I heard he was Nick's ex-partner. But if he's Tobias's bodyguard, he might also be an enforcer of some kind."

"Yeah. This case has so many threads. Could you help?"

"Sure."

She handed him a thick stack of papers. "This is the file on Grace Fontaine's murder and the missing Baby Rose. I printed everything out."

"Wow." He huffed. "I should work out with these. Why are we looking at that again? Thought this was closed."

Mackenzie recoiled, unresolved anger rearing its ugly head. "Yeah, but they might have missed something. It was Lakemore's first sensational case. And Sully's *first* case. Just want to tick all the boxes."

"Sure." Austin didn't think much of it. "Also, we pinged Jennifer's carrier. Should get something by the end of the day."

"Great. Thanks."

Once Austin had left, Mackenzie's mind wandered to Caleb. Despite the simmering animosity in the interactions between Nick and Caleb, she didn't miss the yearning in Nick's eyes. That stormy turmoil when a friend turns foe. When buried memories of trust and camaraderie try to scratch their way to the surface again.

But Austin had a point, and Caleb's behavior yesterday only confirmed the doubt.

With all these thoughts weighing heavily in her head like rocks, she approached Nick's cubicle. There was no one else in the office. She had known him for ten years. But she had also known Sully for ten years and she had been wrong about him.

She had been wrong about her own mother and father and even her ex-husband. Despite being a decorated detective, she had a blind spot for the people in her life that she loved.

Maybe she was wrong about Nick too. Maybe there was a side to him that she didn't know—a side that could betray her.

She began going through the documents on his desk. They were all just copies of Grace's homicide files, Whitney's autopsy reports and an article about the rise of Tobias Mathis. What was she even looking for?

Mackenzie was about to give up when she noticed the corner of a piece of paper creeping out from behind a photo pinned to the board of Nick and Luna.

A shuddering breath rattled through her. She carefully prised out the piece of paper. Only it wasn't paper; it was a Polaroid picture of Mackenzie from a few years ago. She knew he had taken this picture of her but she didn't know he had kept it.

Her stomach folded. Her heart fluttered in her chest. She quickly put the picture back in its place, not knowing what to do for the first time in her life.

TWENTY-TWO

"What do you mean you got an anonymous tip?" Rivera asked sharply.

Mackenzie and Nick were in her office, which was devoid of any clutter or personality. Mackenzie appreciated Rivera's simplistic style. There was a wall of some tokens of appreciation but no personal mementos. No one would think Rivera was even married if it weren't for the faint line around her ring finger. She didn't wear her wedding ring to work.

"Well, it was Zoe from The Farm," Mackenzie explained. "But she sounded scared and begged us not to tell anyone it was her."

Rivera pulled a face. "Are you telling me that the richest hippie in town, Tobias Mathis, is essentially holding fifty women *captive*?"

"Well, it is a cult." Nick pocketed his hands. "He is... charismatic. They are all adults. They are well within their rights."

"Has Zoe made contact again?" Rivera asked.

"No. It was a private number so I couldn't connect with her again."

"Now I'm worried about Zoe." Rivera removed her glasses.

A grave shadow on her face. "What if she's in trouble for reporting this?"

"That Farm is private property. I sent Peterson and more uniform this morning but again access was denied," Nick informed them.

Rivera growled in frustration. "So now we need to get a warrant to verify if someone's been abducted? And on the basis of what? A woman called and said that she *thinks* someone is missing?"

Mackenzie pinched her waist. "But what if she's right? What if we are losing crucial time?"

"Not to mention giving them ample time for a cover-up."

"But what judge will sign off on this?" Rivera countered. "Do we have anything on Hazel Martin? Who is she?"

"She has also had a troubled life," Mackenzie said. "Her parents died when she was fifteen. She bounced around foster homes before crashing on people's couches for a few years before she left for The Farm. A friend had reported her missing three years ago but she later withdrew the complaint when she got a phone call from Hazel telling her where she was."

"Is there a connection between Hazel Martin and the two victims?"

"Nothing besides The Farm. That we could find at least," Nick replied.

"What about her and Grace Fontaine?"

Mackenzie shrugged. "We haven't found any connection between The Farm and Grace Fontaine."

"Have you run a background check on Zoe?" Rivera asked. "Why is Tobias's right hand secretly calling the police? Why hasn't she been brainwashed like the rest of them?"

"Maybe she is just being a Good Samaritan."

A gravelly voice came from the door. Mackenzie turned to find Captain Murphy, looking even more weathered.

"Captain." Rivera shot up from her seat. "Did we have a meeting?"

"No, no." His gait was measured and deliberate. His perpetually grumpy face etched with lines and deep wrinkles. "I was able to establish contact with Zoe. She is safe."

Mackenzie had never been this confused in her life. She and Nick stared at each other. Captain Murphy no longer played a role in investigations. He was long past his retirement age but the man was like fungus sticking to Lakemore PD shamelessly. Most of the time she even forgot that he was around. He had slowly become a ghost who floated the halls of the station spewing spiteful comments and complaining that it was either too hot or too cold.

"How did you reach her?" Mackenzie asked.

"I am the captain. I can do things that you can't."

"Well, did she say anything else?" Rivera said.

"Zoe couldn't talk much, but she did say that no one has seen Hazel since yesterday evening," Murphy replied, looking at Nick. "Hazel will likely show up. Let's wait at least twenty-four hours."

"Captain, we have two dead women from that Farm," Rivera said. "If Hazel hasn't been seen in a few hours, we need to move *fast*."

Murphy was still looking at Nick. It was a subtle thing that Mackenzie had noticed about him from the very beginning. He always addressed the men over the women.

"We need to bring in Tobias Mathis for questioning. He is being uncooperative. Drill him." Rivera's eyes bore into Mackenzie's.

"That's unnecessary." Murphy frowned. "Let's wait twenty-four hours."

"Two women from his Farm are dead."

"But didn't Nick talk to Tobias already? He said he doesn't know anything!"

Mackenzie wondered how Murphy knew that.

"Mack and I talked to him," Nick corrected him gently. "But him not letting us on his premises is reason enough to drag him here."

"This is America. That's his property," Murphy argued.

It was evident that Murphy was going senile. Mackenzie clenched her fists, swallowing words he wouldn't appreciate.

"If Tobias Mathis doesn't come in for questioning, then you tell him that we will go to the media with the link to his Farm," Rivera said decidedly.

Murphy's eyes widened and he finally turned to Rivera. "You wouldn't want a media circus now, Lieutenant."

"I'll do whatever it takes to close this case," Rivera hissed. "Detective Price, Detective Blackwood, bring in Tobias. If Hazel *is* missing, we don't have much time. Whitney and Jennifer weren't held captive. Our killer doesn't want anything from these women—just their eyes."

TWENTY-THREE

There were moments in this job when Mackenzie felt satisfied. That sweet taste of victory. When the badge she wore had more power than the money in someone's bank account. It was a reminder that perhaps the world wasn't so out of control. There was still morality to be salvaged.

When Tobias Mathis appeared at the stairs, he was wearing his smile that he usually reserved for the cameras. Dressed in his classic earthy tones, he radiated a bohemian and eco-conscious lifestyle.

"I want to knock his teeth out. Does he think cameras follow him *everywhere*?" Nick said next to her. "Watch him judge that we are wearing polyester while he wears sunglasses indoors." When Mackenzie didn't reply, he raised an eyebrow. "Mack?"

"Yes." She stared up at him, blinking innocently. Her mind still lingered at the discovery of her picture at his desk.

"What happened to you?"

"Nothing," she squeaked like a mouse and then cleared her throat.

"I think you should lead this interview. He'll lower his guard in front of a woman."

"And why is that?" she snapped.

He rolled his eyes. "Not because you're not strong but he obviously feels threatened by other men. He lives at a Farm with fifty women he knocked up to keep them tied down."

"Oh. I suppose you're right."

"I always am."

When Tobias spotted them, he waved like he was greeting his fans. "Detectives." He lowered his sunglasses to the bridge of his nose and peered at Mackenzie. "I'm all yours."

Mackenzie's expression was stone-like. "Follow us."

"Am I a suspect?" Tobias asked, upon entering the cold room.

The overhead fluorescent lights emitted a harsh light forcing him to put his sunglasses back on. The walls were white, the room bathed in hues of gray. A steel table and chairs were situated in the center. Everything about this room amplified a sense of isolation. Clinical and sterile; it was designed to break people.

"How utilitarian," he added.

"Please remove your sunglasses so that we can see your face," Mackenzie said.

He obliged and took a seat. His chest puffed. His hands on the table. He was sending a message. He had nothing to hide.

"Mr. Mathis, as you know, two women from your Farm— Whitney Smythe and Jennifer Peyton—were murdered." Mackenzie placed the photos of the two bodies on the table to stir a reaction from him.

He turned green like he was going to throw up. "This is too gory, please."

Mackenzie removed the pictures and asked him if he wanted a glass of water but he refused. She and Nick exchanged glances. They both were thinking the same thing— either Tobias was an excellent actor or he was genuinely incapable of killing someone so gruesomely.

But that didn't mean that he couldn't order someone to do it for him.

"Tell me, Mr. Mathis. Does it seem odd to you that two women who left your Farm have turned up dead?"

"It breaks my heart."

"Were you pissed off that they left you?" she pushed. "Did it hurt your feelings or... ego?"

He was flabbergasted. "*No!* Absolutely not. Just because my lifestyle is odd doesn't mean it's wrong. I'm not keeping them there at gunpoint. They are free to leave."

"It's not an easy decision to leave when you are forced to leave your children behind." Mackenzie showed him a copy of a legal contract. "CPS sent this our way. When a woman joins The Farm, you make her sign a custody agreement which gives you custody of the children in the event of separation and deny the mother visitation rights. In fact, you retain the decision-making authority on the child's upbringing, healthcare, and education."

"The agreement went through the family court and they approved it. They acknowledged that the women's past of addiction and substance abuse made them unfit to be solely responsible for their children. The CPS must also have informed you that all my children are well-fed and taken care of," he said, zealousness dripping in his voice. "I'm a good father. The reason we have that clause in the contract is because these women who join us are not balanced. Just because you want kids doesn't make you a good mother. All of them have addiction issues. Once they leave, they can easily slip back into that life without the structure, discipline, and support The Farm offers. I wouldn't want to risk putting a child through that unstable upbringing. Would *you*?"

"And why are you only going after disturbed women? Why choose vulnerable women to procreate with?"

"Because they are the ones who need help and I'm *helping*

them." He explained like it was something understandable. "You can't make society better by ignoring such people. This is how we rehabilitate them. We give them the biggest joy a person can have—being a parent. And at The Farm, we give them the tools to succeed. This clause is written in bold. It's not something I sneak in. Is how I live really a crime?"

"No, but obstruction of justice is a crime," Nick countered. "You didn't let us in last night and you didn't let us in this morning either."

"We are busy preparing for the Harvest Festival. We have orders to ship throughout the country."

"So Hazel Martin is not missing?" Mackenzie challenged.

He blew out a sharp breath. "Look, I haven't seen her since yesterday evening. She didn't show up for our communal dinner."

"And you're not worried?" She arched her eyebrows. "You who sees himself as a savior of these women and wants to rehabilitate them doesn't want the police to investigate her disappearance. The mother of one of your children."

"We don't know if she disappeared. Sometimes Hazel and others leave for a day and then come back. Without telling anybody, of course. They sneak out when they miss that old life of clubbing and drinking." His nose wrinkled in disgust. "Then they realize that that life isn't sustainable."

"So Hazel has disappeared like this before?" Nick asked.

"Well, no," he admitted reluctantly. "Not *Hazel*. She has been with me since she was a teenager! She practically grew up on The Farm. But others... Zoe, for instance. She keeps leaving from time to time for a day or two. But they all come back. They always come back. I'm sure Hazel will too. If she doesn't by tonight, then I promise *I* will call you to The Farm and let you turn the place upside down. I just don't want the police to be there unnecessarily."

"Why? What are you hiding?" Mackenzie smiled cruelly.

"I'm not hiding anything. I'm *protecting*. Our safe haven no longer feels safe when the police start sniffing around. A lot of these women have been in trouble with the law before they joined. It would scare them—the possibility that The Farm is in trouble. That they might lose their home. I have worked hard to build this harmonious community. I can't let some serial killer who likes eyeballs jeopardize the peace."

Mackenzie wondered why everyone in Lakemore was obsessed with peace. How harrowing decisions were made in the name of restoring something that always escaped this town. How many stories were left unfinished in the name of the "greater good".

"In the meantime, could you give us Hazel Martin's phone number?" Mackenzie was ready to write it down. "We can track her phone without disturbing your peace."

He shrugged. "She doesn't have a cellphone. Nobody at The Farm does. Except for Caleb, but that's only because well, he's not really part of the family."

"Bullshit," Nick said.

"It's true. Even I don't. Technology is harmful for us. It hinders us from forming a deep connection with our planet." Something struck him. "Who told you that Hazel was missing?"

"You are free to go for now, Mr. Mathis. I'm sure we'll be in touch very soon." Mackenzie relished not giving him an answer. A fleeting, petty emotion of giving him a taste of his own medicine.

When Tobias left, Mackenzie turned to Nick. "Zoe has a phone. Do you think she'll be in trouble if he finds out?"

Nick nodded. "She might be. But I'm also wondering what the hell is she doing at The Farm if she isn't following any of the rules and is even turning against Tobias?"

Austin poked his head into the room. "Sorry, guys, you busy?"

"No, Tobias just left." Mackenzie gestured at the empty chair across from them. "What's up?"

Austin handed them a piece of paper marked with several highlights. "The GPS information from Jennifer Peyton's cellphone. The activity is normal except for the last two months when she started visiting a strip club pretty often." He ran his finger over the highlights.

"Was she working there?" Nick asked.

"That's the kicker. She wasn't. She has no connection to that strip club and it only popped up two months ago, when Whitney Smythe left The Farm."

The name *Sinsational Nights* sounded familiar to Mackenzie. She dug through her memory.

"Whitney had visited this place too in the last two months," Mackenzie said. "After she came back but not before that. She didn't visit as many times though. Only four times, that's why I didn't think much of it."

Mackenzie assumed that they must have met each other after The Farm—even if they didn't have each other's numbers saved on their cellphones. Why did they pay so many visits to a strip club when they weren't working there? Could it have anything to do with Jennifer's investigation into Grace Fontaine and Baby Rose?

TWENTY-FOUR

"I have so many questions." Mackenzie tilted her head out of curiosity, watching the woman in a slinky dress contort her body in strange ways as she glided up and down the pole.

"Who comes to a strip club at noon?" Nick said, glaring at the group of young men in fancy suits.

"Why? What time do you go to strip clubs?" she teased deadpan.

He pretended to give it some thought. "At fourteen minutes past ten in the evening. Sharp."

"I've read that's the best time."

"Exactly."

Soft rays filtered through the partially drawn curtains but the twinkling lights and mirrored accents cast a sultry haze in the dimly lit room. It reeked of cigarettes and perfume. The lighting did little to mask the grime coating every surface from the sticky floors to the torn upholstery. The stage itself was littered with discarded bills and empty bottles. The staff moved around with purpose, preparing for the night ahead.

They approached the bartender who was busy doing an inventory.

"We're from the Lakemore PD."

"We are fully licensed," he said in a monotonous tone.

"Do you recognize this woman?" Nick showed him a picture of Jennifer. "She used to come here a lot these past few weeks."

The man wore glasses and gave it a long look. "Oh yeah, saw her around. I thought she wanted a job."

"Why did she come here?" Mackenzie asked.

"I think she got a crush on one of our strippers. She talked to her for *hours*."

"Which one?"

He tipped his chin at a group of scantily dressed women giggling at a table. He whistled. "Candy! Get over here!"

The women turned their heads toward the bar. One of the strippers in a cotton pink sequin dress that barely covered her butt hopped over. Her hair was light brown and lay in thick curls around her head. Eyeing Nick, she twirled a strand around her finger and popped a gum. "What you looking for?"

"They're cops, Candy. Cut it."

"Oh." Candy dropped the flirty charade and pouted. "What? Is it Bob? I punched him in the face because he tried stuffing his hand down my panties."

Nick kept staring at her like he was trying to place her. "Do I know you?"

"I would have definitely remembered you, hunk."

Mackenzie took over. "Well, Candy, we are investigating the homicide of a woman who frequented this place. We're hoping you can help us."

"Tracy!" Nick said suddenly. "You're Tracy White."

Candy's mask slipped. She didn't look like a confident stripper anymore. She looked small, almost like a child. Her shiny lips quivered. "Oh my God... you're Detective Nick Blackwood. I remember now."

"Yeah."

Candy hugged her body tight, hiding her exposed skin. An embarrassed flush crept up her neck.

"This is Tracy White, Mack. Remember the case I told you about? Cecily Rodriguez who was never found?"

Mackenzie remembered. She had gone missing in the woods close to The Farm—the pollen from those woods was found on Whitney's clothes. "Yes, I remember."

Candy's gaze fell to the ground. "Well, yeah. That was me. Why are you here? For Cecily?"

"No. For Jennifer Peyton."

Candy's mouth fell open. "What happened to her?"

Nick looked apologetic. "She was killed."

"Fuck." Candy fell onto a chair. "Poor girl. Can't catch a break, can she?"

"You know about her stint at The Farm?" Mackenzie asked.

Candy nodded, giving her a strange look. "How could she live all those years without social media and a freaking *phone*?"

"Did she tell you why she left?" Mackenzie asked.

"Do you mind?" She pulled out a cigarette from her cleavage. "Give me a fireball!" she shouted at the bartender.

"Well, did she tell you why she left?" Mackenzie repeated.

Panic shrouded Candy's eyes as her knees bobbed up and down. "Jennifer found out something about Tobias Mathis. Something that made her feel betrayed."

"What?" Nick asked.

"I dunno. And honestly, I didn't care. She gave me a fifty every time she came to talk. That's all that mattered to me."

"Why did she come to you? How does she know you?" Mackenzie tried not to breathe in the smoke swirling into her nostrils from Candy's cigarette.

"Not the reason your boyfriend knows me." Candy's eyes flitted to Nick.

"He's not..." She gave up. "What do you mean, Candy?"

"Jennifer found me because she found out I kind of knew Garrett Fontaine." Candy took a drag, her eyes almost watering.

"Grace's son?" Nick was puzzled.

"Yeah. She was looking into that family."

"Why?" Mackenzie asked, remembering the web of pictures and news articles she had discovered in the basement.

Candy blew a puff of smoke in their faces. "I dunno. I asked her and she just said she was curious. I think she wanted to become a writer or some shit."

"What did she ask you about Garrett?"

"Just what he was like..." A shadow crossed her face. "Garrett and I worked together in the same community service group. He was peculiar. Never really talked. Just stared at everyone."

"Did she ask about his sister or his mother?"Nick said.

"Yeah, about the whole family. Mostly about the father... what kind of a relationship he had with him, with his wife, with his sister. I told her that I didn't know Garrett that well. In fact, nobody did. He had no friends. I guess he was too traumatized by his mother being murdered in the kitchen while he was asleep upstairs. And then his sister died in those woods. That kind of shit messes you up for life."

Frustration clawed at Mackenzie's skin. Why was Jennifer investigating the Fontaine family and the disappearance of Baby Rose? To the world, that case was closed. A man had gone to prison for the murder of Grace, and fragments of Baby Rose's bones were found in the woods. Nobody outside the Lakemore PD—apart from Russell Grant—knew that Jake Lawson was not the killer—that whoever had killed Grace and how Baby Rose's remains came to be in the woods were still unresolved issues.

What made Jennifer suspect something was amiss?

"Did you know anything about that family? About Barry?" Mackenzie asked.

Candy's eyes tapered as she got lost in her thoughts. The smoke trickled out of her nostrils, dancing and swirling in the air, taking the shape of the tale she told of a very long time ago.

TWENTY-FIVE

THIRTEEN YEARS AGO

Tracy

The sun was sweltering on the hot, sticky day, causing sweat to collect under Tracy's armpits. She squeezed her arms into her body and squinted her eyes against the glare bouncing off the shiny surfaces in the park. People like her scurried around like ants on a mission, picking up crumbs. The air was thick with the aroma of freshly cut grass and the acrid stench of garbage bags filled to the brim. Heat shimmered off the pavement, making distant water fountains look like mirages.

Cecily wiped the beads of sweat from her brow. "Of all the days, *today* it doesn't rain. Hottest day of the year. Ugh."

Tracy picked up discarded candy wrappers. "It's for a good cause, right?"

She shrugged, her lips curving into a sly smile. "Yeah, yeah, good cause and all that. But you know what I'm excited about?"

"What?" She arched an eyebrow.

"Our hiking trip tomorrow." She squealed, her eyes darting to a guy a few feet away who was hauling trash bags into the back of a pickup truck. "I'll finally make my move."

"Didn't his fiancée leave him like a week ago?"

"Yeah, and he needs a shoulder to cry on."

As they continued picking up trash, Cecily suddenly bumped into someone, causing her to stumble. A flicker of irritation flashed in her eyes when she realized who it was—Garrett Fontaine. But she quickly plastered on a fake smile. "Excuse me."

"What was that?" Tracy whispered to Cecily, looking over at Garrett. He was always a solitary figure, present at every event and activity but never interacting with anyone and carrying an invisible weight. His dark hair fell over his forehead, obscuring his gaze. He kept his eyes low, but whenever Tracy saw his eyes settled on her she would instinctively look away.

There was something both frightening and tragic about him.

"He's always staring." Cecily sighed. "I was nice to him *once* and now he's like fixated. Keeps watching."

Tracy stared at Garrett's back. He was a puzzle piece. It filled her with unease that no one would ever know what he could have been. His tragic past had branded him forever. "Poor guy. Dead mother and sister."

"No excuse."

Tracy's gaze shifted and she gasped. "Look, by the park's edge."

Cecily followed her line of sight, spotting a parked car with a man at the wheel. It was Barry, Garrett's father.

"Why's he here again?" Cecily mused. "It's so weird that he chaperones his twenty-seven-year-old son."

"I remember seeing him at the soup kitchen last month. He was just... watching." The memory unsettled her.

"One time, he was standing outside during one of our meetings the *entire* time. A whole two hours. Next to a tree."

They continued cleaning under the blazing sun. But

Tracy's eyes kept moving to Barry—his aging, harsh face always watching them, his presence looming. She shivered at the sudden cold flash despite the heat, as she felt his eyes on her.

TWENTY-SIX

Candy propped her legs on another chair, leaning back and staring at the ceiling. "He was always around too much. Garrett was just sad but his father was a creep, always following his son."

"Afraid that he'd lose the only person left in his life," Nick noted.

Candy shrugged. "What's the point? I heard Garrett died in a car crash anyway a few years later."

"Did Jennifer mention anyone else? A woman named Whitney, perhaps?" Nick probed, his chair angled further away from Candy to distance himself from the smell of cigarettes.

"I don't recall. Maybe? She talked mostly about her son. She missed him and desperately wanted to get back to him."

Mackenzie was conflicted. On one hand she knew about the legal contract that forced Jennifer to leave her child behind but on the other hand, she couldn't help but feel anger toward Jennifer for putting herself in such a position.

"Did she ask you anything about what happened between you and Cecily?" Nick asked.

Candy's face twitched. Her nostrils flared. She put out the

cigarette and blinked incessantly to keep the tears at bay. "It came up when she found out I was the girl who came out of the woods alive."

"She didn't know that was you?" Mackenzie shook her head in disbelief.

"Nope. She was surprised, and well, she got curious about that too."

"I wasn't the detective on your case, but I remember you, Tracy—"

"Don't call me that." She cut him off with gritted teeth. "Tracy White also died in those woods."

"What do you mean *also* died? From what Nick told me about that case, Cecily was just declared missing."

Candy smacked her fist on the table. "Damn it. Where's my shot?" she snapped at the bartender. "Give me Xanax."

She snatched the pill and shot glass from the bartender, glaring at his back as she downed a shot with the pill. She was visibly shaking, opening and closing her fists.

Nick pulled his chair closer to her and leaned forward. "I remember seeing you ten years ago, Tracy." His baritone deepened at her real name, always knowing which buttons to push. "I was at the station when you used to come in for questioning by Detective Stephens. I saw how worried you were about your friend. Did something else happen in those woods?"

Candy turned her head, tears spilling from her eyes. "I... I just want to forget. Don't make me go back there... what does that have to do with Jennifer being dead?"

Because Mackenzie didn't believe in coincidences anymore. That's what Nick was thinking too.

"That's for us to figure out, Tracy. Do you know what happened to Cecily?"

She stared at Nick—he had trusting eyes. Despite the hardness of his face, his eyes reminded Mackenzie of oceans in the dark. Bottomless pools of ink. "She's dead."

"How do you know that?"

Candy squirmed in her chair, looking nothing like the confident woman who didn't bat an eye when she took off her clothes on stage. "I've tried so hard to forget about that time... I can't even say my own name anymore after what happened..."

"Something is bothering you, my child. Let it all out." Eleanor held Mackenzie tight in her arms, after the latter had awoken in the middle of the night screaming.

But she couldn't. Her mother had made her promise not to tell anyone. No one would understand. They both would go to jail. A sob was stuck in her throat as she shook her head in the crook of Eleanor's neck.

"Never underestimate the power of unspoken words, Mackenzie. They will build up like plaque inside you until you say them out loud and release the poison."

"I found her that night. I found her body," Candy conceded, horror mounting in her eyes. "She was lying there on the ground with all that blood just pouring out of her. It was so dark, and we were in the middle of the woods. I couldn't get any reception on my phone."

Shapes took form in Mackenzie's mind. She envisioned how that night played out. She knew how dark the woods in Lakemore could get. How the trees and the rocks came alive and made eerie sounds. How the mud felt soft between the toes and easily swallowed a body. How it smelled like cedar, pine, and blood.

"I ran away, out of the woods, to get help," Candy continued. "But I got lost and then someone hit me on the head."

Nick frowned. "I don't remember that part. You were injured?"

"I lied that I tripped in the dark. I was attacked." She instinctively touched her forehead. "I was definitely attacked."

"Why didn't you tell anyone? Why did you lie?" Mackenzie asked.

"Because when I woke up in the hospital, they told me that Cecily was *missing*! That they had searched the woods and found nothing. I was so confused. I didn't know what to do. A part of me wondered if I had imagined the entire thing. But then later that evening when I went home, there was a package for me... someone had taken pictures of me over Cecily's body."

Mackenzie's eyebrows crashed together. "Who sent them?"

"I don't know. They were anonymous. Probably the person who attacked me in the woods. But those pictures were damning. And I had already lied to the police that I didn't know what happened to her. So I didn't say anything. And I never found out who sent me those pictures."

"Was there a note with those pictures?" Nick asked.

"No. There didn't need to be. It was obvious what they meant."

"Do you still have the pictures?" Mackenzie asked, hopeful.

"I destroyed all of them..." Candy said. "The only proof of my guilt."

Alarm bells were starting to ring in Mackenzie's head. Jennifer had found Candy in an attempt to gather more information about the Fontaine family because she was investigating the disappearance of Baby Rose. And then Whitney visited the woods where Cecily was found dead. Why did Jennifer and Whitney suspect the two crimes were connected?

"Sully just texted me," Nick said to Mackenzie after they had let Candy go. "Tobias Mathis called and said that Hazel hasn't returned. It's been twenty-four hours since she was last seen. We can officially declare her missing."

TWENTY-SEVEN

Morality was an artificial construct. Self-preservation was human nature. Mackenzie knew that everyone had a conscience that whispered to them what was right and what was wrong. But it was shockingly easy to dial down the volume. It was easier to surrender to the fate of something eating you alive on the inside than something that could change the outside.

Was self-preservation such a deeply imbibed instinct that nobody stood a chance?

Mackenzie had carried her dark secret her whole life. It had grown inside her over the years, spreading like an infection, seeping into every relationship. It was only when she said the words aloud to Nick that she realized what it was like to breathe.

She had chosen self-preservation to hide the ugly truth. That was what Sully had done too. Except Sully's lies had framed someone innocent. But *was* he innocent? Innocent of that particular crime perhaps—but he was not an innocent person...

"Do you think if Sully had framed a good person, things

would be different?" Mackenzie asked Nick as they drove to The Farm.

Nick took a moment to reply. "He never would have agreed to do this to a good person. And if you ask me, even Mike Ortiz wouldn't have suggested it in the first place."

"That wasn't my question."

A muscle in his jaw ticked. "Yes. Then he would have been morally wrong too. Now he's just... ethically wrong."

"So morality trumps ethics?"

"Is this a philosophy class?" he grumbled.

"No, I'm just trying to understand."

"My father and grandfather were always debating this when I was a kid. Grandpa had said something interesting—morality has to do with living with ourselves and ethics has to do with living in society. I guess that's why Sully has managed to get past all these years." Nick's eyes clouded over with a faraway look. "Somewhere he can justify it to himself. He just doesn't want to disappoint everyone."

Mackenzie wasn't sure if Nick was talking about Sully or himself. "Did anything else happen between you and Caleb?"

His knuckles whitened as he gripped the steering wheel. "What do you mean?"

"I mean are you ready to talk about it? Instead of shutting me down."

Nick's lips pressed tight in a thin line. "I told Jenna to send the information on Hazel to the police at Riverview and Tacoma. She's also tracking down her next of kin."

Mackenzie stiffened. The tension between them would simmer—burning questions, broken promises, misunderstood intentions, they would cackle in the air. This time, though, she sensed an icy barricade that left her feeling cold and alone. She pivoted her focus to Hazel and messaged Peterson to send the information to local bus stops and train stations.

When The Farm came into view, Mackenzie prepared

herself. The sky bled deep purples and blues as the fading light receded on the horizon. Stars began popping like a sprinkle of snowflakes. The sprawling fields of swaying grass and crops became shadowy silhouettes. The huts blended seamlessly into the background. Last night when Mackenzie had arrived, it was darker and the huts looked like gatekeepers. But now soft lights emanated from them, casting an inviting glow.

Tobias and Caleb were standing at the edge of The Farm deep in conversation. They broke off abruptly when the headlights swept over them.

"I told you, Detectives, I will be the first to sound an alarm the minute we suspect something is wrong." Tobias greeted them, like he was expecting a pat on the back.

Caleb maintained a distance, a toothpick perched between his lips.

"Where and when was she last seen?" Mackenzie asked, ready to tear her way through The Farm.

"Caleb and I talked to all the women." Tobias guided them through the cobble-stoned path. "She was last seen during a team-building exercise after lunch around four in the afternoon."

"What happened after that?" she asked.

"When Hazel didn't show up for our communal dinner, Zoe went to check her room and didn't find her there," he recalled. "I asked Caleb to search the premises, which took a few hours."

Blades of grass brushed against Mackenzie's skin. A constant hum of insects buzzing, crickets chirping, and leaves rustling surrounded her. Unlike yesterday when The Farm looked like a splat of blackness in the middle of nowhere, she could feel the energy pulsing. A waft of strange smells hit her even before she had reached the clearing where some women stood, dressed in long dresses of earthy tones. Her chest constricted at the sight. A sea of worried faces—former addicts, some of them still bearing hollowed eyes and spots on their skin, now they looked like puppets, like caricatures. They'd gone from being controlled by alcohol and drugs to being run by Tobias Mathis. They still didn't know the meaning of freedom and free will.

"Detectives." Zoe stepped forward, taking charge. "You have our cooperation. We want our sister back—safe and sound."

Mackenzie nodded. Zoe always spoke with undercurrents of something that Mackenzie couldn't quite pinpoint. She always looked at them in a way that gave the impression she was yearning to say something else but couldn't. "Where does Hazel usually stay?"

Zoe guided them to one of the huts which had some rooms. Tobias and Caleb were right behind them, further heightening Mackenzie's senses. Zoe pushed open a door and yanked on a string that lit up the rows of fairy lights hanging from the ceiling.

It was a standard room—a bed without a headboard, a table with two chairs, and a closet. The walls were adorned with drawings and crafts made by someone young—the technique still raw but bursting with sincerity.

The first thing Mackenzie noticed was that the bed was made. Everything in the room was tidy. "Did anyone enter this room?"

"No," Tobias replied. "We just opened the door to check if she was in here, but I instructed everyone to stay out so as to not tamper with anything."

"Very considerate of you," Mackenzie muttered under her breath but nobody heard her. She and Nick put on their gloves and began to inspect the room.

"After that team-building exercise, which direction did she head in?" Nick asked, opening the closet and going through her clothes.

"Her son, Jackson, said that he saw her walking toward her room. Apparently, she had said that she wanted to take a nap," Zoe said.

"Where is Jackson?" Mackenzie asked.

"He's sleeping right now," Tobias interjected. "He's only seven years old. We haven't told him yet."

Mackenzie glanced at Hazel's pictures. They were all taken when she was working around The Farm, from writing the bottle labels to carrying a smoke gun to the beehives. A tall, slender woman with blonde hair and freckles.

"Did Hazel ever mention Whitney and Jennifer?" Nick asked.

"Just the usual. Occasionally, we remember the sisters who left us but nothing other than that, from what I remember," Zoe said.

"How was her mood in the last few days?"

"Normal." She shrugged. "She's been at The Farm for the last eight years. She is well settled in this life."

Mackenzie understood what Zoe was trying to tell them— Hazel had no reason to run. But if Whitney and Jennifer were killed after they left The Farm, why was Hazel targeted?

"What forensic evidence do we have that can link Hazel's disappearance to Whitney and Jennifer?" Nick whispered to her.

Mackenzie stared at Hazel's face. The damage from the drugs had receded with time; after all she had been clean for the past eight years to be still a part of The Farm. But there was something heartbreaking about her. She looked subdued. Like something from her had been snatched and she was an incomplete version of herself. Her eyes brimmed with peace as well as unfulfillment.

"Wait a minute." Mackenzie's spine jerked upright. She had spotted something. Her head whirled to the entrance where

Zoe, Tobias, and Caleb were peering in. "Could you please leave us alone?"

Distrust dripped from Tobias and Caleb's faces, but Zoe was quick to obey. She ushered them away.

"That woman is a question mark if ever I knew one." Nick turned to Mackenzie. "What did you find?"

She directed his attention to the pictures. "Notice that Hazel is left-handed?"

All the photos of her writing, carrying supplies, eating—she favored her left hand. "Okay…"

"Everything on her desk is positioned on the opposite side. The pens, the erasers, the stapler, the notebooks…"

Nick connected the dots and went back to the closet with sliding doors. "These doors… they opened left to right and all her clothes are on the right side."

Mackenzie placed her hands on her waist. "Why would a left-handed person have their entire room organized like it belongs to a right-handed person?"

He clicked his tongue. "Also, doesn't this room look a little too clean? Tobias didn't let us in for twenty-four hours and allegedly had Caleb searching The Farm."

"There's no way they didn't enter the room to cover something up."

Nick's mind was racing when his eyes locked on something. He retrieved something from next to the side table. A toothpick.

"What's that?" Mackenzie asked.

His jaw clenched hard. His nostrils ballooned. "Caleb. Asshole is always chewing on one."

"It's just a toothpick. He'll deny it."

"That's why we'll run a DNA test on it. He was convicted of assault a few years ago. His DNA will be on file."

. . .

Back at the station, the air was buzzing with activity. Sully and Rivera were engrossed in an animated conversation in the conference room. Mackenzie pretended to fiddle with the vending machine, but her eyes were trained on her two superiors battling it out. It was late evening but neither showed signs of deflation or exhaustion.

Rivera leaned on the table, pinning Sully with a serious look. Sully was seated, his hands clasped in front of him. His burly frame facing away from Mackenzie. But the way he kept rubbing his palms together told Mackenzie that he was being backed into a corner.

"Heard that Sully has been making mistakes." Troy appeared out of nowhere. "Since Mad Mack is being nosy."

"I'm not being nosy... but what kind of mistakes?"

He tried not to laugh. "I don't know. Something to do with budget and some warrant submitted without his signature... the boring administrative shit. Wonder why he likes it."

Perhaps that's why Sully avoided being on the field. It wasn't laziness; it was to evade the memories of what he did. It was the same reason she didn't go to the woods behind Hidden Lake for many years.

"Well, *this* fight is probably about that Cecily Rodriguez disappearance... sorry, murder," Troy corrected himself. "I heard through the grapevine."

"Why is Rivera so angry?"

"Because first the Grace and Baby Rose Fontaine case was unofficially reopened and then this one. Rivera doesn't understand why two old cases are being revisited. Makes the department look bad." He was walking away but halted. "By the way, Daddy has been walking around grumpy. Are Mommy and Daddy fighting again?"

"How your wife stands you I'll never know." She shook her head, defeated, and ignored Troy's chuckle.

It gave her some validation that she wasn't the only one who had observed Nick's slow descent into madness. She saw him standing outside under the awning, facing the light drizzle.

Mackenzie stepped outside to join him. A cold shiver spread over her skin. It was just the two of them and the pitter-patter of the rain which formed puddles and swirling pools on the ground.

"How did you do it?" she asked.

He didn't turn around. "Do what?"

"Hold on tight to me when I was pushing you away." It was easier to talk to his back. "Because when you push me away, I feel like punching you in the face."

He chuckled, his shoulders quaking. "It was frustrating, though violence never crossed my mind."

She stood next to him, observing his face. "Then what did?"

"You don't want to know." Nick put an unlit cigarette between his lips, avoiding her eyes.

"Why not?"

"Because everything between us will change." He finally locked eyes with her. Her belly squeezed at his smoldering eyes. And then he looked away, playing with his lighter. "It will when you find out what I did. And I can't have you look at me the way you look at Sully now."

"Nothing will change." She moved closer, surprising him. "You mean something to me."

Mackenzie had no idea where this strength was coming from. Her breath was shallow. Like her lungs had been punctured with many holes. Nick was equally surprised. Only he would appreciate her being this brave.

He took a deep, shaky breath. "That Cecily Rodriguez disappearance. The night it happened... I lied about something."

"What?"

The words came out strangled. "A cam picked up Caleb's car in the vicinity of the woods that night. He said he had lent his car to a friend and that he was hanging out with me that night."

Mackenzie's lips parted.

"He told me he didn't remember that night as he was high. But he convinced me that he had nothing to do with Cecily... so I lied when I was questioned about his alibi. I lied."

A rock fell in the pit of Mackenzie's stomach. His chest rose and fell as he waited for her reaction. She inadvertently took a step back and immediately regretted it.

His face fell. The little hope in his eyes vanished. "How could I have told you, Mack, knowing you'll hate me like you hate Sully?"

He marched past her before she could reply.

TWENTY-EIGHT

"The community is reeling from the recent developments in the ongoing investigation of the brutal murders of two women, both found with an eye violently removed. Tonight, we bring you the latest update as a new name emerges in connection to this chilling case." Laura talked into the microphone, as she walked through one of the parks near a lake. "Hazel Martin, a local resident, has been reported missing under mysterious circumstances, raising concerns that she may be linked to these heinous crimes. Law enforcement agencies have intensified their efforts to uncover any leads or connections between Hazel and the previous victims. The Lakemore PD remains tight-lipped about the details, leaving the public in a state of unease and uncertainty. We reached out to them for a statement, but our requests were met with silence." She raised her eyebrows. "We urge everyone to exercise caution and take necessary precautions until more information is made available. Stay tuned for more developments."

Mackenzie turned off the television. Well, the news was out. She was surprised that the connection with The Farm hadn't been discovered. But perhaps it was only a matter of time. She turned on the blender and let the white noise fill the deafening silence of her empty house.

She didn't sleep well last night. She had woken up with sore muscles, which meant that she was tensing in her sleep. An observation courtesy of her ex-husband. But there was this chaos building inside her. And Nick's revelation had fanned it.

He had lied during an investigation about the alibi of a person of interest. He had broken the law. He had protected his partner. Sully had protected the peace of the town and Barry. And now these heinous crimes were linked and at the forefront again.

Amidst her tangled mess of feelings toward Nick, there was one question that was blaring like a siren since his confession. Caleb was around those woods the night Cecily died. Whitney was in those woods the day *she* died. Jennifer had been talking with Cecily's friend. Hazel had gone missing. All roads lead to one destination.

Caleb Mercer.

But why? What did he want? He had come across as a vagabond who enjoyed starting fires, but he didn't strike her as a sadistic serial killer. Could that façade be hiding something more sinister?

Sweat from her morning run lingered on her skin, making her clothes sticky. She was guzzling down the thick green smoothie when the doorbell rang. Half-expecting it to be Nick, she swung open the door to find Austin, his eyes swarming with excitement and cheeks pink from the chilly air.

"What happened?"

He brandished a thick file. "I think I found something in the Fontaine murder you asked me to look into."

Mackenzie's heart stopped. Had he found out that Sully and Ortiz framed Lawson? Was Sully going to be in trouble? "What?"

"Barry lied." He pushed past her and headed to the kitchen

island. He shrugged off his jacket, overflowing with that rush when another piece of the puzzle was slotted into place. "Barry gave a statement that he left work at 6:30 p.m. to get home to take his wife out for dinner." He flicked open the file to a page that had a map of Lakemore thirty years ago.

The Fontaine house was circled in red and so was Barry's office, roughly ten miles away. "On average, it would only take him ten minutes to get home."

"That's correct, let's assume rush hour and it took him say... fifteen to twenty minutes?"

"That's fair." Mackenzie nodded.

"Sully and Ortiz reached the Fontaine house after responding to the 911 call at 7:10 p.m. And five minutes later, Barry arrived. It took him forty-five minutes to cover the distance from work to his house."

She knew what he was getting at. "Yes, but he said he stopped by Floral Delights to pick up some flowers for his wife."

Austin smiled haughtily. "He didn't. Floral Delights was closed that day because of the rainstorm."

"So why did Barry take that long to get home?"

"Exactly."

Mackenzie recalled Candy's words—how even though Garrett was a loner, it was Barry who was always hanging around, trying to babysit his adult son. How something about Barry made her skin crawl. Was it possible that Barry had something to do with the murder and Baby Rose's disappearance? But what motive could he have?

"What if Baby Rose wasn't his biological kid?" Austin proposed, reading the doubt on her face. "What if Grace had cheated on him? I don't know about you but I've seen cases in which the husband snaps and even punishes the child."

Mackenzie couldn't dismiss the possibility. Otherwise why would Barry lie?

"This doesn't add a wrinkle in your investigation, does it?"

Austin tried to keep his tone light. "I see you and Nick have been tense."

"Yeah, it's just his ex-partner Caleb." Mackenzie's tone was measured. "His involvement is bringing up tumultuous emotions."

"It's unfortunate when you think you know someone but you really don't."

Mackenzie nodded. Her head heavy with spinning thoughts. Her throat was clogged with a hardening lump. Is this how Nick felt about her when she'd confided in him about what she and Melody had done? Did he feel conflicted and confused but was better at hiding it?

And then there was Sully. That innocence in him that always shone through was tainted now.

Her phone rang. "Hey."

"GPR and cadaver dogs have picked up human remains in the woods," Nick reported. "They are excavating the remains. You need to get here."

Lakemore's woods were like beasts—always awaiting their next meal. If you spent enough time here, the wildness was easy to get under your skin. The Farm was another beast, but visible to the naked eye, starting from the frayed edges of the woods. As Mackenzie entered the belly of one of many beasts in town, she felt prying eyes on her.

She had never been afraid of the woods until she'd left a part of herself in there more than twenty years ago. That's how these woods grew—they collected pieces of your soul and whispers of your darkest secrets. It wasn't the buried bodies that you needed to fear.

The rain from the night before had left the ground all mushy and soft. Her boots squelched as she navigated the uneven terrain. The tall pines formed a canopy. The moss covering all the rocks and tree trunks glistened.

Gloom coated the moist air. She never thought she'd miss the sun.

By the time she reached the site, the tips of her fingers were numb. The ground sloped downward where the excavations site and a white tent were set up. The forensic experts and officers worked amidst towering trees and dappled sunlight. The area was scattered with equipment, from trowels and brushes to shovels and GPR. Cadaver dogs on a leash continued to bark. Soil was being scooped into evidence bags and cameras were recording snapshots.

Nick was in his trench coat, standing over Becky and Angela, the state's leading forensic anthropologist. They were standing inside a hole that had been dug to access the remains.

Mackenzie approached them. She knew they had found bones, which is why Angela had been called.

"What do we have here?" she asked.

A human skeleton was in the hole. Its hollow contours made it look like a macabre sculpture. The bones were weathered, worn over time, some off-white and bleached, the rest tinged with brown. The texture looked both flaky and eroded. Something turned over in Mackenzie's gut. But after years of seeing many bodies in all stages of decomposition, it was hard to be fazed.

"The wide and circular pelvis indicates a female," Angela announced. "The narrow nasal aperture and prominent nasal bridge along with moderately developed zygomatic arches suggest the victim is likely to be of European descent."

"How long has she been dead?" Nick asked.

"I can't give you an estimate on that right now since a dead animal was buried above her. That would have interfered with the decomposition process."

Mackenzie was taken aback. "A dead animal above her?"

"Yeah, we found *two* skeletons. The top one belonged to a skunk."

"Ew. Weren't these woods searched for a body?"

"No," Nick scoffed. "We don't bring out this expensive equipment to search for buried bodies when there has been no sign of a murder."

Mackenzie shivered when a gust of wind blew. Nick took off his coat and threw it around her shoulders despite her protests. Becky tried to hide her smile.

"I'm guessing you need to take the bones back to your lab for cause of death?" Mackenzie asked.

Angela nodded. "I do. But Nick was just telling me about your case with the missing eye?"

"Yes..."

Mackenzie's eyes darkened. "Same MO. This female's left eye was violently removed."

Dr. Angela Weiss had once correctly deciphered that a victim was a swimmer who had broken his arm when he was seven years old. She was never wrong.

"How can you tell?"

"There are bone fractures and lacerations around the left eye socket in the maxilla, which are not present in the right eye socket. I can confirm this once I see those tissues under a microscope but I'm quite certain."

"Great. Our serial killer has four victims spanning three decades," Mackenzie grumbled.

Her statement cast a shroud of impending doom. Mackenzie and Nick felt it seep into their bones. Their insides held captive by the unknown. They had another victim.

Grace Fontaine. Cecily Rodriguez. Whitney Smythe. Jennifer Peyton.

And Hazel Martin was missing. She could be dead already, her body waiting to be discovered.

TWENTY-NINE

Hazel Martin's face was broadcast on all the news channels in town. Her face cluttered the front page of newspapers. The neighboring towns had been supplied with her details. Posters with her picture were printed by the sheriff's office and put up at all bus and train stations.

"She has no next of kin," Officer Peterson said, downcast. "Her ex-roommate was listed who hasn't heard from her in years and said that Hazel didn't have a family. She used to be a meth head."

Mackenzie's forehead crumpled. "Oh, just her son. Jackson." She was holding the poster of Hazel. Usually, the Lakemore PD didn't have the budget to use glossy paper. They always had to rely on regular paper, which was frequently washed away in the rain. But for Hazel, they were able to use glossy paper. She'd heard that Sully was pushing hard and was able to get Captain Murphy on his side.

"Did you know that they coat the paper with a thin layer of clay which gives it its glossy appearance following heat and pressure?" Peterson said.

"No, I didn't." She smiled. "You're doing great, Peterson."

"Am I?"

He was so young, still fresh out of the academy, radiating that desire to be someone's hero. Her eyes lacked that luster when she had joined the police. She didn't want to be anyone's hero—it was too late for that. She just desperately wanted to fix something that was broken inside her. She ached for Peterson—this job was going to shatter that naivety. If the violence didn't get to him, the betrayal of those around him would.

"Mack!" Nick half-jogged down the hallway. "Clint did it."

"Did what?"

"He cracked Whitney's phone and found her messages. She was talking to Jennifer Peyton through a dating app."

Mackenzie slammed the box on the steel table and yanked out stacks of papers that were clipped together. They were in a room in the basement where the temperature had nosedived due to the heating failing, and voices bounced off the walls. Chinese takeout boxes were spread out over the table.

"I printed out copies of Whitney's messages." She slid a copy each toward Nick, Peterson, and Jenna. "We are looking for any mention of Tobias, Caleb, Cecily, Tracy, Grace, Baby Rose, Barry... anyone related to the case. The messages go all the way back to when she first left The Farm and purchased a phone. We can't miss anything."

Determined, everyone began leafing through the pages with their highlighters ready. Mackenzie perched next to Nick who was absorbed by the task in hand. He threw a glance her way and opened his mouth to say something. But realizing they weren't alone, he went back to reading Whitney's messages.

When her stomach rumbled, Nick pushed a box of noodles her way, his nose still buried in the papers.

"Austin discovered that Barry was most likely lying about his alibi when Grace was killed," Mackenzie said.

"Candy also didn't like Barry very much, did she?" Nick pointed out.

"I thought that the trauma of losing half his family like that probably screwed him and his son up. But what if there's something else? Peterson, you tailed Barry, was there anything suspicious about him?"

Peterson stared into space. "No... he lives the life of a hermit. Gets flowers every Sunday for the three graves behind his house."

"That doesn't mean anything," Mackenzie said.

"That's harsh," Jenna commented.

It irked Mackenzie as it perpetuated a stereotype about two women not getting along but there was always friction between them. A tendency to rub each other up the wrong way. But she ignored Jenna's jab. People were capable of both love and hate.

"Does he have a criminal record?" Nick inquired. Peterson shook his head.

Mackenzie went back to dissecting Whitney's messages. She was very active on three dating apps. Two of them were the popular ones. But the third was an app just for locals. It was over eight weeks ago when Whitney and Jennifer were matched.

"Both of them were looking for men *and* women on these dating apps?" Nick sounded surprised, but quickly added, "Nothing wrong with that of course, except what are the chances they'd match considering their shared history?"

"And if they left The Farm and wanted to get in touch, why didn't they? There is no evidence of them even meeting up despite the fact they were both still in Lakemore," Jenna added.

"Because they were scared of someone," Mackenzie said, a theory starting to take shape. "Someone was stalking Whitney. Someone ransacked Jennifer's house. What if they knew that they were being watched, and that's why they came up with this convoluted way to communicate undetected?"

"That seems like a stretch, doesn't it?" Jenna said. "That's paranoia…"

"But these are two women who were part of a cult. They were convinced by a man to have sex with him, sign away custodial rights of their children, and live on a Farm without direct access to the outside world. Their personalities are malleable. They could have been brainwashed into believing that Tobias's reach was wider than what it actually was."

"Or maybe they were right to be paranoid. Two of them are dead and one is most likely dead."

Mackenzie's insides rattled at the possibility. None of the women showed evidence of being held captive—what chance did they have?

Her eyes flicked through the messages between Whitney and Jennifer.

W: How have you been?

J: Still can't sleep. How was it for you?

W: I can't breathe sometimes. But at least this way only I suffer and he won't cry, missing me.

It struck Mackenzie that they were talking about leaving behind their babies. She continued reading their intimate exchange. She was used to invading the privacy of victims and suspects. But it felt wrong to intrude on a mother's pain.

J: Remember we are doing this for them.

W: Yes… when this is all over then we'll get our children back.

J: It's the only thing that keeps me going. I promised her that I would come back for her.

Mackenzie wasn't even aware of the tears cascading down her cheeks. She furiously wiped them away before anyone noticed. She was Mad Mack.

W: What did Candy tell you?

J: How weird Garrett and Barry were.

W: We knew that already.

J: But also Candy's name is Tracy White. Her friend went missing in the woods ten years ago.

W: Calling you asap.

"They were using the dating app's call feature," Peterson noted, dejected. "We can't know what they were talking about on that call."

W: I can't stop thinking about him. I can't believe I did this.

J: We are doing this for them. So that we can bring them home.

W: But what if staying was better? At least we could have been there for them. What if they feel we abandoned them?

J: It won't get to that, Whitney. We will be together again before they realize we are gone. This is for their future. They can't stay on that Farm forever. It's not healthy or normal.

W: I suppose. I got in touch with our contact. I'm meeting her tomorrow.

J: Let me know how it goes. I'll stay on Candy.

The words "our contact" arrested Mackenzie's attention. Jennifer and Whitney's investigation into Grace and Baby Rose had led them to Candy through Garrett. But who was this other person they were talking about? She flipped through more pages and conversations, mostly about them missing their children, and struggling with life.

Until she zeroed in on a name that made her suck in a sharp breath.

J: What did Violet tell you?

W: Calling you in 5.

Violet. Mackenzie had met the timid, fidgety daughter of Mike Ortiz when she had accompanied her father. But what did she have to do with any of this?

THIRTY

The farmers' market was bustling. As soon as Mackenzie stepped into the warehouse, she couldn't hear herself think. The walls were lined with stalls decorated with vibrant banners, selling locally grown produce, fresh flowers in bloom, and artisanal goods. Vendors advertised their goods, competing with each other for customers who in return bargained with them. Lively chatter echoed. The air was infused with the aroma of fresh bread and freshly brewed coffee.

In the array of stalls, Mackenzie's eyes were drawn to the largest stall at the back. Selling rows of honey jars, fresh berry jam, pumpkins, corn, turnips, and radish, a few women dressed in long, earthy robes stood collectively, politely smiling at customers, and working systematically. Their mannerisms seemed rehearsed and measured. Their faces displayed subdued emotions. They were clones of each other. The light within them was dim and stifled.

But Mackenzie's eyes were drawn to a different stall between towering sunglasses and pyramids of fresh fruit. A wooden sign said "Fresh Catches by the Ortizes". Wooden crates brimmed with crushed ice, glistening with seafood. Shimmering silver fish were carefully arranged on beds of ice. Salmon, halibut, and Dungeness crab.

Violet stood behind the stall, packing fish for a customer. Her father wasn't with her. She was frail and soft-spoken. Her expressions were demure, unlike the other vendors who were loud and animated. She reminded Mackenzie of a meadow. But the way Violet hauled a big fish with ease, her biceps toned, showed that she was determined.

Her eyes darted around nervously, avoiding direct contact with the customers. It was as if she was more comfortable with the fish than with people. One of the customers stared at her curiously and whispered something into her companion's ears.

"Poor girl." Mackenzie glared at the couple. "She's just minding her own business."

"Violet?" Nick got her attention, approaching the stall.

Violet's eyes lost their focus for a second before they panicked like a deer caught in headlights and she blinked. "Oh. Dad isn't here."

"I know. We're here to talk to you," Mackenzie said. "Something you want to tell us?"

She swallowed hard, clasped her hands, and bowed her head, like a schoolgirl about to be told off. "I'm sorry... I... I'm so sorry."

Nick felt sorry for her. "Let's talk now. You must have been watching the news?"

"Yes." She fixed her glasses. "Hazel."

"We found an exchange of messages between Whitney and Jennifer that were all about you." Mackenzie tried to keep the accusatory tilt out of her voice. "You met with Whitney?"

"Yes... yes..." She folded her arms, scratching them, her words barely audible. "Two or three times."

"Why? How did you know her?" Mackenzie asked.

Violet turned away and busied herself with mundane tasks. She spoke more clearly, her back turned. "I didn't. She found me. Here, actually. Came to me because I'm Mike Ortiz's daughter."

"They were looking into the disappearance of Baby Rose, and Grace Fontaine's murder by extension," Mackenzie expanded.

"That's right." Violet's shoulders fell. "They found out that the lead detective on that case was my dad. They also knew about Sully, but he was just a uniform back in the day. So Whitney was interested in what my dad had to say."

"Did they ever talk to him?"

"No. Well, Whitney came *here* to find him. But she found me and we got talking and..." She turned around then, looking at everyone but them. "I suppose that I was an easier source than my dad. She wanted me to find out."

Mackenzie retrieved her notepad from her jacket. "What questions did she ask you?"

"Just details about the investigation. They were interested in the evidence against Jake Lawson." Crooked teeth dug into her plump lower lip as she recalled the details. "How and when they found the remains of Baby Rose. A lot of questions about Barry."

She and Nick glanced at each other. Barry Fontaine. The two women were circling in on him.

"Did you ask your dad anything?"

"No." Violet's face fell. "I know my dad. This case has always haunted him. It was his last one before he retired, and the fact that Baby Rose was found dead... it wasn't easy for him."

"Then what was Whitney expecting from you?" Nick asked.

"To indirectly fish for information?" she suggested. "Check his old notes?"

"Did Ortiz keep any of his notes?"

"A few. But there was nothing new in them really. That's

what I told them too. Well, except for how bad Barry and Grace's marriage actually was."

"What do you mean?" Mackenzie asked.

"All those stories in the newspapers about their perfect married life was a lie. Barry's friends and coworkers reported several public arguments and fights between them. I told Whitney about it. That was the only interesting thing I found out."

"Why did you agree to help her?" Nick asked. "If you knew how much it affected your dad, what motivated you?"

She let out a nervous chuckle, her hand shaking as she tucked a strand of hair behind her ear. "I was curious. My dad is very protective of me. He always kept me away from everything scary or dangerous. Didn't want me to be exposed to how messed up the world was."

Mackenzie remembered how Ortiz and his wife had been trying for years for a baby. When his wife finally got pregnant, Ortiz decided to retire early to be there for his daughter. She wondered if Ortiz was filled with shame with what he had done, distanced himself from this life and anything that reminded him of it. She wondered if he wanted to protect her from a shade of life that could corrupt an innocent person.

"Did Whitney mention a stalker?" Nick asked. "Or somebody called Jennifer?"

"She did mention Jennifer once. A stalker... no, not really." Her eyes glazed over as she stared into the empty space behind them. "But she was worried about the investigation. Said that leaving The Farm didn't necessarily mean that you were disconnected from it. But I thought maybe she was talking about her daughter."

"Did she tell you what made her and Jennifer look into that old case?" Mackenzie asked.

Violet's face darkened. "It's because of what they found in the vault."

A spark of curiosity flickered inside her. "What vault?"

"On The Farm, there's a vault in Tobias's hut. It's under lock and key. Nobody knows what's inside it. She said that a friend got into it and found something, after which she started looking into the disappearance of Baby Rose and roped her in."

Mackenzie's thoughts sprinted. What could Tobias Mathis have in that vault about Baby Rose? What was the connection?

THIRTY-ONE

"How do we get into that vault?" Nick asked out loud, throwing a dart that landed smack in the middle of the board.

"We plan a heist," Mackenzie replied dryly. He grinned but she was only half-joking.

They were in the lounge where some of the officers and detectives hid for a much-needed break. The room was strewn with couches, a pool table, a dart board, and a ping-pong table. Troy and Finn were campaigning hard for a foosball table. It was after much effort that the lounge was populated with something other than the vending machine.

In the recent past, the crime rate had decreased. There was peace in Lakemore. Until from the bleakest recesses of the town, darkness began to fall again. Four women dead. One still missing.

"Are there any leads on Hazel?" Mackenzie asked, the sides of her head pulsing with stress.

"Sheriff's office has been following up on tips, but they're all bogus." Nick hit another bullseye. "No sightings reported in Tacoma or Olympia."

"What if she's dead?" Mackenzie croaked.

Nick's hand froze in mid-air. When he landed the next shot, it bounced off the board. "Then we make sure no one else from that Farm goes missing. At least there's a pattern between the victims."

"Not between Grace and Cecily."

He exhaled and ran a hand through his hair. "Did Angela get back to you on cause of death?"

"Not yet. But I think she'll have something for us in a few hours. Becky messaged me to say they have cleaned the bones."

"Does Becky have cause of death for Jennifer?"

Mackenzie shook her head. "She's getting frustrated. Angela has agreed to consult after she finishes post on Cecily Rodriguez."

"What's the injury again?"

Mackenzie recited from memory. "A high-velocity injury to the ribs that caused internal bleeding. But it wasn't a bullet."

He widened his eyes in exasperation. "Good luck to her with that one."

"We need to talk to Barry. Confront him about his alibi," she decided, purpose flooding her veins. There was no point in ruminating in thoughts. Moving forward was the only way to quell that eddy of fear in her belly. She touched Robert's watch on her wrist.

Mackenzie was flailing in the freezing lake. She gulped air, and water pummeled into her mouth. A force was dragging her down.

"Keep moving, Mackenzie," Robert said, treading water. "You just have to keep moving and you'll never be afraid."

They were formulating a plan when a uniform came in with Zoe and a young boy.

"Zoe?" Mackenzie couldn't hide her surprise.

Zoe smiled, her hands clutching the boy's shoulders. "This is Jackson, Hazel's son."

Jackson was a skinny boy, wearing pants and T-shirt made out of fabric in earthy tones just like his father. His dark hair formed a messy mop. His eyes were almond shaped.

"Hello," he said.

"He really wanted to meet you," Zoe explained.

"Tobias let him?" Nick was skeptical.

"He doesn't need to know." She winked at them. "Besides Jackson is good at keeping secrets, isn't he?"

Jackson nodded eagerly.

How was Zoe able to defy Tobias? While he was deeply entrenched in the minds of the other women to the point that Whitney and Jennifer continued to live in paranoia after leaving, Zoe seemed oddly detached.

"How can we help you, Jackson?" Nick said. "We are doing our best to look for your mom."

Jackson looked up at Zoe, as if waiting for some kind of permission. She nodded at him encouragingly. "Jackson, remember what we said about secrets? That sometimes it's okay to share your dad's secrets if it helps your mom."

"Dad will get angry," Jackson said in his sweet voice. "I don't want him to get angry."

"Well, then our trip here can be a secret we don't tell anyone." She waggled her eyebrows.

Jackson hesitated for a moment before turning back to Mackenzie and Nick. "There are some cameras around The Farm."

"Cameras?" Nick repeated.

"I heard Dad and Caleb talking about it when one of them stopped working."

"Does anyone else know about these cameras?" Mackenzie asked.

"No," Zoe replied for him. "Tobias never told anyone about them."

"Did you see any?" Nick prodded. "Where are they?"

"I have seen at least five. They are up in the trees, hidden by foliage and leaves. Not possible to find unless you are looking for them."

A creepy sensation unraveled in Mackenzie's gut. The more she discovered about Tobias's activities, the ickier she felt. How did his empire keep expanding while he held so many women hostage? But this wasn't the first time a hero was unmasked as the villain in this town. She had come to an unnerving conclusion—that perhaps everybody was rotten deep down.

Either everyone was evil or they were cowards.

"Thanks, buddy. We'll look into that right away." Nick gave him a fist bump. Jackson smiled shyly. Then when he looked at Mackenzie expectantly, she tipped her chin up in a curt nod. The corners of his mouth fell and he stepped back into Zoe's arms, scared.

"Of course you nod at someone and scare the daylights out of them," Nick muttered in her ears.

She nudged him in the ribs with her elbow. When Zoe and Jackson turned to leave, she said to Nick, "Can you look into getting access to the cameras at The Farm?"

"Yes..."

"I have to talk to Zoe. Something's going on here." She didn't have time to explain and rushed after them. Turning around the corner, she saw Jackson getting something from the vending machine with Zoe nowhere in sight. She searched for her face in the crowd at the station and did a double take when she found her.

In a corner, Zoe and Captain Murphy were engaged in conversation. On the surface, it appeared to be friendly. But Mackenzie noted a certain tightness on their faces and the forced rigidness in their postures.

After a few minutes, Zoe called Jackson over and parted ways with Captain Murphy. He watched her walk away with a thoughtful expression until his eyes collided with Mackenzie's. His eyebrows pulled together and he went back into his office, huffing and disgruntled.

"Mack!" Nick came up behind her. "I was just told by Rivera that we can't file for a warrant to get the camera footage."

"Why?"

"She said Murphy has been closely monitoring this investigation and the word of a seven-year-old boy isn't probable cause."

"But Hazel was last seen going to her room before she disappeared. We need access to The Farm to see who abducted her."

"There's no sign that that's a crime scene." He sucked in his breath. "There were no signs of a struggle in the room."

"Because they had *hours* to clean anything up." She pressed him with a look. "How are we supposed to get access to the vault if we can't even get the security footage?"

The sound of Nick's phone ringing interrupted them. His eyes grew large at the notification. "The DNA on the toothpick came back. It belongs to Caleb."

"So he was in her room. He is Tobias's enforcer. Maybe he enlisted his help to tamper with evidence in the room," Mackenzie said.

"Well, I have an idea. I think I can convince Caleb."

When Caleb arrived at the station, he seemed on edge. His hands were inside his pockets, but Mackenzie could tell they were clenched. He tried tucking his neck in, hiding in the collar of his beige jacket. His mouth moved around the toothpick he incessantly chewed. Mackenzie wondered if it was a nervous tick. The longer he sat in the interrogation room, the more his chewing increased and his careless façade began to chip away, brick by brick. His hands twitched. He squirmed in his chair. He stole glances at the mirror, the other side of which stood Mackenzie and Nick in a dimly lit room.

Nick leaned on the doorframe, the muscles on his arms bulging and ropey.

"Are you sure you can handle this?" Mackenzie asked, crossing her arms. He had lied for Caleb once already.

He gave her a flat look. "Seriously?"

"Yes."

His face fell. "Mack, if he's guilty, then I won't let him get away with it."

Her throat closed. "He knows which buttons to push. You already lied for him once."

"He was my partner." He winced like she had slapped him. "He had a really bad childhood. I could never imagine that he was potentially involved in something like this."

Mackenzie wanted to volley more questions at him, but before she could form the words Nick turned and walked away. Even if Nick didn't have a soft spot for Caleb anymore, he could still overcompensate and make a mistake.

She watched Nick barge into the interrogation room. Everyone around her was personally tangled with this case. She was the only one who could afford to be objective.

As soon as Caleb saw Nick, he rolled his eyes. "Of course, it's you. Why am I here?"

Nick remained standing. He tossed the evidence bag on the table. "That toothpick has your DNA all over it. Guess where we found it?"

Caleb shrugged, disinterested. "Where?"

"In Hazel's bedroom." He tilted his head. "Now tell me, what was it doing there?"

"I don't know." Caleb let his hands fall to the side. "Is this even ethical?"

"What is?"

"*You* interviewing *me*." His eyes darted to the mirror and he spoke to Mackenzie directly, as if he could sense her in the other room. "Detective Price, shouldn't you be doing this?"

Mackenzie's nostrils flared. She thought of creative ways to wipe that perpetual smile off his face.

"I'm going to ask you again. What were you doing in Hazel's bedroom?"

"I was there to check on her after no one had seen her for a while. Might have dropped it then. No big deal." Caleb leaned back, throwing his arm over the back of the chair, and swaying his knee.

Nick circled him. "What happened to you, man? Doesn't it hurt to come back to this station as a suspect in a murder investigation?"

Caleb's face flashed with fury. "Is that why you brought me here? To try to embarrass me in front of your girlfriend?"

He snorted. "Where were you the night of Whitney's murder?"

"I must have been at The Farm," he said with a straight face.

"What about Jennifer's murder?"

"At The Farm."

"Can anyone verify that?"

"I'm sure Tobias can." He challenged him with his eyes. Mackenzie felt the simmering tension between them through the wall. "Anything else?"

"What about the night Cecily Rodriguez was killed?" Nick asked with a cruel smile.

Mackenzie was seeing shades of Nick she didn't want to see. That streak of brutality stemming from betrayal.

Caleb was aghast. "She's *dead*?"

"We dug out her bones, man. In those woods." He watched him closely, his eyes soft.

"What do you want from me, Nick? You regret doing what you did for me?"

"Should I?"

This wasn't the plan. Mackenzie tapped on the glass to drag Nick back on track.

Caleb laced his fingers together on the table and scowled. "I know nothing about Cecily. I don't remember that night."

"We want access to the security cameras on The Farm for the two days leading up to Hazel's disappearance, including the day *itself*."

Caleb smirked haughtily. "Got a warrant?"

"No. But you will get us those videos."

"Why?"

"Because if you don't then we will tell Tobias that we found your DNA in Hazel's bed and clothes."

Mackenzie drew a sharp breath. This was personal and she felt like an intruder in an interaction that was fraught with history and emotions she couldn't fully grasp.

"*What?*" Caleb was appalled. "I know you. You won't do that."

"I lied for you once already." Nick returned a mirthless chuckle. "What's another lie to get to the truth?"

"Just because Tobias has been cooperating without lawyers doesn't mean he can't afford the best in the country. I dare you to lie and get away with it this time."

"Well, we could at least *imply* that. I can imagine Tobias's reaction already. I can tell how protective he is about those women..."

Caleb ripped the toothpick from his mouth and cursed under his breath. "I'll get you the tapes. Just don't tell him anything. He's crazy possessive about them."

"Did Tobias tell you to hide the evidence regarding Hazel's abduction?"

"Listen. Hazel was Tobias's favorite. She was the only one practically raised on The Farm. He's deeply affected by this."

"You cooperate with us and we'll cooperate with you. Are you aware of a vault at Tobias's lodgings?"

The defiance burning in Caleb's eyes gave way to fear. "What vault?"

Nick threw a glance over his shoulder. Mackenzie also noted the shift in Caleb's demeanor. "We know Tobias has a vault on The Farm. Do you know what's inside it?"

Caleb's chest heaved. "Nick, stay away from the vault."

"I just told you that if you cooperate with us then we'll cooperate with you." Nick glowered at him.

"I don't know where it is. I've never seen inside it," he insisted. "I swear."

Mackenzie didn't know how much they could trust this troublemaker. But this was the first time she'd seen him lose control like this.

"Then why are you telling me to stay away from it?"

"Because I know how crazy protective he is about it. There's something inside it that Tobias doesn't want *anyone* to find out. Not even me."

But according to Violet, Jennifer had gotten into that vault. Something that had sparked a chain of events that linked two murders spanning thirty years. Mackenzie pondered over what Tobias could possibly be hiding inside it. If it had to do with Baby Rose and Grace, what was the connection between Tobias and the Fontaine family?

When Mackenzie's phone trilled with a notification from Angela Weiss, she went back to her desk still ruminating over various possibilities.

She opened the mass spec report that Angela had sent her and gave her a call as instructed.

"Hello, Detective Price?" Angela's stern voice came from the other side.

"Hi, Dr. Weiss. I have the report open that you just sent me."

"Good, good," she said. "All right. She was stabbed to death. Stab wounds are evident on the ribs, manubrium and clavicle, ulna, and radius. But Dr. Sullivan told me that you were interested in information regarding the tool that was used to remove the eyeball as it pertains to some open cases you have. We sampled the connective tissue, in particular periosteum and fascia, along with the lacrimal glands and surrounding ducts. We detected metal particles in significantly more quantities than other expected compounds associated with decomposition and the soil in which the victim was buried."

Mackenzie checked the analysis results herself to confirm. "Bronze."

"That's right."

"Are you sure, Dr. Weiss?"

She didn't seem to take offense. "Absolutely. We used SEM-EDS which is highly accurate. The sample is bombarded with an electron beam which generates an X-ray profile of the element. It doesn't destroy the sample so we tested twice to verify. It matches the profile from the forensic analysis during Grace Fontaine's autopsy."

Mackenzie hummed, her thoughts racing ahead. The same weapon was used to remove the eyes of Grace Fontaine and Cecily Rodriguez—two murders that took place fifteen years apart. Both had one person in common—Barry Fontaine.

THIRTY-TWO

Mackenzie panted like her lungs were drawing air from straws. Her feet slapped the concrete, the sound echoing in the barren streets. She never listened to music when running at night. She imagined a hand clamping her mouth shut and being hauled into the dark woods of Lakemore. The air was sticky and harsh to breathe. Even though the sidewalk was flat and there was no wind, she felt like she was running against the flow.

It was a moonless, cloudy night. Many of the lampposts were not working, and the other ones flickered. There was nothing more nerve-shredding than the woods at night. The darkness was thick and velvety, and the sky itself hung lower than usual, pressing down on her.

Darkness was closing in all sides. It would smother her, snuff out the life.

She came to a halt and so did her spiraling thoughts. Her lungs collapsed onto themselves as she caught her breath. A hot ache pulsed through her legs.

Was Hazel Martin the latest victim of this darkness?

Lakemore PD had even dispatched patrols around The Farm. It was a precautionary measure since all three women were either members or former members. Tobias Mathis wasn't happy with this scrutiny and interference but technically couldn't complain as nobody was trespassing on his property. Nick was at the station going through the footage that Caleb had been able to send. There were at least seven cameras. But there was no way to verify if there were any more. The sheriff's office had been following up on any tips but the hotline set up for information on the whereabouts of Hazel Martin was no longer ringing off the hook. The leads were drying up and so were the prospects of finding her alive.

Mackenzie found herself on the path where Whitney was last seen alive. It annoyed her no end that they only had a partial snapshot of her running before the camera was knocked out by the storm.

The road stretched ahead of her like a wavy, gray ribbon. Pine trees bordered each side. The sound of insects buzzing grew louder. There wasn't a single person around, and not a single set of headlights cut through the darkness. Her pulse thrummed under her skin. She double-checked that her Glock was tucked into her sock.

She began running down the road, placing herself in Whitney's shoes. She didn't know why or what to expect. But she imagined someone chasing her, someone who terrified her like they did Whitney. As she ran at full speed, she saw a wraithlike figure of Whitney running alongside her.

Mackenzie stopped. She noticed something. A traffic mirror was positioned at the curve of the road. If Whitney was running on this road, she would have passed that mirror. It would have caught her reflection and that of the person behind her. The traffic camera didn't have a view of the mirror. But she remembered seeing a power distribution shed. She hurried back down the road and found it sitting a few yards into the woods.

Patches of moss and cracked shingles clung to the sloped roof. The dilapidated structure made of weathered wood and corroded metal was full of holes and crevices, through which vines snuck in and out. But it was a functioning unit. Multiple conduits were lined outside, electrical cables entered and exited the structure and ventilation grilles were strategically placed.

There was a camera above the reinforced door of the shed, facing outwards—not at the road where Whitney was running but it would have the view of the traffic mirror.

Mackenzie jumped up in a frenzy and called Peterson. "Find out the utility company for the area where Whitney was found dead and get their security footage for the night. I have a good feeling."

A few hours later, Mackenzie was back at work after taking a shower. A fresh pot of coffee was brewing in the break room. The bin was overflowing with Chinese takeout boxes. Yawns were stifled. Eyes were rubbed. Necks were cracked.

But sleep eluded Mackenzie when she arrived at the station with a renewed sense of hope. She found a bespectacled Nick sitting at his desk, peering at the screen. She didn't realize he wore glasses.

"You got glasses?" she asked.

He jumped. "Mack! What? Yeah." He removed them. "Just for reading."

"Old age catching up," she said to his dismay. "What are you watching?"

"Went over the footage Caleb sent and I found only this one video capturing Hazel. It's from the day Whitney was killed. She met Hazel."

Surprise registered on Mackenzie's face. She pulled up a chair next to him. "Whitney visited those woods that day Cecily was found."

"Yeah. One of the cameras on the border of The Farm covers that section of the woods." He dragged the cursor back and replayed the video from that day. "That's Whitney standing there at three in the afternoon."

A blurry figure of Whitney stood in the woods, wearing the same clothes she was found dead in. She kept checking the time on her phone and kicking rocks, clearly waiting for someone.

Around fifteen minutes later, Hazel came into view. Her long hair reached her waist. In a jarring contrast to Whitney's clothes, Hazel was dressed in the long, earthy dress like the other Farm girls.

They began talking to each other. It was hard to make out any words from the video but after five minutes or so, Hazel began shaking her head profusely and stepping back from Whitney. Whitney took a step forward, raising her hand to touch Hazel but the latter flicked it away. Hazel's shoulders were shaking and then she turned and ran away from Whitney. Whitney called after her but then turned and walked away in the opposite direction.

"What the hell were they talking about?" Mackenzie voiced what they were both thinking.

"Maybe Whitney and Jennifer were trying to get Hazel to leave The Farm too. They had realized that Tobias was a psycho and wanted to be free. And that's why Tobias killed them."

"But Hazel was upset by what Whitney had to say."

"Hazel practically grew up on The Farm, remember?" Nick said, chugging his third coffee. There was no way he was sleeping tonight. "She's hardwired to be loyal to Tobias as that's the only life she's ever known."

Mackenzie followed his train of thought. "But perhaps Hazel started thinking later that Whitney and Jennifer were right. She might have questioned staying with Tobias so he had reason to get rid of her too."

"Exactly."

"It's a good theory. How do we prove it?"

The door to Sully's office opened with a creak. Mackenzie

was surprised that the sergeant was still around. He was usually the first one out the door, determined to get home to his wife and wash away the grisliness of the job.

"Detective Price," Sully hollered. "In my office, now."

Nick shot her an incredulous look. "No idea what that's about."

She rolled her eyes and headed to Sully's office, her head held high in defiance. She had successfully avoided Sully since his devastating confession. But when she entered the office, ice filled her chest.

Rain pounded on the windows, juxtaposed against the knee-deep silence of the office. It was tidy with no unnecessary boxes or token of his latest hobby. There was only a bottle of Scotch and a sculpted glass.

"You drinking on the job again?" She crossed her arms.

He twisted open the bottle and poured himself a glass. "Technically, I'm off duty."

"Why did you want to see me?"

Sully took a sip. "How much longer are you going to avoid me?"

She scoffed. "We're professional and cordial at work."

"You're also my goddamn friend," he snapped.

Mackenzie's heart cracked open. It was a simple statement, a simple relationship. But it held enormous weight for someone whose only companion was loneliness.

"You framed someone." Her tone dripped with disappointment. "It doesn't matter if he deserved it or not, but how could you have done that?"

"I've lived with that every single day." His eyes were round and haunted. "Just locked it away somewhere. And now it's everywhere in my head."

"So you feeling guilty is supposed to make it okay?"

Sully gritted his teeth. "What makes you the authority on any of this, Mack?"

"What I feel doesn't come from some misplaced sense of self-righteousness." Her face turned red. "It comes from the fact that I don't know you *at all*."

"And who knows you?" he whispered.

Mackenzie staggered backward. His gaze was stinging, poking holes in her standoffish, prickly façade.

"Don't you think I know that you are hiding something too, Mack? You've been working for me for a decade. Don't think I'm a fool for not seeing you being haunted by something every day. Guilt recognizes guilt. But I've never cared about your past."

"Whatever I did in my past?" The blackening memories of her arms hurting from lifting the legs of a dead body threatened to resurface, but she pushed them back down. "I can promise you that I never *framed* anyone and I *never* broke the law as a police officer."

"Then I envy you, Mack."

"You envy *me*?"

"It's easier to live with the guilt you can justify."

Mackenzie's shoulders sagged. The torment on Sully's face was undeniable. His fat mustache hadn't been trimmed. His round jaw was dotted with facial hair. Dark circles lined his weary eyes. He desperately needed a haircut. He took another sip of Scotch.

"Why haven't you told anyone what I did?" Sully asked.

"Because you're my friend."

His stare was somewhere between dumbfounded and crushed. It was the last thing he expected from Mad Mack. She always had logical reasons not emotional.

"A time comes in the life of every officer, Mack. A time when they have to decide between following the law and doing what they feel is right. I hope that time doesn't come for you. Because if it does, it will be nearly impossible for you to ignore your gut feeling."

Mackenzie's eyes drifted to the window. She saw her reflection in the darkness. Perhaps that darkness twisted people's minds. It fractured any sense of right or wrong. Perhaps Lakemore truly was doomed.

There was a knock on the door and Peterson popped his head in. "Detective Price, I got something for you."

Mackenzie excused herself from Sully's office. "What's up?"

"I got the footage from the utility company."

"That fast?"

"I might have threatened the guy," he admitted sheepishly.

She patted his arm. "Good job. What do we have?"

"You're right. The mirror does capture Whitney running away. But she wasn't running away from a person. It was a car."

"A car?" she repeated. "Did you get the license plate?"

He beamed. "I did. I just ran it through the DMV. It belongs to Russell Grant."

Russell Grant—the private detective Barry hired thirty years ago.

THIRTY-THREE

NOVEMBER 9

"WASIS confirmed there are no priors." Mackenzie took long strides as they walked down the narrow dirt path to Russell's house.

"He might not have a criminal record," Nick replied, "but he is ex-police. And runs a gym."

"Which means he's familiar enough with protocols to be a sly killer."

Nick pushed his sunglasses further up the bridge of his nose. His dark hair blew slightly in the faint breeze. Finally, the sun had decided to shine upon Lakemore after a few bleak days. Perhaps, this was the day they would find Hazel alive.

"What do you think his motive was?" Mackenzie asked.

"Maybe he got so obsessed with what went down with Grace that something flipped in his head." Nick shrugged.

"You don't think he killed Grace?"

On either side of them, tall grass swayed. Their golden hues contrasted against the blue skies. Behind them followed five uniforms, all ready to execute the search warrant against Russell.

"The weapon used to remove the eye is different. I have a feeling we are dealing with two killers," Nick said.

The words lingered in her mind. She strongly suspected the same, especially considering the fact that the last two homicide victims knew each other and were killed in quick succession, unlike the first two victims—Grace and Cecily.

A modest house made of whitewashed panels appeared at the end of the path. A front yard spread out before the house. Sunlight filtered through the branches of nearby trees, creating a patchwork of light and shade on the ground. Next to the house was a pond, shimmering under the sunlight.

Mackenzie knocked on the door. Footsteps scuffled. The door opened. Russell stood there in his pajamas, his muscles bulging under his clothes, his height towering over both Mackenzie and Nick.

"What's going on?" He opened the screen door and eyed the cops standing behind.

"We have a search warrant for your property, Mr. Grant." Mackenzie handed him the documentation while Nick gestured the uniforms to begin scoping the area. Two circled the house and three pushed past an annoyed Russell.

"Why?" He scowled.

"Because we have you on video chasing Whitney in your car moments before she was killed. Not to mention your car model matches the description given by her friends," Mackenzie said. "I don't think that's a coincidence."

There was a sharp sound of a drawer crashing to the floor. Russell jumped and yelled at the uniform to be careful with his things. He looked at Mackenzie and Nick, frazzled. "I didn't do this."

"We literally have you on camera, Mr. Grant. We are looking for Hazel Martin. Where is she?" Mackenzie said.

His eyebrows knotted. "I don't know! I didn't kill Whitney! I was following her, yes, but I didn't kill her."

"You didn't say anything about that before," Nick said.

"I didn't want any trouble!" His desperate eyes searched their hard faces. When he realized they weren't budging, he rubbed the back of his neck and shifted his weight from foot to foot. "I was following Whitney. I got an anonymous note a few months ago. That's why."

When Mackenzie and Nick remained impassive, his restlessness heightened. "I'm not lying. I still have that note. Can I show it you?"

Nick motioned to Peterson to shadow Russell while they waited. Seconds later, Russell emerged with a piece of paper. He handed it to them. "This was left on my porch."

Mackenzie read the letter. She felt like someone had hollowed out her chest with a knife. Scribbled on the paper in black pen were the words:

Baby Rose is alive. The answer lies at The Farm.

THIRTY-FOUR

An hour later, Russell was sitting in the interrogation room. Despite his large frame, his face looked small. A thorough search of his house hadn't yielded any evidence pertaining to Hazel or Jennifer.

"What happened to the note?" Rivera asked. "Did you send it for analysis?"

Mackenzie nodded. "Dusting it for prints and DNA other than Russell's."

"Could this be a joke?" Rivera said, her eyes bouncing between Mackenzie and Nick.

Nick stood next to Mackenzie, leaning his arm against the frame of the mirror. "I don't know."

"What do you mean? Jake Lawson was convicted and bones were found in the woods a few weeks later which belonged to a human infant. That and the fact that there was no other trace of Baby Rose despite a massive search, led to the conclusion that she died in those woods. Maybe this letter was sent by some conspiracy theorist," Rivera said.

Mackenzie hid her discomfort in front of Rivera. Baby Rose's bones were found. But this case was already twisted with

Sully's and Ortiz's corruption. What if there was more deception to uncover? Nothing about this case was as it seemed.

The door flew open and Sully barreled in, his face swelling and puffing. "She's alive?"

"We don't know that." Mackenzie spoke in a measured tone. "I've asked Dr. Angela Weiss to look at the pictures of her bones to verify."

Rivera eyed Sully scathingly. "What the hell is going on with you, Sully?"

But Sully was in a daze. Like a parched man, seeing the hint of an oasis, all his attention was directed at the possibility that Baby Rose was still alive. That she hadn't been eaten by animals. That perhaps the story of the Fontaine family would have *some* kind of happy ending.

"It was his first case, Lieutenant," Nick jumped in. "It obviously means a lot to him."

Rivera glared at them all. "I'm not a fool, Detective Blackwood. And I sure as hell don't care that you're the son of a senator. I don't care what happened thirty years ago and I don't care what happened fifteen years ago. What I care about is here and now, the case that's under *my* supervision. I want no mistakes. Is that clear?"

Sully nodded almost like a petulant child getting scolded. "Yes, Lieutenant."

"Now grill him," she ordered Mackenzie and Nick.

When they entered the room, Russell jerked upright, desperation clouding his face. "I swear I have *no* idea who's killing these women. I don't know what happened to Whitney after that night."

"Why were you chasing her?" Mackenzie asked flatly. "We have you on video."

He tsked in irritation. "I wasn't chasing her! I was following her. She arrived at the party and was hanging out with her friends. At some point she slipped away and I didn't realize where she had gone. I was driving, looking for her, when I saw her running and screaming. She had this gash on her head."

"You didn't see who was after her?" Nick wasn't convinced.

"No!" His forehead crumpled as he leaned forward. "A storm broke out. I rolled down my window and even shouted, asking her what was going on. But she was catatonic. She was so afraid. Maybe she thought I was after her too."

"And when did you lose her?" Mackenzie asked.

"She ran into the woods. I could have stopped the car and gone after her, but the weather was getting rough, and frankly I..." He sighed. "I thought she was back on drugs and having an episode. I saw shrooms and acid at the party. Figured she was tripping."

"Did you see anyone else?"

"No. That's why I didn't say anything before because I didn't know anything that could help you. Please believe me."

"We will believe you once we verify your alibi for the night of Jennifer's murder too," Mackenzie warned. "Now tell us about the note."

"It was left on my porch. I don't know who put it there and I don't have any security cameras."

"You believed what was written on the note?" Nick asked.

"Yeah. I did. I knew Jake Lawson was innocent. So I didn't think it was a stretch of the imagination that more than one thing had gone wrong in that case."

Unease danced on Mackenzie's skin. She felt Sully standing on the other side of the mirror, listening with bated breath and also hope.

If Baby Rose was indeed alive then Sully might see it as his redemption.

"And what led you to Whitney?" she continued.

"She was the same age that Baby Rose would be today. She had blonde hair. She left The Farm and it was around that time that I got the note. I was just watching her when I could..." He sat, deflated. "Maybe she was the one who left the note. Or maybe she was Baby Rose."

"Did you ever follow Jennifer Peyton?" Mackenzie presented him with a photo of Jennifer's body, hoping to get his reaction. He was a large man, capable of abducting and handling an adult woman. But the gruesome sight of the body made him flinch and gag.

"No! Please!"

She withdrew the picture.

"Look. I swear I didn't do this. This case haunted me. It haunted everyone." He pointed a finger behind them. "I bet it has haunted your sergeant too. When I read that note, it might have scared the living daylights out of me, but it gave me hope. That maybe Baby Rose was out there somewhere and that a two-month-old girl hadn't been left in the woods to be eaten by animals. I thought maybe Barry might finally find some solace in his life after losing everything. Father and daughter reunited thirty-one years later."

"Did you tell Barry about this note?" Nick quizzed.

"No. Not at all. I didn't want to get his hopes up."

There was a loud knock on the mirror behind them. Mackenzie gestured to Nick to continue questioning their suspect. She returned to the room where Rivera and Sully were watching closely.

Sully handed her his phone. "Dr. Angela Weiss is on the line for you."

"Hello, Dr. Weiss. Did you get a chance to look at the bones?"

"I did." Something about her tone made the hair on Mackenzie's arms stand up. Like she was preparing for a blow. "These bones are not human, Detective Price."

"What?"

"These belong to a racoon."

Her tongue was suddenly too heavy. "A racoon?"

"The bones were originally identified as the infant's hand. But this is a common mistake. The phalanges of a racoon are almost identical to that of an infant. I suspect an inexperienced forensic anthropologist or perhaps the lack of better equipment at the time led to this misidentification."

It was concluded thirty-one years ago that the only remains of Baby Rose found in the woods were her hand after she was eaten by some wild animal. A hollow pain spread across Mackenzie's chest as brick by brick her composure was worn down by a heartbreaking but hopeful realization.

Baby Rose was alive.

THIRTY-FIVE

"So that's why Whitney and Jennifer were looking into Baby Rose's disappearance. 'The answer lies at The Farm'. They got into that vault and found the evidence. One of them must have left that note for Russell, hoping to involve more people to get to the truth." Mackenzie tapped a pen to the side of her temple.

With every tick of the clock that the whereabouts of Hazel Martin remained unknown, Mackenzie felt a crushing pressure mounting in her temples. Jackson's face was seared into her memory.

Two mothers failed trying to get back to their children. Now Mackenzie felt like they were the only ones who could save Jackson from losing a mother too. The thought of failing left her with jangled nerves.

"Is that maybe why Whitney was talking to Hazel that day?" Nick suggested. "Did she think that Hazel was Baby Rose?"

"Hazel was on The Farm the longest. It could also be that Whitney was recruiting Hazel's *help* to find Baby Rose."

"Why not ask Zoe? She seems to have more freedom than the other women to investigate."

Mackenzie didn't have an answer to that. She didn't have an answer to a lot of things, much to her dismay. Her hip dug into the edge of the table. "We have to inform Barry that his daughter might be alive."

Nick stroked his chin. "Also confront him about his alibi for the night of his wife's murder."

She recalled Barry's slumped shoulders and sagging face. There was nothing but dimness in his eyes. A body that moved languidly without any purpose or fire, merely operating on instincts living next to the graves of his entire family. A part of Mackenzie wanted to give him hope, a reason to live. But Candy's words about Barry being too watchful and his shady alibi made her suspicious.

"Even if he did kill his wife because of their tumultuous marriage, why would he kill *three* other women over a span of thirty years?" she asked Nick.

"Maybe he liked it, Mack. Violence is in our design. We are predators. Once you kill once, ignite that dormant instinct, it's hard to live without it. For some people, that is."

She mulled over his words. Lakemore PD couldn't afford to have an in-house profiler but Nick was pretty good at it. Austin swung by the conference room, his tie loose and sleeves rolled up. "Hey, I just heard back from the lab. There were no prints or DNA found on the letter."

Mackenzie tossed her pen across the table, her mouth flattening. "Great. They were careful."

Nick was puzzled. "I don't get it. If either Whitney or Jennifer left that note, then why did they make sure not to leave their prints? Did they not want to get caught?"

Rivera stopped by. "Detective Kennedy, are you not working on that homicide at the old-age home?"

"We closed it. Justin's making the arrest."

"So now you're itching to get on our case?" she teased.

He shrugged. "What can I say? These two end up walking into the most interesting ones."

"Happy to switch next time around." Nick raised his mug to him before taking a sip.

"We've had to let Russell go for now," Rivera informed them. "Since there is no evidence to link him to the murders. But I've asked patrol to keep an eye on him. Do we know who left the note on his porch?"

"No prints. No DNA," Mackenzie reiterated.

"Let me have a look at it again." Rivera put on her glasses as Nick pulled up a photo of the note on his laptop. "This is absurd. Can we track what paper it was or what kind of pen was used?"

"It's generic white paper and a black ballpoint pen," Nick said.

Rivera scrutinized the handwriting. "That handwriting looks familiar."

"Whose is it?" Mackenzie asked.

Rivera shook her head and took Nick's laptop, typing something. "I was watching this segment on Tobias's company the other day. I think I saw it there..." After a few minutes, her eyes widened. "There it is!" She turned the laptop and all four of them peered closer at the screen. It was paused at a frame where Tobias was talking to the camera, and behind him was a stall selling pottery and candles. "Look at the letters—R and F specifically. *That's* the handwriting." In front of the stall, there was a blackboard with the words The Farm and what they were selling written in chalk. Rivera went back a few seconds to show them the writer.

"Zoe," Nick whispered, the corners of his eyes creasing.

Mackenzie's jaw tightened. "What's up with this woman?"

Rivera straightened. "All right. We need to split up to move fast. Detective Kennedy, why don't you run a background check on our mysterious Zoe. See what you can find."

"On it." He left the room.

"You two. Go grab Zoe and bring her in for questioning. Meanwhile I'll go and break the news to Barry—"

"No, I will." Sully was standing at the door. He looked like he had cleaned up. His hair was combed and his mustache trimmed. "I should talk to Barry."

Rivera gave him a curt nod. "Take Peterson with you."

Mackenzie knew that Rivera didn't fully trust Sully with this case yet. His unusual behavior had been blaringly obvious. But it was Rivera's finely tuned instincts that knew his bad mood was more than just the general nature of the job.

"So Zoe knows that Baby Rose is alive." Nick walked alongside Mackenzie, putting on his blazer.

"She might have access to the vault considering her special status at The Farm. The vault contained information that Baby Rose is alive. That's why Whitney and Jennifer were investigating."

"But why would Zoe care about any of that? And how did she know about Russell?"

They stepped out of the building into the parking lot. Mackenzie was riled up. Determination coursed through her veins. Zoe knew more than she was letting on. Maybe she held the key that would crack the case open.

Outside, clouds raced each other in the dull sky. Wind blew with abandon, sweeping the concrete ground, rustling leaves, and tousling their hair. Mackenzie had to rub her eyes when dust flew into them. The town was painted in gray hues.

Sully and Peterson were heading toward Sully's car on the other side when a deafening blast shattered the peace.

Everything happened in quick succession.

"Ahhh!" Mackenzie cried. Her body ducking. Nick instinctively covered her with his body.

In the blink of an eye, Sully's car erupted into a fireball, a blinding inferno. The force of the explosion sent Sully and

Peterson hurtling backward through the air. Commotion ensued. Several officers ran out of the station to Sully and Peterson who were lying on the ground. The car was engulfed in roaring flames. Fragments of hot metal rained down on the ground like confetti.

The heat distorted the air. Mackenzie felt it on her cheeks as she watched the scene, her heart pounding.

"He has no pulse!" one of the officers surrounding Sully and Peterson yelled.

And Mackenzie sank into Nick's arms.

THIRTY-SIX

"Who did this?" Mackenzie Price whispered to herself. Her loaded words were drowned out by the roar of thunder. Forks of lightning sliced the gloomy, gray skies. The air was cinched with humidity as rain refused to fall.

Mackenzie's eyes took in the sea of sad faces standing around a freshly installed tombstone on the green patch of land. The cemetery was dotted with tombstones of all shapes and sizes on the rolling green hill.

It wasn't too far from here that her mother, Melody, had buried someone they loved one wretched night twenty years ago in an unmarked grave. Mackenzie could spot it in the distance behind a tree. Her chest tightened. The priest spoke about life and death, about love and loss, and the blistering reminder that despite the differences in what we looked like, where we came from, and our experiences, all of us shared the same destiny: one day we lose everything.

Nick's warm hand clasped hers. "Peterson was one of us. We will find whoever killed him."

Peterson was so young, so kind, always spitting out facts and eager to clear his detective exam.

A faint sensation of comfort spread through her. That sense of surety and strength that she wasn't alone. But underneath the pain she felt from watching a family cry uncontrollably as they took turns throwing soil on the coffin, a beast was waking up inside her.

Anger. A hungry monster that wanted to claw its way out of her chest and kill the person who had ripped apart this family.

Her eyes flitted to Robert's grave behind the tree. There was someone standing by the tree, dressed in black, and leaning against the thick trunk. The figure was blurry in the distance, partly hidden in the shadows. They watched the funeral from afar.

"Nick, who is that?"

Nick followed her troubled gaze and squinted his eyes. "I don't know. It's a cemetery, Mack."

The figure turned and began walking away. Maybe Nick was right. She was becoming paranoid. She had every reason to. Someone had come after *them*.

But then the figure halted in front of Robert's grave. Mackenzie forgot to breathe. They bent down and placed a white rose.

Mackenzie untangled herself from Nick.

"What happened?" Nick asked.

"I have to go." She slipped away from the crowd and walked toward the mysterious figure.

At the edge of the cemetery when they were far from prying eyes, the figure stopped and turned around.

It was Zoe.

Mackenzie froze. "What are you doing here?"

"I came to pay my condolences." She looked different, dressed in a black raincoat over her standard long, beige dress.

"How do you know about him?" Mackenzie gestured at the white rose that Zoe had placed on Robert's grave. She hadn't had a chance to visit since this case started. It had weighed heavy on her. Every time she came here and talked to him tears would cascade down her cheeks.

Even after all these years, the tears hadn't run dry.

"You are famous ever since that documentary aired. I thought I'd do some research."

"Who the hell are you?" Mackenzie spat.

Zoe chuckled but it didn't reach her eyes. "You should ask me *why* I'm here."

"Why then?"

"To warn you." Zoe's smile dropped.

"Warn me?"

"The explosion in the car," Zoe said. "I have a feeling that happened because you were getting closer to the truth."

The drizzle grew stronger, falling on Mackenzie's back like icy needles. She struggled to keep her eyes open. "Lakemore PD will be investigating the explosion. They'll find out whoever was behind it."

"I'm sure they will." Zoe wasn't concerned. "But I'm worried about you, Detective Price. Whoever is behind this might consider you a serious threat."

A tingle ran down Mackenzie's spine. "Are you threatening me?"

"Not at all. You are a popular name in Lakemore. You have a reputation. If I were the killer, I'd be worried about you being on the case. I would do everything in my power to stop you." She began backpedaling. "All I'm saying is that if I were you, I would be cautious."

"Wait." Mackenzie studied Zoe for a moment, looking for any signs that could help her solve the enigma she was. "You knew about Baby Rose being alive and left an anonymous letter for Russell Grant tipping him off? Why?"

Zoe's practiced composure dissolved. She stirred in surprise. "I know Russell was hired as a private detective back then. I thought he'd be interested in going back to the case. Being a Good Samaritan."

"Why not tell the police?"

"The police would have needed some evidence before pouring their resources into that investigation." She shrugged. "I didn't need that with Russell."

"How did you know she was alive?"

"There are things in that vault, Detective Price." A shadow crossed Zoe's face that made Mackenzie's blood curdle.

"You have access to it?"

"Not alone. Tobias doesn't trust anyone completely. I do have a lot of freedom. But breaking into that vault is not something I can do alone. It's at least a two-man job." The tilt in her voice dripped with implication. "Or a two-woman job."

"We can't get a warrant for anything on Tobias. Two warrants have been rejected already."

Zoe nodded, contemplating. "If only there were a way to get into that vault without a warrant."

"Evidence has to be admissible. I'm an officer of the law. I follow protocol."

Work was a sacred place for Mackenzie. Everything outside of it had been corrupted and she was determined to preserve one aspect of her life. To keep it pristine and away from the stain of lies. Because some lies were sticky. They became a grimy layer underneath every interaction. It was why she couldn't look at Sully in the same way. Because his lie was there, lurking under every word they exchanged, every expression they shared, every breath they took in the same room.

Even with Nick—even though his lie hadn't been as big. It had awakened the dormant demons inside her that whispered: *what is he capable of?*

"I understand that your hands are tied while you're still a cop."

What an odd thing to say, Mackenzie thought.

"I would give you one piece of advice," Zoe continued before Mackenzie had a chance to reply. "Any warrants for Tobias might be getting blocked but warrants for Barry Fontaine's financials won't. I have always wondered if there was more to him losing his blossoming business after his wife was killed."

"Mack!" Nick's voice traveled through the rain. Mackenzie turned to find him walking toward her holding an umbrella. When she turned back to face Zoe, she was gone. "Who were you talking to?"

Goosebumps sprouted on Mackenzie's skin. "I have no idea."

THIRTY-SEVEN

"Ladies and gentlemen, it has been four agonizing days since thirty-one-year-old Hazel Martin went missing. As the search intensifies, hope begins to dwindle even as the police are leaving no stone unturned in their investigation. This is the *third* woman from Tobias Mathis's organization to be targeted. We are here today live with Mr. Mathis." Laura angled her head to the left and the camera panned to Tobias seated next to her. While Laura was dressed in a silk blue blouse, her auburn hair blow-dried, and lips painted with gloss, Tobias was wearing his loose-fitting, brown garments, trying hard to look the part of a humble, relatable man despite the millions in his bank account. It made Mackenzie wrinkle her nose in disgust.

"Mr. Mathis, thank you for joining us today."

"Thank you for having me. Though I would like to make one respectful correction, if I may. I don't have an organization. We are a family. I haven't lost employees; I've lost people I love."

Laura's smile was tight. "Do you have any theories as to why three of your... family members were targeted? Two dead and one missing."

"I don't know." The camera focused on his face. His expression leaked remorse. "I have asked myself this very question every second of every day since Whitney was killed."

"Do you have any enemies? Your company is a growing force to be reckoned with. Your company hasn't gone public yet, but you were already forcing out a lot of competition. Could this be an extreme way to damage your brand?"

His lower lip jutted out as he shrugged. "I don't have enemies, Laura. I have treated everyone with respect. My competition are big corporate companies who don't have much to lose by losing Lakemore as a potential market."

Laura tried to hide her frustration. It was evident that even she was becoming agitated by his masked arrogance. "Why do you only include women in your *family*, Mr. Mathis?"

"The world is an unkind place especially to women, Laura. I'm sure you know fears that I can't imagine, have had experiences I will never fathom. Despite the great strides women have made in this country, the truth is that they still face more discrimination, more resistance, fewer opportunities and most importantly—inferior *safety*. That's why I made the decision to uplift that section of the society. Offer them safety, structure, community while they develop new skill sets."

Mackenzie rolled her eyes and canceled the window on her computer. "That's insulting."

"I want to throw up at how sanctimonious he is." Nick was sitting at his desk behind her, drinking his coffee. His white shirt, usually crisp, was wrinkled.

The atmosphere at the station was subdued. A dampening force had settled upon them like a heavy blanket. It had been two days since they buried one of their own. They were all going about their day, but there was no laughter, no joking around and many thoughtful gazes. Mackenzie had found herself expecting to find Peterson loitering around the water cooler or getting lunch from the break room, reciting one of his fun facts. Often, she turned a corner expecting to see him walking down the hallway. Her heart stuttered for one fleeting second when she thought she saw him, but it was someone else.

Jenna's boots clacked on the floor. "Morning."

Mackenzie looked up to find her hollowed eyes and hair in disarray. "How are you doing, Jenna?"

Jenna had spent a lot of time with Peterson. Today for the first time, Jenna didn't regard her sourly. "I've been better." The corners of her mouth pulled down when she revealed an evidence bag. "Peterson was working on this."

"What's that?" Nick asked.

"It was retrieved from Jennifer's basement where her entire investigation into Baby Rose took place. It's some nonsensical poem. I don't think it means anything, but Peterson was obsessed with it. He thought it meant something."

Mackenzie and Nick leaned in to read what was written on the piece of paper.

"Whispers of stars in the midnight sky, echo through the realms where dreams die..." Nick read aloud. "A poem about night and secrets? Why was Peterson interested in this?"

She shrugged. "Beats me. But I felt I should say something. He would have wanted me to."

Mackenzie took the evidence bag from her. "Thanks, Jenna. I'll look into it." When Jenna left, she stared at the poem. Ten lines of words pulsing with something ominous but seemingly nothing to do with the case.

"Maybe Jennifer was into poetry?" Nick suggested.

"Maybe." But she wanted to give Peterson more credit. He was bright and creative. Perhaps there was something in this poem that had caught his attention.

"I have to talk to Clint. He's been pinging me." Nick sighed.

Mackenzie nodded absentmindedly as she began writing down the words on another piece of paper, her mind dissecting them to try to decipher what was hidden. Her toes clamped and unclamped in frustration as she rearranged the words and looked them up to check if there was a double-meaning or a connection to Grace or Baby Rose.

Austin's hand blocked her view. She jolted.

"Sorry, I called you twice," he said.

"I was absorbed in something."

He was leaning over the divider that separated her cubicle from Troy's. "Remember that warrant that came through on Barry's financial records?"

"Yes."

"Thirty-one years ago, a few weeks *after* Grace was found dead, Barry made some unusual large wire transfers from his business account over two years." He showed her a document displaying lumps of money starting from ten thousand dollars to almost one hundred thousand. "Back then he said that the wire transfers were part of his investments and asset management strategies."

The offshore company in Panama was called Golden Gate Investments Ltd. Suspicion spiked in her. "Let me guess, this company doesn't exist."

"You're right. I'm still hunting that down. I've asked Special Investigations for their help."

"That's a good idea. Austin, did you run that background check on Zoe? What's her full name again?"

"Zoe Anderson." His eyes flashed. "I found nothing. She's not on any database."

Mackenzie registered surprise. "DMV?"

He shook his head. "Nada. And somehow Murphy found out and chewed my ear off about wasting resources on this." When someone called him over, he excused himself, leaving Mackenzie with a chaos inside her that she couldn't tame.

She went back to the puzzle Peterson had been working on. There were grooves on the paper from folding it. But they didn't just run vertically and horizontally. She began folding the papers along the same diagonally running lines. Letters from different words formed. None of them made any sense. But she kept trying different combinations of folding the paper. The words pieced into letters forming a new word upon every fold. She was starting to lose hope when she spelled out something that made sense.

FOURSIXTWOONE

Mackenzie sat back, her mind reeling. Could this be a coincidence? If not, what did this number mean? She scoured through her memory, all the case files she'd spent hours studying. But she hadn't seen that number before.

She felt a hand on her shoulder. She jumped and turned around. Nick stood there, holding a laptop. He stared at her, tortured and angry. Then he showed her a video.

It was a video of Mackenzie going into the woods after Whitney at the time and date of the murder.

It took several moments for the video to sink in. A wave of confusion crashed over her. Her insides tightened in protest. Before her brain could formulate a response, Nick leaned into her ear and whispered: "Play along."

"Huh?"

And then Nick said the words loud enough for everyone to hear, words that she had dreaded hearing since she was twelve years old. "You're under arrest for murder."

THIRTY-EIGHT

Mackenzie was convinced she was truly going mad. Her thoughts were thrashing and clashing into each other. She tried to catch a thought, an emotion, something. But there was only numbness, stinging numbness that soaked every pore on her puffing face. Her breath turned shallow. Panic spooled through her. Nick escorted her down the stairs to the holding cell. Whispers spread like wildfire throughout the building.

They all saw her in cuffs. They all saw her being arrested by her partner. They all saw what she truly was deep down, what her mother had forced her to be—a criminal.

She felt like she was walking underwater. Her vision rippling, voices drowning. The sound of the metal door opening was sharp and then she was shoved into the cell by Nick.

"How could you do this?" Nick gripped the bars on the cell so tightly his knuckles turned white. His face taut and eyes blazing. "Why?"

"I didn't do this," Mackenzie croaked.

"Like hell you didn't!" he roared. The officer on guard watched them nervously. Nick clocked him a glance. "Get out."

He swallowed hard and fled.

Once they were alone, Nick turned to her. "Someone sent an anonymous video."

"It was Caleb. I saw him at the station and he was *smirking*."

"That asshole," he cursed. "It's obviously fake. Why is he targeting you?"

"Zoe had warned me that something might happen."

"That's why I put on that show. All warrants against Tobias get blocked, Murphy is protecting Zoe, Peterson died in a car explosion and now you're being framed. I don't know who to trust. I wanted a public spectacle to let Tobias think he won."

Mackenzie chewed her lip. "Well, once you dig deeper, Clint will be able to prove that the video is a fabrication. So this won't stick. What's the point of this?"

"I don't know." He rubbed the back of his neck. "To send a message? For us to back off? To slow us down?"

"Or maybe not." A thought snagged.

"What are you thinking?"

She opened her mouth to tell him but then remembered he couldn't be complicit.

The sound of approaching footsteps grew louder and Sully barreled in. "What's going on? What the hell is on that video?"

"We're trying to figure that out." Nick scratched his head.

Worry was etched on Sully's face. "Mack, don't worry. We will analyze that video right away. You—"

"No."

"No?" Nick and Sully cried in unison.

"Suspend me."

"Are you insane?" Sully growled. "Of course I know you're innocent."

Mackenzie faltered. Her train of thought brutally disrupted when shame cut her deep. She stared at the two men standing on the other side of the cell, their eyes burning with anger for her, their belief solid that she could do no wrong despite the evidence. They hadn't even questioned her.

While she had so easily doubted them.

"Mack? Are you in shock?" Nick said.

"No." She brushed it off. "Follow protocol, Sully. Suspend me. You need to focus on finding Hazel."

"You're onto something." Nick's eyes narrowed. "But you're not telling me."

"You're not the one in a holding cell. Do what you've got to do."

Sully groaned. "All right. Pending further investigation, you're suspended. Your badge and gun."

Mackenzie unclipped her badge and removed her Glock. "Here you go."

"Book her and hold her for the next twenty-four hours," Sully ordered before leaving them.

"What is it that you can't tell me?" Nick whispered, his eyes searching hers.

But she was defiant. "Trust me. Go. I only have twenty-four hours."

"I understand." As he left, he deliberately knocked over the items on a desk. One of them was the key to the cell. It was within Mackenzie's reach. Nick looked at the key and walked out of the room to engage the officer on duty in a conversation.

Mackenzie moved swiftly. She wedged her hand between the bars to reach for the key. She didn't have long. The muscles in her arm burned; the key was just at her fingertips. Finally, she grabbed it. Nick continued chatting with the officer outside, buying her time.

She unlocked the door but made it look like it was locked and then slid the key away from her. By the time the officer returned, he didn't suspect that the holding cell wasn't actually locked. He stole a glance at her, eyeing her curiously.

For years, she had carried a dark secret—when she was only

twelve, her mother convinced her to bury a body in the woods. She dreaded that someone would find out, that they would look at her differently, that she would feel the way she felt that night.

Like a ghost.

Her worst fear was realized today. It was liberating. It freed her, undid something inside her.

She sunk to the floor and placed her hands on her knees. Once the officer's shift was over, she was going to slip out of here. She was going to break into Tobias Mathis's vault and find out what was in it that led to Whitney and Jennifer getting killed, and Hazel being taken.

THIRTY-NINE

Mackenzie was without her gun and without her badge. She was suspended from duty and now committing an actual crime of escaping custody when the officer on the graveyard shift had fallen asleep. Her heart beating wildly in her chest, she jogged into the night, knowing that soon they would be hunting her down.

But if her instincts were right then this night would end with her proving her innocence and finding out what was hidden in that vault.

After all, she was suspended. She didn't have to follow protocol to find evidence and worry about making it stick in court.

The moon was milky white and the wind whispered through the desolate streets of Lakemore, carrying a chill that seeped into Mackenzie's bones. She regretted not wearing her jacket. Her toned arms were exposed and sprinkled with hair that was standing up straight. Dark clouds loomed overhead. The flickering streetlights revealed boarded-up shops. As she ran toward The Farm, the buildings began to disappear and the wilderness grew denser. The smell of damp earth infused the air. The shadows around her intensified.

Thirty minutes later, The Farm came into view. It always left her with an icy feeling in her chest, seeing it at night. Vulnerable women living in some trance. She wanted to shake them out of it. But the two women who had shaken out of it were dead.

It wasn't easy to leave.

She spotted Tobias's hut right in the center. It was the tallest one, towering over the rest. She navigated through the maze of grass and weeds around her. She was trespassing. But tonight she was a criminal anyway.

Reaching the main hut, she slowed down. Cold sweat matted her scalp. Crickets chirped around her. There was no one around. It was too late. Everyone must be asleep, including Tobias Mathis. But where was the vault? What if he woke up? She was raking her mind for options when a voice came from behind her, making her gasp and her heart gallop.

"Detective Price?" Zoe said in a soft voice. "Well, I don't think I can say detective anymore."

"How did you—? Oh. Caleb."

She held up a lantern that cast a glow on her dark face. "Tobias is asleep. He smoked a lot tonight, so I highly doubt he's going to wake up."

"And where is the vault?"

"Just a few feet from him. It opens with a combination. A four-digit code. I don't know what it is, though."

It made sense now. FOURSIXTWOONE. "I think I do."

Zoe didn't question how. "Remember I told you this is a two-person job?"

"Yes."

"It's because of the alarm system. The vault has two doors. One is glass and then there's a metal one," Zoe explained. "The metal door will open with the number combination. But the glass one can only be unlocked with a voice print. If you force it open, an alarm will go off throughout The Farm."

"How do we mitigate that?"

Zoe pointed to another hut. "I will have to be there to disable the alarm systems. I got wire cutters and electrical probes to bypass the sensors. For *you*..." She flaunted a glass suction cup. "I got this."

Mackenzie was at a loss for words. "How are you this prepared?"

"I'm always prepared."

Zoe's enigma was getting on her nerves. Her instincts were telling her that Zoe was an ally but then her words and actions had disarmed her at the funeral. She didn't like not knowing. Especially when she was working with someone. "Let's be clear about one thing. As much as I would love to have arrested you for your riddles and vague statements, I can't. But if I find out you had anything to do with the murders and Hazel's disappearance, I will forget all your help and throw you in prison myself."

Mackenzie glared at her. She was taller and older. But Zoe wasn't even slightly rattled by the threat. "Why don't we finish what you're here to do? You can arrest me after you get your badge back, *Ms.* Price." She nodded at the hut. "We don't have a lot of time. Last thing I want is Caleb seeing us."

They shared an understanding, a common goal even if the motivation was hidden. Mackenzie made her way to Tobias's hut. The door was slightly ajar, perhaps to let the cool air in because as she crept inside, she was enveloped by heat from the scented candles. Inside it was as she remembered—weathered wooden walls and pillars adding to the rustic allure. In the middle was the large bed where Tobias had had sex with a woman while others watched and chanted.

He was sleeping. His naked form was splayed on the bed. His breathing was even. Bile rose in her throat, thinking about what this man did. Convinced people to enable his perversion and packaged it as something deeper and meaningful to profit from. The vault was in the far corner, last time concealed behind a pillar. A steel door behind a glass one.

Formidable, impregnable, and keeping something coveted.

She tiptoed past him to the vault and kept checking over her shoulder to ensure that he was still out. Reaching the vault, she swallowed. A charge built in the air. Nerves danced in her stomach.

This was it. If there was a time to turn back now, then this was it. She was knowingly breaking the law. This time as an adult. This time it was on her. Before she could convince herself otherwise, she proceeded to open the door with the suction cup. She positioned it on the smooth surface of the door, ensuring a tight seal. Gripping the handle firmly, she applied steady pressure, gradually lifting the glass door without a sound. Once the opening began to expand, there was a sharp squeak of the alarm ringing.

It only lasted a second before it was silenced. Zoe must have disabled it. But that one loud moment made Mackenzie's breath hitch in her throat. She looked over at Tobias. He had changed positions, now lying on his stomach. But soon his breathing returned to normal.

Once the opening was large enough, she slipped inside. Now she was facing the metal door with a touchpad. With trembling fingers, she punched in the code.

4-6-2-1

With a click the door was unlocked.

"Thanks, Peterson," she whispered.

Her hands were clammy as she opened the door as quietly as she could and stepped inside. It was a compact space. There were two shelves with files and folders neatly arranged. Each bore the weight of someone's identity and secrets.

Mackenzie's eyes scanned them for a familiar name. They locked onto a file in the corner.

Barry Fontaine.

Quickly she grabbed it. There was no other file for Grace or Garrett or even Baby Rose. This must be it. Something inside this file convinced Zoe, Jennifer, and Whitney that Baby Rose was alive. With her mission accomplished, she was about to leave when she spotted another name of interest.

Caleb Mercer.

She hesitated. She hadn't come here for this. But Caleb *was* a suspect. She plucked that one too and exited the vault, only bothering to close the metal door. Whenever Tobias woke up, he would know he had been robbed.

She stuffed the files under her shirt, tucking the bottom into her jeans. She padded across the hut to escape. Finally, she was out in the night. The cold, sharp night. She wandered away from Tobias's hut to the edge of the clearing, looking for Zoe when the blow came to the back of her head.

FORTY

Searing pain shot down her neck in hot strings. Her knees softened and she buckled. Someone scooched down to search her. They were after the files. It took Mackenzie a moment to gather herself and to register who her assailant was—Caleb.

She pressed forward with her arms into the ground, lifting her weight and kicking back into the soft part of his knees. He stumbled, almost losing his balance. Once there was some distance between them, she rammed into his left knee with her shoulder, sweeping him off the ground. He landed facedown with a groan. But he swiftly regained his balance.

He was trained in combat, just like she was. He was also a man with an advantage over her when it came to strength. But she was no amateur—and she knew how to take down someone bigger.

He threw punches at her but she deflected with lightning-fast jabs. She was pure body and muscle. No thought. Just an animal who had to survive. When he punched her in the gut, she was unable to block it entirely. But the files tucked into the front of her jeans softened the blow. His eyes grew large when he realized that's where the files were.

Wisps of long golden hair fell down in his face. His face was as pale as the moon. They circled each other, muscles coiled. Mackenzie ducked a wild swing, delivering a swift uppercut that rocked Caleb's jaw. He staggered back and retaliated with a roundhouse kick.

It sent Mackenzie flying, landing on the ground, her skin split open by the rocks and twigs. She grabbed a fistful of mud. Before she knew it, he was right in front of her, his hand brutally tearing her hair away from her face, forcing her to look at him. When he turned her head, she shoved the mud into his eyes.

"Fuck!" He stumbled back, his face contorting as he tried to rub the dirt from his eyes. She had a small window to overpower him. With a final burst of energy, Mackenzie landed a powerful kick to his abdomen. And then an elbow to the side of his head around his temple. That was a crippling one.

He fell to his knees. She punched him in the nose, drawing blood that shone brightly against his pale skin. And finally she went around him and put him in a chokehold. His body resisted and writhed, trying to shake her off. But she exerted more pressure. Slowly his strength began to fade, his body growing sluggish. His desperate grip on her arms slackened.

She uncoiled her arm from around his neck and let him fall flat on his face. He had passed out.

When the adrenaline began to recede, the pain started to trickle in. Her arms ached from the punches she had blocked. Bruises began popping up all over her skin. Soreness spread. But at least the files were safe.

Where the hell was Zoe?

Her eyes searched the darkness as she tried to catch her breath and will her body to stand up. There was a sound of footsteps and rustling behind her. A flashlight pointed at her and she winced.

"What the hell happened?" It was Nick with five officers

behind him. When he saw Caleb on the ground, his face darkened with fury. "Are you okay?"

"Yes. I'll live."

One of the officers went to Caleb to check his pulse and call for backup.

Tobias's hut lit up like a lightbulb. The door opened and he came storming out, fastening his robe around him. Sleep left his eyes when he saw the scene before him. A bloodied Caleb passed out. A bruised Mackenzie panting. And Nick with a small group of police officers on his premises. The panic in his eyes told Mackenzie that he must have noticed the vault had been broken into.

"What the hell is going on?" he barked. "How dare you enter my property?"

Mackenzie had never seen him angry. He always maintained that aura of a calm messiah. But the vault was his Achilles heel.

"We can if we're pursuing a criminal." Nick shrugged. "Mackenzie Price escaped from a holding cell and we tracked her location by GPS to your Farm."

Tobias was dumbfounded. "*What?*"

"And then we arrived here and saw a physical fight. Looks like we're going to have to investigate. Plain view doctrine." Nick winked as he pulled her up and cuffed her again. "You're under arrest *again*." Then he dropped his voice so that only she could hear. "Are you hurt?"

"Not badly. Just have to ice them."

"Did you get what you came for?"

"Yes."

FORTY-ONE

Mackenzie sat with her legs up in the interrogation room with an ice pack that she pressed against all the bruises on her arms and shoulders. By the time she was driven back to the station in the back of the squad car, it had started raining.

Even inside this clinical, impersonal room that looked and felt detached from the rest of the world, she could hear the rain beating down and thunder clapping. The noise put her at ease, made her feel connected to the world. She looked at her reflection in the mirror across from her.

She couldn't recognize herself. Her red hair in disarray. The humidity had left them in wild curls. Her face smudged with dirt. She wasn't in her classic pantsuit. Just a black tank top and blue jeans. It was so unlike her to be this carefree and relaxed. Maybe because tonight she wasn't *Detective* Mackenzie Price. She was just Mack.

The door opened and Rivera walked in, followed by Sterling Brooks—Mackenzie's ex-husband and an ADA.

She took her feet off the table, straightening up, her mouth falling open. "Sterling?"

He was as good-looking as always. Tall and muscular with

dark skin and curly black hair. His icy blue eyes that drew her in all those years ago were piercing. He pressed his lips in a thin line. "Mackenzie."

She frowned at Rivera. "Where's Nick?"

"Outside. I told him to sit this one out because he's obviously biased." They took a seat across from her.

"In case you didn't notice, *he* was the one who arrested me in front of everyone."

Sterling cleared his throat. "I was called to discuss whether any charges need to be filed against you for murder." He made a face like the mere possibility of it was ridiculous.

"Clint analyzed the video, and it was fabricated," Rivera informed her. "You were framed."

"Yeah, I know."

"Why did you go to The Farm tonight?" she asked. "You must have known that once we had taken a good look at the video it would be deemed as fake and you would be released. You just had to spend one night in the holding cell."

"I... didn't know how long or easy it would be to prove my innocence so I took matters into my own hands."

"And you went after the vault to prove your innocence?" Rivera raised an eyebrow.

"All warrants for The Farm kept getting rejected. I had an opportunity, I took it. Is Tobias filing a complaint against me?"

"No." Sterling sighed. "He isn't. The last thing he wants is more police attention. Did you see anything else in that vault?"

She knew her ex-husband. He was hiding something. "Files and folders with names. I don't remember seeing any name I recognize though."

He nodded gravely and jotted something down. "All right."

"There's also the matter of you escaping custody," Rivera said. "Even if you aren't going to be charged with murder, you did break a few laws. Including theft."

She dropped the two files that Mackenzie had taken from

the vault. One for Barry and one for Caleb. Rivera looked pissed. "What am I supposed to do with this unit where everyone lies?"

"You can watch the tapes. I'm not hiding anything."

"Mr. Brooks, how should we proceed?"

Sterling watched Mackenzie with a softness that she hoped Rivera wouldn't notice. But Rivera noticed everything. Is that why Rivera had called Sterling and not some other ADA? So that she could follow protocol on paper but also make sure Mackenzie didn't get into any serious trouble?

"It has come to the attention of the DA's office that potentially a mistake was made when Jake Lawson was convicted thirty-one years ago," Sterling offered in a neutral tone. "Even though there is no one in the DA's office from that time anymore, it is still an embarrassment to the office that we would like to be corrected. If this file on Barry Fontaine provides any new information on the case of the homicide of Grace Fontaine and the disappearance and death of Baby Rose, then the office won't be bringing charges against Detective Price for the crimes of trespassing, breaking and entering, and theft."

"That's a generous offer," Rivera commented.

"It's a fair one. If we focus more on punishing petty crimes at the cost of something as serious as murder, we'll be doomed. We're just thinking about the big picture." He bit back a smile.

Mackenzie mouthed him a thank you. He nodded. They were together for six years before he had cheated on her. He was ready to move mountains to earn back her trust and forgiveness. Despite her cinching anger, his earnest efforts had almost convinced her. But that was before she realized that she wasn't the kind to mend broken bonds. Sitting across from him and knowing they had each other's back filled her with warmth.

Once Sterling had left, Nick and Sully entered the room, wheeling in a television set with a CD player.

"Do you need ibuprofen for the pain?" Nick asked her as he plugged in the TV to the power outlet.

"I'm fine."

Sully fell onto the chair Sterling had occupied. "There were two CDs in that file you stole from Tobias's vault."

Nick pushed the first CD into the player and fiddled with the remote until a scene appeared on the screen. The camera was fixed on a tree in the woods.

"Tobias loves monitoring the woods, doesn't he?" Rivera hissed through her teeth.

Apparently, Tobias's habit of surveillance went way back. Tobias had capitalized on the secrets that the woods of Lakemore spoke about on stormy nights. The time and date on the video from fifteen years ago. Nick's face was ashen when he relayed that that was the night Cecily Rodriguez officially went missing.

Mackenzie squinted, leaning forward, trying to sear every piece of information in the video into her memory. It had been raining hard. The ground was matted with sodden leaves. The trees were battered by the rain, their branches bending out of shape. Wind whipped the night into a frenzy, wicking away the leaves and sending them into a flurry before they were slammed into the soil. It was dark but there was a cabin in the frame. Porch lights flickered, casting a glow and throwing light onto the surroundings. The audio kept blipping in and out. Prongs of lightning lit up the screen.

A few seconds into the recording, a figure ran into the frame.

Caleb Mercer.

He clung to a tree and sunk against it. Panting and shaking. His clothes were drenched. His blonde hair dark and sticking to his skull.

"What the hell is he doing?" Sully growled. "Never liked that one. No offense, Nick."

"None taken," he replied. His eyes flicked to Mackenzie. There was an edginess in them. Edginess tied to the lie he had told Bruce about Caleb's alibi that night.

Caleb spots the cabin. He scans the woods, his brows tied in a worried note. As he inches closer to the cabin, more light falls on him.

Mackenzie's insides scrunched into a fist. There was blood on Caleb. His shirt was covered in it. His hands were covered in it. There were even streaks of it running across his face. He stared at his hands in horror. His shoulders rose and sagged, drawing scraps of air. He kept twitching. He was probably on something.

He broke down the cabin door and disappeared inside. The video continued for a few more seconds before the screen went black again.

Nick pulled at his hair, pacing the room with his fingers locked behind his head. His worst fear had been realized.

Silence hung in the air.

"So Caleb was in the woods that night." Rivera's seething voice was the one to tear through the stillness first. "Isn't this the night of the Rodriguez girl's disappearance?"

"Yes," Nick answered.

"And hadn't you given a statement to the detective in charge that Caleb was with you that night?" When Nick didn't reply right away, Rivera shook her head and stood up. "Do I need to open an investigation into you, Detective Blackwood? Murphy might care about your political lineage, but I don't."

"He was with him for part of the night," Mackenzie chimed in. "That's what Nick told me. They weren't hanging out all night. But the time is unclear to him. Right, Nick?"

Nick shot Mackenzie an indignant look but she reciprocated with defiance.

Rivera sighed, exasperated. "Play the second tape."

Nick inserted the second CD into the player and pressed the button.

This time the camera was facing a baby crib in a living room.

Sully's face was bone white. "That's the Fontaine house."

There was a date and timestamp on the video. Thirty-one years ago, the evening of the murder of Grace Fontaine. The time was six forty-five in the evening and Baby Rose was asleep in the crib.

"They had a camera installed in the house?" Nick asked Sully.

"To my knowledge, they didn't."

Within seconds, a figure approached the crib. A man. He bent down to lift Baby Rose out of the crib. Once he had her in his arms, he looked around, scared.

Barry Fontaine.

A strangled sound escaped Sully's throat as he struggled to find his voice. "He... he arrived before we did."

Barry opened the screen door that led to the backyard and left with Baby Rose.

"That's why his alibi didn't make sense. He did reach home on time but then he left and pretended to come back," Mackenzie said.

Ten minutes later, Barry returned to the living room without Baby Rose. He looked flustered. He was shaking and squirming. His eyes darted to the camera and he wiped his mouth. He climbed on top of a chair and disconnected the camera.

Thickening silence suspended in the air. Mackenzie took in what she had witnessed, trying to rearrange all her theories about what went down that night.

Nick was the first one to talk. "He took his own daughter into the woods. That's where he took her, right?"

"You can access the woods through the backyard. That's the path we suspected Jake Lawson took." Sully looked lost.

"But how does it prove that Baby Rose is alive?" Mackenzie questioned. "This just proves that Barry left her in the woods and not Lawson."

Nick unclipped a picture from the file. "Some pictures were taken that evening."

He presented them to Mackenzie. There were three pictures. One of Baby Rose in her blanket in the woods, tucked inside a hollow trunk on the ground and concealed by shrubbery. The second was of a man with black boots and khaki pants standing next to her. The third picture showed the man's feet pointing the other way like he was walking away—and no Baby Rose or blanket on the ground.

"Someone took her from the woods!" Mackenzie whispered. "Zoe and the others saw this evidence at some point. That's how they knew Baby Rose was alive. That's what started everything."

"Too bad who took her isn't visible," Nick said, staring at the pictures and then frowning. "Interesting."

"What?" Mackenzie's interest piqued.

Nick poked his finger at the last picture. "Am I crazy or are these shoeprints not the same size?"

Rivera eyed the picture and nodded. "I've read about this condition that some people have."

"This should narrow down our pool of suspects. Someone took her and hasn't come forward," Sully said. "Get Clint to get the sizes of these shoes."

"Talk to Barry tomorrow. All of you," Rivera ordered. "Prepare a warrant for Caleb. He is covered in blood and lied."

"Am I still suspended?"

"Until tomorrow morning, you are. Go home and sleep off all your rule-breaking. Tomorrow, I want *Detective* Price back at work. And one more thing to all of you." Rivera placed her hands on the table. She meant business. Her voice carried a sharp edge. Purposeful and harsh. "Three crimes nearly fifteen years apart—why do I have a feeling that it was a seemingly white lie that grew out of control that has led to the events we are at today?"

FORTY-TWO

Mackenzie needed a bath and a good night's sleep. Her muscles protested whenever she moved.

"Do you want me drop you home?" Nick was at her side, hands in his pockets.

"Maybe. I'm hurting too much to be able to drive."

Rivera's words kept haunting her. They were supposed to be on the good side. Reasonable and rational minds. They had undergone extensive training to ensure that the value system was a part of their being, imbedded so deep into their psyche that they viewed the world through a different lens all together.

But they were fallible. They were just as flawed and tempted as the people they had the authority to throw into jail.

"What happened to Caleb?"

"He's at the hospital. I didn't get a chance to talk to him." He looked uncomfortable.

"Did I really knock him out that hard?"

His grin was lopsided. "He'll be out in a couple hours."

"How do you feel?"

Nick was always an anchor to her. That solid presence in her life she turned to. For the first time, he appeared so lost and baffled. A naivety she didn't know he was capable of. "I think I'm still processing. I... I swear, Mack. I swear on my kid. The Caleb I knew and worked with? There was not a single thing about him that made me suspect that he could *kill* someone. He was fucked up from his upbringing and had an addiction issue. But that didn't make him a killer. Well, at least that's what I told myself back then."

"Why would Caleb kill Cecily Rodriguez?"

"Some connection we have yet to unearth."

"And why would he remove her eye like that? And what are the chances that it was the same bronze residue left in Grace's eye socket?"

"Why are you defending him?" He spread his arms. "A few hours ago, you two were beating each other to a pulp."

"Before you assume the worst and blame yourself, consider the facts," she volleyed back. "You and Sully are too close to this to be impartial. I'm just trying to manage expectations here."

"Yeah." His hand went straight to his lighter and he started playing with it.

They were walking out of the station when Nick's phone rang and he excused himself. They stood under the awning. The stormy night had dimmed into a light drizzle. There was no thunder. Just a smoky blackness and soothing rain. The asphalt glistening.

Mackenzie studied his features as he spoke on the phone. The sharp lines of his face, the black hair with a sprinkle of gray on the sides, the long nose and coal black eyes. Something expanded in her chest. Had she been blind this entire time?

"That was Becky." He crossed the distance between them after hanging up. "She analyzed the contents of Jennifer's stomach. Mack?"

"Huh?" She shook her head and focused. "Yes, Jennifer's stomach. What was in it?"

"A bluefish common to Washington. Dinoflagellates consistent with salt water in the river."

"Okay..."

"But she also found didymium, a ciliate and oomycote," he recited. "Who named these things anyway?"

"That's a mold found in freshwater."

His lips twitched. "Why do we need Google when we have you?"

"I like to read. But that means that the body was moved. It was thrown into the river afterwards."

"Yes, so it's a long night for me." He thumbed his phone. "I'm calling you an Uber."

When the car arrived, he opened the door for her. She hesitated before getting in. She looked at him, not realizing how close they were standing. He was distracted, his mind being stretched in different directions as it processed Becky's information. But for a second, he snapped out of his thoughts and noticed her staring.

Mackenzie thought she was either going to throw up or implode. She quickly climbed into the car and closed the door behind her.

Mackenzie didn't have butterflies in her stomach. She had spiders. Like spiders were crawling up the walls of her stomach and filling it with cobwebs. She stared at her reflection in the mirror. She was wearing a white dress. She was getting married.

"I want to throw up."

"You can always say I don't." Her grandmother, Eleanor, said from behind her, sitting in a wheelchair. She was as skinny as a whippet. She had lost all her hair trying to fight the cancer. There was only sagging, wrinkly skin stretched tight over her bones now.

"I can't." Besides, this is normal, she told herself. And was this dress too poofy?

"You just need to ask yourself one thing, Mackenzie," Eleanor said. Dementia had feasted on her brain. Old age had left her body and brain withering. But she had flashes of clarity. Moments when her brilliance would shine through.

"What's that, Gran?" She lowered herself to Eleanor's level. The only true parental figure she had.

"Can you have difficult conversations with him? Because getting married isn't just about enjoying life, it's about facing life. You have been yearning for normalcy and you found him. And don't get me wrong, he's a good boy. I'm fond of him. But if you can't be ugly with him, then this marriage doesn't have a future."

Mackenzie knew something was wrong. The thought of walking down that aisle filled her chest with panic. But surely, this was just cold feet. Every bride felt this. Besides, the wedding was bringing up complicated emotions. It hadn't been easy watching Sterling's family show up for their big day while she only had her grandmother.

But Sterling was a kind man. He loved her and chased away the demons that held permanent residence inside her brain.

"Can you talk to him about things that scare you?" Eleanor clasped her hand with more force than Mackenzie knew she was capable of.

Before Mackenzie could lie to placate her, the door swung open. Nick was standing there, looking dapper in a tuxedo. He did a double take and blinked. "You look... poofy."

"Seriously?" She huffed.

"I just imagined you getting married in a white pantsuit. It suits your personality more." He grinned and then his eyes softened. "You look great, Mack."

"Thanks."

"I heard you don't have your something borrowed."

"I don't." She scratched her head and looked around. "Maybe I can borrow something from the hotel."

Nick rolled his eyes. "It should be something meaningful." He offered her his gun.

"Are you insane?"

"I removed the magazine. Obviously. It's empty."

Mackenzie checked it and tucked it in her garter. Finally there was something about this wedding that felt like herself.

"Go get him." Nick smiled.

Mackenzie emerged from the bath, her chest rising and falling with each deep breath. The scalding water cascading over her body provided temporary relief, an embrace of warmth for her weary muscles and tender bruises. Steam enveloped the bathroom, creating a veil of mist that danced across the mirrors, distorting her reflection. Leaning against the lip of the tub, she closed her eyes, the memories resurfacing vividly behind her eyelids, like scenes from a forgotten film, lingering in the steam-filled air.

After soaking in the bubbly water, she rinsed herself off and wrapped a robe around her body. She wondered if Nick had figured out where Jennifer's body was before she was thrown into the river. Perhaps that location would help them find Hazel.

She wandered downstairs, deciding to indulge in a midnight snack when the doorbell rang. It was half past midnight. She dragged her feet to the door. When she opened it, she froze.

Nick stood there. In the dead of night.

She was suddenly self-conscious. Her skin flushed. She was just in her robe. Her hair still dripped water. "Hi."

"I just realized something."

"What?"

"We're not technically partners tonight since you're on suspension... do you want me to leave?"

Mackenzie's heart twisted and beat like a jackhammer. Her throat was dry. But still she managed to murmur. "No."

He beamed before his hands held her face and he kissed her.

FORTY-THREE

NOVEMBER 13

The next morning Mackenzie woke up to an empty bed. The curtains in the bedroom flapped. She must have left the window open. The events from last night came crashing down on her with a force that left her feeling both dizzy and heated. She showered and got ready in a daze. The reality of what had happened was yet to sink in. But for now as Mackenzie climbed down the stairs, her veins thrummed like it wasn't blood flowing through them but bubbles.

When she saw Nick sitting at the kitchen island, drinking his coffee, and staring intently at his laptop, she squeaked, startled. "You're still here?"

"No, I'm a jackass who'll leave after we sleep together. Smoothie?" He directed her attention to her Kale smoothie next to the blender. "Not going for a run today?"

"I feel like I got a good workout last night." She guzzled her green smoothie, giving her a morning boost.

"Wow. I never pictured you as the flirtatious one."

"I was referring to beating up your ex-partner." She deadpanned. "Where is Caleb now?"

"Holding cell. We are charging him with assault. Sully tried talking to him this morning about that video we found yesterday but he lawyered up really quick."

"How do you feel about that?"

"We all make mistakes. But lying to protect him was a choice." His face was grim.

"Would you have done things differently?" She traced the rim of the glass with her pinkie.

"If knowing what I know now, I would have. But back then? Probably not. It's hard to ignore your gut feeling."

Mackenzie recalled Sully's words. *A time comes in the life of every officer, Mack. A time when they have to decide between following the law and doing what they feel is right. I hope that time doesn't come for you. Because if it does, it will be nearly impossible for you to ignore your gut.*

"Bingo." Nick looked at the screen. "We got a few hits."

"About what?"

"Remember that freshwater mold found in Jennifer's stomach? Sheriff's office sent us a list of all of the water bodies in Lakemore where that mold can be found. The water source has to have the same sediment, larvae, archaea too."

"Okay, how many do we have on the list?"

"Nine."

"That's not bad. Let's dispatch teams to search the neighboring—"

Nick turned the laptop to show her the catch. "It's 400 acres."

"Oh!" Her eyebrows shot up. "Well, that's discouraging. We need something more to narrow it down further."

"Yep." He checked his watch. "We should head out to see Barry. Sully should be on his way too."

As they got ready, Mackenzie broached the awkward topic. It had been years since she'd had a conversation like this. She felt too old for this. "What happened last night... I go back on duty today... *officially*."

Nick put his tie around his neck and shrugged. "That doesn't have to change anything."

She stuttered and waited for the earth to open up and swallow her. "You said last night that I was on suspension so I assumed that—"

"Oh, that was before how I realized how good it was!" He grinned.

She rolled her eyes and swatted him on the arm before pushing past him. "I don't want anyone at work finding out about us."

"Why not?"

"Just. I have a reputation." She tipped her chin high and squared her shoulders. "I like to maintain it."

"You're right." His face was serious. "Can't have anyone know how freaky Mad Mack can get." She glared at him ready to charge. "I'm kidding!"

Mackenzie and Nick arrived at Barry's cabin with Sully's car in tow. The cabin was veiled by the mist and surrounded by towering evergreens. Moss clung to tree trunks, rocks, and fallen logs, its velvety texture a contrast to the dilapidated cabin with rough, weathered wooden walls. Decaying leaves formed a carpet as Mackenzie's boots swished through them.

Barry sat on a rocking chair, staring into the wilderness where shadows seemed to dance. He failed to notice two cars pulling up in his driveway. Mackenzie found it hard to believe how Barry could have perpetrated the crimes. He only ever displayed one emotion—resignation. He came across as too detached to care about anything. Like a huge part of him was somewhere else already and he was waiting for the rest of him to follow.

Behind she heard the sound of footsteps shuffling and was surprised to see Ortiz with Sully.

"Mr. Ortiz?" Nick was surprised as well.

"I called him," Sully explained. "We were both a part of this."

Ortiz clearly didn't want to be there. His body was hunched into his coat, his hands inside his pockets, and his head hung low. He avoided making eye contact. At least Sully was bravely facing the wrongs of his past.

Ortiz just wanted to hide forever and lock it all away.

"You should lead, Sully," Nick said gently. "Finish what you started."

Sully braced himself. His fists curled and uncurled at his side. He looked so unsure of himself, but when Ortiz patted his shoulder, he stood upright and marched forward, ready to face his troubling past again.

"Barry?" Sully said.

His expression was blank. "Officer Sully."

"It's Sergeant now," he scoffed like it was a joke. "We need to talk."

Barry's eyes trailed to the rest of them standing on his porch. "What do you want now?"

"You left Baby Rose in the woods."

His shoulders fell. His Adam's apple bobbed as he squirmed. "I... did."

"Why?"

His breaths became ragged. He almost fell over, clutching his chest. Sully rushed to him, helping him to sit upright, while Ortiz stayed back, trying to hide behind Nick. Tears welling in his eyes at the sight of the shell of a man who was once a business magnate.

"Why did you lie, Barry?" Sully pleaded, leveling with him. "You came home before we got there. Why didn't you call the police right away?"

Mackenzie recalled Barry and Grace's tumultuous marriage and how he kept a close eye on Garrett to the point that his classmates noticed his looming presence. Did Barry snap at his wife and punish his daughter? Did he obsess over Garrett because he was the only person who was *his*?

"Because I wanted to protect my son." Barry said aloud the secret he had been holding on to for thirty-one years. The trees swayed when a gust of wind blew, making fallen leaves dance momentarily.

"Your son?" Ortiz's voice broke.

"Garrett. He killed her. He killed Grace."

FORTY-FOUR

THIRTY-ONE YEARS AGO

Barry Fontaine

Barry stepped through the door holding a bouquet of roses, a smile playing at the corners of his lips. He'd been looking forward to this evening, a quiet dinner with Grace at their favorite restaurant. The last few days had been fraught with fights and tension. Grace was tired—she had given birth to Baby Rose only two months ago and Garrett's issues were escalating.

Only yesterday, when Baby Rose had hurt herself Garrett had made her cry instead of helping her. Barry had wanted to thrash the boy, beat some sense into him. Like the old days before everyone began throwing around words like "trauma" and "abuse" too casually. But Grace had stopped him.

Again.

Begged him to never give up on Garrett.

Again.

"Promise me, Barry." Tears filled Grace's eyes. "Promise me you'll always take care of him."

Barry sat at the edge of the bed, rubbing his palms. "Grace, he's not normal. He needs treatment."

"He needs our kindness!" She sobbed. "I carried him. I made him. He's just lost. But our boy is in there."

"What if tomorrow he does something really bad?" He finally looked at her.

Grace swallowed hard, wiping her nose. Fierce determination burned in her teary eyes. "I don't care what he does. We protect him, no matter what. We stand by him. Because that's what a parent does. Our first loyalty is to him, not to anyone else. Not even to each other."

It was a discussion Barry had been having with her for too many years now. Now he just wanted to create good memories.

"Grace, sweetheart, I got something special—"

He faltered, stunned by the chilling scene that greeted him. Grace was sprawled across the kitchen floor. The roses fell from his grasp, their petals brushing against the cold tiles.

And there in the midst of the tragedy stood his son, Garrett. The boy's face was twisted, a mix of confusion, fear, and something darker that Barry couldn't understand. A bronze weapon, stained crimson, dangled from Garrett's trembling hand.

Barry's voice cracked. His heart pounded against his ribcage. "Garrett, what have you done?"

"I'm sorry, Dad." His voice quivered. "I was tired of her always watching me, always staring at me."

Barry's eyes shifted back to Grace's body. He saw the empty socket where her eye should have been. His heart skipped a beat, realization crashing over him like a tidal wave. Horror and disbelief tangled in his mind.

"My God! What have you—"

"I wanted to know how it feels to have someone really see you." His voice was too young to say such words. Barry's legs gave way. His son was unrecognizable. And then Garrett said the words that Barry knew he would remember till the day he died. "I wanted to steal her sight."

FORTY-FIVE

"He was only twelve," Sully said in disbelief.

Ortiz folded in half, leaning against the railing, and heaved. "Jesus Christ."

Mackenzie's stomach churned.

"He was always different. Never normal. Grace and I were always fighting. I wanted to send him to military school. Since he was two years old, he would throw violent tantrums. He would scratch and bite and hit us." Barry sobbed. "And the worst part was that he did it all with a straight face. No tears. No anger. Nothing."

Mackenzie was jolted by the revelation. Her thoughts thrown into disarray by Barry's confession.

"When Baby Rose was born, Grace thought maybe a change in the family dynamic would help him. But it didn't. We were always protecting her from him. We even installed a camera in the house."

That explained the footage where Barry was seen taking his daughter from the crib.

"We never saw that camera," Sully recalled.

"I got rid of it before the cops arrived. I couldn't let the police take my boy away... he was still my boy, my son," Barry cried. "I thought I could fix him. Grace wouldn't even want to send him to military school, let alone ruin his life by going to juvie. I knew Garrett would be taken away and be prodded and tested and locked up. And I just... couldn't. I needed *time*. I needed to think what to do. I still hadn't processed anything. I just operated on instincts. My instincts to keep whatever was left of my family together—"

"He killed your wife," Nick pressed. "He was clearly a danger to everyone at that point, including you and Rose."

"I know." He snapped. "When Garrett was ten years old, he burned Grace's hand. On purpose. I was livid. I'd had enough. I was ready to send him away but Grace begged me not to. We fought for hours. She *begged* me." He wiped away a stray tear. "Begged me to never let our family scatter. Made me swear to never give up on Garrett, no matter what. *We are supposed to love them unconditionally* she said to me. It was all I could think about. Somehow keeping my promise to her. Somehow just getting through that day and dealing with Garrett later without involving anyone else."

"Then why did you put Rose away in the woods?"

"I panicked. I wasn't thinking straight. I thought it would throw everyone off. I was going to go back into the woods and get Rose and make up some story. But I was surrounded by cops all the fucking time!" he bellowed, eyes bulging. "By the time I managed to sneak away, she wasn't there. And then they found her bones."

"You left an infant in the woods?" Nick couldn't help himself. "Are you serious?"

"I didn't know the woods were that dangerous. I found a cozy spot for her. She was asleep. I was going to go back and get her after giving my statement to the police and move her to another property I owned."

"Did Garrett kill Cecily Rodriguez?" Mackenzie asked.

Barry nodded, horrified. "He would stare at her and her friend. I kept a close eye on Garrett because I knew what he was capable of. I couldn't turn my son in but I could keep him on a tight leash. I was hoping that with age and the loss of his mother, he would change. That violent tendency would die. But it didn't. He did it again."

I wanted to steal her sight.

"And what did you do then?" Sully asked.

"One night he called me into the woods. Said he couldn't stop the urge. He said Cecily reminded him of Grace. Positive and cheery, so unlike his own mind. He wanted to steal her sight too, to see the world the way she did. To understand. He kept rambling all night while I buried the body. No body. No investigation."

And that's what happened. With no trace of Cecily, there was only a brief search after which it was concluded that she had fled town. She was twenty-two years old. There hadn't even been any sign of abduction or foul play. Even her friend, *Candy*, was too afraid to come forward with the truth.

"You didn't turn him in?" she snapped.

"Because I'm a parent." Barry gritted his teeth, his nostrils flaring and spit spraying. "Because when you're a parent your first instinct is to protect your child and to believe that your child can be saved, even from himself. I can tell you're not a mother."

She pursed her lips and looked away. This wasn't the first time someone had thrown that in her face like it was meant to be a scathing insult.

"Your son killed *two* people," Nick reminded him with a sharp edge to his voice. "He was a menace. How could you let this go on?"

"He was all I had left." He broke down in tears. "My wife was dead. My daughter was gone. I only had my son. Despite everything he was still my kid. He had Grace's eyes. He... there were moments when he was normal. When that fog lifted... giving me just a sliver of hope. I was selfish, Detective. I was selfish because I was trying to preserve whatever was left of my family. This... empty life." He looked around. "It's my punishment."

"But Tobias Mathis found out what you'd done," Sully said. "How did he know? Did he blackmail you?"

Barry nodded. "I knew him before he became who he is today. When he was just a scrawny teenager who enjoyed being a peeping tom. Surveillance wasn't as big back then as it is today. But he always had the best equipment. In fact, he was the one who installed that camera in my home. I didn't realize that he could see whatever happened in my home too. He'd even put cameras in the woods. Odd hobby."

"Tobias used to put cameras in the woods back in the day?" Nick repeated. When Barry nodded, Nick's eyes flew to Mackenzie's.

They were both thinking the same thing: the camera in the woods that had captured someone taking away Baby Rose and Caleb fleeing thirteen years ago covered in blood. Tobias had clearly continued this habit of watching people by equipping The Farm with surveillance technology.

That's how Tobias amassed his wealth and bought Caleb's loyalty.

"He sent me a video of me grabbing Baby Rose from her crib after the murder. He drained me dry. But it didn't matter at that point. I'd lost everything anyway. And not long after that, Garrett died in a car crash. I guess life punished me by leaving me all alone." Barry looked up at the sky, at the flock of birds that tapered across. "All I have left are memories, memories of Grace, Baby Rose, and even Garrett."

"I'm sorry, Barry." Ortiz swallowed hard. "I'm so sorry."

"Why? Don't you think I deserve this?" His smile was hollow. "Because I kept holding on to my monster son."

Ortiz shook his head, fighting back tears. "No... no, you don't."

Mackenzie waited with bated breath. Sully's mouth opened and closed and twisted as he tried to formulate the words. "Baby Rose didn't die in those woods, Barry."

Barry stiffened and stared at him. "What?"

"Those bones we found weren't human. Someone else got to her before you did."

"Who? Who took her? Where is she? Where is she?"

Ortiz and Sully tried to placate him. They gave him reassurances that they would find her. But Barry's body was convulsing. He was hyperventilating. His body was reacquainting itself with an emotion that he had been deprived of for over three decades—*hope*.

"I think I know what happened," Nick muttered to Mackenzie. "I think Tobias took Baby Rose and raised her on The Farm with a new name. He had the motive to kill them. But why would he use the same MO as Garrett?"

"Only Tobias can answer that. But if that's the case, then Hazel might still be alive. I would like to assume that he would hesitate to kill someone he practically raised."

"Raised and then impregnated?" Nick's face darkened. "Asshole deserves a bullet in his head." He stared at his phone with a deepening frown. "Caleb just made bail. He's out."

FORTY-SIX

NOVEMBER 14

Beams of sunlight filtered through the open blinds and pierced Mackenzie's eyelids. She cracked them open and griped. She had fallen asleep at her desk again. She snapped her spine as straight as an arrow, wiping the drool from her chin. Over the years, there had been many occasions of her falling asleep at the station. Fortunately for her, she'd had the sense to keep a bag of toiletries at work.

The search for Hazel Martin was ramping up despite the leads bleeding dry. The radio cackled with the news asking people for help. The posters on the lampposts of Hazel were washing away with the rain. Mackenzie watched through the window as a uniform put up brand-new posters.

How long they would stay up in this downpour was anyone's guess. She scanned the woods beyond the parking lot, wondering how the weather was their biggest enemy.

Footprints and tire tracks were often washed away as soil rearranged itself every few hours. Posters didn't stick to surfaces. The dense foliage and thickets draping most of the landscape made it easy to conceal bodies and evidence.

"Good morning." Nick was back without his tie.

"Did you spend the night here too?"

He nodded, still groggy. "Yeah, but I slept in the break room before Troy tried to tickle my ear with a feather."

She tried to gather her thoughts again. "Wait, I had found something last night."

"What?"

She showed him pictures of Garrett in his bedroom. "Do you see this trophy on the shelf?"

It was shaped like a cone with a sharp, pointy end. A prize Garrett had won for some science fair in elementary school.

"It's sharp enough to be the murder weapon and it looks like a bronze finish from the picture."

"I'll ask Peter—" He caught himself. "*Jenna* to pick it up from Barry's. He still hasn't thrown anything away of his family's."

Peterson's absence was like a hiccup. It derailed trains of thought, rattling through Mackenzie, rude and disruptive before forcing her to return to her normal state.

"Sounds good." Her voice was thick and she cleared her throat.

"I think I found something too." Nick smiled conspiratorially. He placed snapshots of the video in Caleb's file, focusing on the cabin. "It wasn't clear in the video so I printed out different frames to see if we could salvage something. Do you see this?" He circled something hanging above the porch of the cabin.

Something dangled, flying wildly in the storm. It was visible only in a few of the snapshots when it swung under the light. "What's that?"

"It's a red ribbon. That's a visual symbol the Boy Scouts use in Lakemore to mark cabins used for bird watching. It's like an aviary. It houses bird identification charts, field guides, you get the gist."

"Boy Scouts includes bird watching?" She raised a skeptical eyebrow.

"It teaches patience," he said defensively. "But this red ribbon identifies habitats for some birds that are challenging to find in this region, like Black Swift or Marbled Murrelet."

"So you know the location of this cabin?" she asked hopefully.

"Unfortunately, there are a lot of cabins with this marker but I cross-referenced it with that list the sheriff's office provided us with of freshwater bodies." He unrolled the map of the town. "And bingo! There's only one. There's a creek that runs nearby. Just a few yards out west."

"What are we waiting for?" She put on her jacket. "Shall we go?"

"Yeah, I was just waiting for Clint to track down who the cabin belongs to. The Boy Scouts haven't used it in over twenty years according to their website."

"Nick!" Clint was rarely seen outside his office in the basement where he had built a fort for himself with his big monitors. His tall neck made him tower over everyone around him. "It's definitely not abandoned. The utility bills show it belongs to Caleb Mercer. He's been paying for it for the last thirteen years."

Nick was livid. "Every time I cut him some slack thinking he isn't a murderer, he goes ahead and proves me wrong."

Mackenzie was fueled with determination. She checked her Glock and tucked it into her waistband. Her instinct told her to bring a pocketknife too. The cabin was where Jennifer's body had been before being thrown into the river. It was the same cabin that Caleb had run to, covered in blood, on the night of Cecily's murder. Hope flickered inside her that she was closer to finding Hazel—alive.

. . .

Mackenzie followed Nick as they ventured deeper into the woods. Rain cascaded, creating a relentless drumming upon the forest canopy. It drowned out every other sound. All she could hear was the rain thumping down on Lakemore one more time. It was like static in her ears—all that white noise. Fat droplets splattered into her red hair and clothes. They pelted against her eyelashes often blurring her vision. The frigid air chilled her to her bone. Her clothes clung to her body, drenched, and suddenly weighing a hundred pounds.

"How much further?" She had to yell to make herself heard.

Nick stopped and turned around, his black hair covering his forehead. "What?"

She gestured at her watch. "How long?"

"Two more minutes. Almost there!" he shouted back. As he made to set off again and almost slipped on the slick fallen leaves on the ground.

Mackenzie steadied him and they resumed their journey, climbing uphill and using branches for balance. It was a treacherous landscape. The ground punctuated with dips, bumps and fallen trees. Thickets and shrubberies stretched out like tangled webs scraping Mackenzie like they wanted a taste of her.

The cabin finally came into view. Surrounded by green foliage that shimmered in hues of green and emerald. They exchanged a glance and nodded. Undeterred, they inched closer to the cabin when Nick stopped suddenly. She almost slammed into him.

"What?"

He pointed at the window of the cabin. A man was standing there. The back of his head golden. His arm was raised. Was he holding a gun?

Caleb.

Mackenzie gestured to Nick to circle the cabin and head for the window while she planned to enter from the front.

Nick nodded. They parted ways. She had her gun ready in

a tight grip. When she stepped onto the porch, a shiver ran down her spine. Finally, she was sheltered from the rain. Her breaths formed misty clouds. Her teeth chattered from the cold.

She kicked down the door and stormed in. "Lakemore PD. Freeze!"

The sight made her stop in her tracks. There were three people in front of her.

Hazel Martin on her knees—blindfolded, gagged, hands and legs tied together. At the sound of Mackenzie, she tried screaming for help, her body writhing to be freed.

To the right was Caleb. The gun in his hand pointed at someone who also had a gun aimed right back at him.

Mike Ortiz.

FORTY-SEVEN

Mackenzie froze. Her brain tried to compute the situation. What the hell was Ortiz doing here? Why did he have a gun? She blinked hard, trying to get her head around the sight before her. She focused on what mattered most—Hazel was alive.

That was good. They weren't too late.

"Detective Price!" Ortiz exclaimed, delirious. "Thank God you're here. I have been following Caleb. He has been holding Hazel captive."

"What are you doing here?" Mackenzie asked but Caleb talked over her.

"What the fuck are you talking about?" he fumed. Spit sprayed out his mouth. "What do you think you're doing in *my* cabin? I came here and found you and Hazel!"

"He's lying, Detective Price," Ortiz insisted. "He's doing all of this for Tobias Mathis. He couldn't hold the women hostage or kill them back at The Farm so he does his dirty deeds here."

"Quit lying, asshole! I haven't come to this place in months!" He gritted his teeth and looked at Mackenzie. "I had no idea Hazel was here. I don't use this cabin often."

Nick's face appeared in the window across from Mackenzie. There was a back door. When their eyes met, she shook her head just a fraction. She wanted him to stay put. He gave her a curt nod.

She didn't want him barging in yet because in his desperation Ortiz had given himself away. How did he know that someone was *killed* here? To his knowledge, Jennifer's body had just washed ashore.

Her heart thundered in her chest. Adrenaline swarmed her senses. She clicked the safety off and pointed the gun at Ortiz.

His eyes enlarged. "What are you doing? It's *him*. Tobias Mathis's lapdog. I've been following him to redeem myself. After I goofed up all those years ago—"

"How did you know someone died here, Ortiz?"

Ortiz gulped and staggered back, waving his gun between them. "I assumed that was his plan! Look under that floorboard." He tipped his chin to a board on the floor that had been lifted up on one side. "He's got money stashed there. He's been stealing from Tobias!"

Mackenzie tightened her grip. She would have shot him in the kneecap. But not only was a panicked man with a gun dangerous, Hazel was in the room. Bound and helpless. Then there was Caleb—the unpredictable element.

"If you just got here, then how do you know what Caleb's keeping under that floorboard?" Mackenzie hissed.

Ortiz was digging himself into a deeper hole. The air continued growing sharper in the cabin. The palpable chill biting into her skin. She knew that this wasn't going to end well. There were too many factors going against them. But before she signaled Nick to even the field, she wanted to extract the truth.

"Why did you come here, Caleb?" Mackenzie asked, her gun still aimed at Ortiz. But there was a warning in her eyes.

Caleb's eyes thinned, a resolve taking hold. "You shouldn't have stolen those files from the vault. I'm sure you saw what Tobias has on me. How he forced me to become his *lapdog*." He spat out the word. It was the insult Nick had hurled at him too. Clearly, it had cut him deeply, coming from a man who was once a friend.

"Why were you covered in blood that night?"

"I don't remember!" Tears welled in his eyes. "For the life of me, I can't remember. I was high as a kite. I don't even remember what I took that night. And suddenly I realized there was blood over me. I ran, still strung out, and found refuge here. When the news of a missing teenager broke, I lost my shit."

"And then Tobias blackmailed you with this footage."

"He likes to keep an eye on the woods, he says. He says having power in the woods means having power over Lakemore."

The words rang true. Everyone in this town had left a part of their innocence buried somewhere in the woods.

"So you came here to get your money and skip town?" Mackenzie guessed. "But you didn't kill Cecily Rodriguez. It was Barry Fontaine's son. He had confessed to his father."

"You're lying, bitch!" he hissed through his teeth. "I'm not that naïve. You know what? Maybe I *am* here to get my money and leave and maybe Ortiz is here to kill Hazel or whatever the hell he wants to do. You're just a nuisance, aren't you?"

Mackenzie's stomach dropped. Caleb's arm moved. Now the gun was pointed at her. He pulled the trigger. The bullet scraped Mackenzie's knee. Pain exploded in her leg. She almost buckled, still holding onto her gun for life.

Right then, the backdoor blasted open. In lightning-fast speed, Nick tackled Caleb to the ground. The force of the impact momentarily dislodged the gun from Caleb's grip, sending it skidding across the floor. Nick threw punches at Caleb, each blow landing with a resounding thud.

Fear gripped Mackenzie as she watched them struggle. Blood guzzled out of her wound, soaking her jeans. But she knew the bullet had only scraped her; it wasn't lodged inside her. She took deep breaths, powering through the burning pain.

Hazel cried hysterically, still devoid of her senses. Ortiz still had his gun. She mouthed him to drop it but he kept hesitating.

That's what sealed his fate. He was guilty.

With a sudden burst of strength, Caleb got ahold of Nick's gun. Everyone froze. Mackenzie's heart pounded. She aimed the gun at his foot and shot.

The deafening crack of the gunshot shattered the silence, the bullet whizzing past Caleb, embedding itself into a nearby wall. The bullet didn't hit him but the shock of it made him drop the gun.

There was another cry. In the commotion, Ortiz had managed to get hold of Hazel, his gun pressed against her temple.

"Let me go, Mackenzie," Ortiz said, sweat beading all over his face despite the cold.

"I can't do that."

While Nick and Caleb continued to beat each other up, Mackenzie focused on Ortiz. He pulled Hazel with him, out of the cabin into the pouring rain. With her leg still throbbing in pain, she limped after them. The adrenaline diluted the pain. She would rest later. Right now, she had to save Hazel's life.

Her injured knee protesting every step as she pursued Ortiz through the relentless downpour. Rain unleashed upon her, trying to smother her again, washing away the blood that was trickling down her leg. In her trembling hand, she tightly gripped the cold metal.

Ortiz held Hazel next to him, the gun pointed at her. But his face was etched with desperation not cruelty. His eyes scanned the woods. It would be difficult to escape in these harsh conditions.

Mackenzie's voice rang out, cutting through the rain-soaked air. "Mike, it's over. Let Hazel go. She's the same age as your daughter." Her words hung heavy in the air. "Think about Violet." Ortiz took a ragged breath. "Hazel has a kid. Jackson. He's waiting for her. Don't do this. You're a parent yourself!" she yelled above the noise of the rain, inching closer.

Conflict brewed behind Ortiz's eyes. She could see it. It was saying Violet's name that softened him. He was a father. There was still hope. But then he tightened his grip on Hazel. She was losing him.

"Please, Mike. There's no way out of this. Let her go. You don't have to go down this path," Mackenzie urged, her eyes locked on his, searching for any glimmer of surrender. "I know you don't want to do this."

"I don't." He faltered for a moment. But then the rain intensified and his face clouded with resolve. "But I have to. Drop your gun, Mackenzie. Otherwise, she dies in front of you. Do it now."

He clicked the safety off.

Mackenzie hesitated. With a heavy sigh, she lowered her gun to the ground but picked up a piece of rock at the same time and closed it in her fist. Because of the rain, he hadn't noticed. It was a calculated risk. Ortiz knew Mackenzie wouldn't be able to follow him.

Her knee was bleeding, growing heavier and stiffer.

His hold on Hazel loosened. In a split second, Mackenzie threw the rock at Ortiz. It hit him on the head, providing enough of a distraction for her to brandish the knife from her sock as she lunged at him.

The moment his hand went slack on Hazel, she crawled away. With a swift motion, Mackenzie slashed across his chest, his startled cry of pain piercing the air.

Ortiz stumbled backward, dropping his gun in the chaos. Mackenzie wasted no time, her instincts taking over as she slammed his head against a moss-covered rock. Ortiz crumpled to the ground, his consciousness slipping away into the darkness.

"Oh my God." Mackenzie was on the ground now, clutching her knee. She found the strength to get to Hazel. "It's me. Detective Mackenzie Price."

Hazel's face was streaked with tears when Mackenzie removed her blindfold and cut through her restraints with the knife.

"Jackson—"

"He's fine," Mackenzie reassured her, handing her the phone. "Call 911 and give them our location. I need to go in and find my partner."

Gasping for air, Mackenzie limped back into the cabin, cutting through the thick rain. Once she was inside, she saw Nick and Caleb still fighting.

She searched for the gun on the ground. There was one on the other side of the room. She tried to get to it when both Caleb and Nick ended up diving through the window —headfirst.

"Nick!" Mackenzie cried. Nothing mattered. Not even the pain. She somehow ran to him. Tears clogging her throat. Worry hijacking her thoughts. Her insides liquefying into acid burning her from the inside out.

He grunted in pain, standing up. There was a cut on his brow. Blood ran down his face. Mackenzie relaxed in his arms. "Thank God." She pressed her forehead into his head. "I was so scared."

They turned their attention to Caleb. His head was hanging on the other side of the window. His body curled over the windowsill. He was too still. A sharp piece of broken glass was lodged into the side of his neck. Blood left his body in buckets, trickling down the wall of the cabin, merging with the rainwater, turning it scarlet red.

Caleb Mercer was dead.

FORTY-EIGHT

The curtain was torn back, and the doctor with salt and pepper hair sighed upon seeing Mackenzie. "Detective Price, you again."

"Hey, Doc," Mackenzie greeted him bashfully. The throbbing ache in her knee was already dulling.

He retrieved a pen from his front pocket and clicked it. "You know in my career of over twenty years, I haven't seen anyone else in the emergency room as often as I see you."

Her face heated. "It's an occupational hazard."

"I'm sure it is," he quipped sarcastically, reading the chart. "The bullet grazed your patella and exited. Luckily there was no foreign substance left in the bone and the CT scan shows no fracture, which is a surprise but maybe your body is just used to it. I'll prescribe you some prophylactic antibiotics to reduce the risk of infection, and regarding your wound management..." He narrowed his eyes at her. "You know what to do, right?"

"Yes."

A Cheshire smile broke out across his face and he tucked her chart under his arm. "Great. I'll go help out the other unlucky souls."

"Mind if I slip into the next room and speak with Mr. Ortiz?"

"Go ahead. He should be awake. He just had a concussion and minor injuries." He shrugged, leaving the door open on his way out.

Mackenzie grabbed a cane one of the nurses had left in her room and limped out of the room. She wasn't allowed to bend her knee, it felt like this heavy, swollen, thumping weight that was pulling her under. The hallway stretched ahead, lined with painted white walls and informational posters. Hushed steps of doctors and nurses on the gleaming linoleum floor caused her to ricochet to the moment that always played in her mind when she ended up in hospital.

Mackenzie dropped like a deadweight onto the steel chair that squeaked in protest. Her heels stuck together, her fingers interlinked in her lap, she sat rigid and straight. She stared blankly at the tiled floor with markings giving direction. She knew she was surrounded by noise—wheels rolling on the floor, pagers beeping, phones trilling, and the announcements on speakers.

But it was silence that blared in her ears.

She was trapped in a bubble. Her eyes scanned around till they latched onto a spot on the wall across from her. It looked like dried blood. A smudge of brownish-red liquid left behind by some bleeding patient as they were raced to the operating theater.

A door opened and closed.

Heels clicked.

She was jolted from her thoughts and stood up. Her grand-mother was walking toward her from the other end of the hallway.

Mackenzie's vision swam. Her grandmother's frame was blurry. Her face hidden by the glow from the lights in the ceil-

ing. It wasn't until she reached close enough to touch her arm that the image of her grandmother took shape.

"Mack?" Her gray eyes were teary.

Mackenzie clutched her arm. "What happened?"

Eleanor's fat lip quivered. She hesitated when she spoke. "Mack, she was in an accident."

She gulped and nodded. "I... how?"

"Why don't you sit down?"

"No!" Her voice came out shrill.

"The police are investigating, but it looks like her car slid on black ice and hit a pole."

Mackenzie squeezed her eyes shut and fell onto the chair again. Vaguely, she registered Eleanor's comforting hand, rubbing circles on her back.

"How is she?"

"She's been in surgery for over two hours now." Her eyebrows were stitched together. "One of the nurses just gave me an update. There's been severe brain damage. They're doing everything they can but... but it's not looking good." Her voice broke at the last word.

Mackenzie's chest swarmed with what felt like buzzing bees. She wanted to run. She wanted to move. All her life she was afraid. First of her father's drinking and then of her father's corpse. But this anxiety was different, more visceral. She was going to be an orphan soon. But it wasn't that thought that was making her chest implode.

It was the realization that soon she was going to be the only one left who was guilty of that night.

"I'm so sorry, Mack." Eleanor's voice cut through her thoughts. "I... I don't know what to say anymore."

"I don't either."

"Do you want to eat anything?"

"I don't know."

She looked up at her aging grandmother. Tall, broad, and

muscled from doing manual labor in a factory for decades. Even as her fiery eyes misted with tears and the corners of her mouth pulled down, there was a strength to her. Her comforting hand never wavered. She didn't break down. She held herself together, like a stubborn vase with cracks.

As Mackenzie rested her head on her grandmother's shoulders, she wondered why strong mothers have weak daughters.

The door to Ortiz's room was cracked open. The guard standing outside gave Mackenzie a nod. She caught a glimpse of Ortiz lying on the bed, his hand cuffed to the side rails. He stared at the ceiling, his breath choppy. He was crying. When Mackenzie made her presence known, Ortiz wiped away his tears.

"What do you want? You got me," Ortiz grumbled. Mackenzie hopped into an armchair. When she almost lost her balance, he instinctively reached out. "Careful!"

She froze and sunk down into the chair slowly. His mask of indifference climbed back up on his face, hardening it like stone. "Hazel was taken to the other hospital to be treated for severe dehydration among other things."

His stare was passive but Mackenzie noted the twitch in his jaw. "I see."

"Why did you do this, Mike? Why, after all these years?"

"I didn't want my daughter finding out what I'd done." His chest deflated. "When I found out those women had been in touch with Violet, I suspected they'd found out what went down all those years ago. My daughter means everything to me, Detective Price. I couldn't have her know the corrupt man I was. I wouldn't have lived down that shame."

"And why did you gouge out their eye? To throw us off?"

"Yes."

But that didn't make sense. Why would Mike mimic the same MO as before? It was solely because of that that they were able to link the new murders to the old ones and ultimately find out what Ortiz and Sully had done. If Ortiz had just killed them, it would have been harder to connect the crimes. He could have gotten away with it all.

"What did you use to remove their eye?"

"A letter opener."

"Where on your premises would we find this letter opener?"

"It's in the shed where I do some woodwork."

"And why didn't you kill Hazel?" she prodded, her instincts waking up from a slumber to detect an aberration. A dissonant note in the music. An off stroke in the painting.

"I..." Raw emotion took over. "I... thought she was Baby Rose. That's what Whitney told her. She was the right age. I hesitated. I felt like I owed her after my botch. But I also couldn't let her *go*. She came to find us, asking questions about Grace. Luckily, Violet wasn't home."

"And Violet didn't suspect anything?"

"I have done *everything* in my power to keep her away from the darkness of this world." He wagged a finger at her. "You keep her out of this. She's naïve."

"How did you kill Jennifer?" She crossed her arms.

"What do you mean? You don't know?" he scoffed, an edge to his voice.

"Why don't you tell me?"

"I shot her in the chest and threw away the gun."

A sick feeling grew in the pit of her stomach. Her phone rang. Her eyes were trained on Ortiz when she answered. "Price."

"Mack, I just talked to Hazel," Nick said in the backdrop of telephones ringing and footsteps shuffling. "She only remembers small details. Like Ortiz knocking her out. Smell of camphor."

"I see. What else did Hazel say?" Mackenzie asked on purpose to study Ortiz's reaction. He stopped breathing.

"Nothing."

"Can you check Ortiz's alibi for the night of Whitney's and Jennifer's murder? We'll need it to build our case."

"I'll get Jenna on it." He hung up.

Ortiz swallowed incessantly, panic mounting in his eyes. "I was at home, Detective Price. You won't find anything."

She struggled to stand up again, trying not to put any weight on her injured leg. "Just doing my due diligence. Something you should have done thirty-one years ago to avoid this clusterfuck of a situation we are in now."

"You'll need physical therapy if you don't keep that leg immobile for some time. It's a tough spot." He caught himself and looked out of the window into the glittery blackness.

Something was wrong. He was too paternal to have killed two women his daughter's age. His story had too many holes. His explanations lacked a consistent emotion. Becky was clear that Jennifer didn't die from a gunshot wound. The striations on the bone weren't consistent with a bullet. Could Becky be mistaken? Or perhaps it was wishful thinking. She turned away to head out when she noticed something.

His shoes. One of his shoes had significant padding inside for a more secure fit. Saliva thickened in her mouth.

In those pictures found in Tobias's vault, the man who had picked up Baby Rose from the woods wore shoes of different sizes. One was size 8 and the other size 10. It coincided with the time when Ortiz had revealed to Sully that his wife was pregnant and had conveniently moved all the way across the country away from all the attention on a missing infant. It suddenly came to her: Sully never *saw* Ortiz's wife pregnant.

Her scalp prickled when the realization sunk in. Violet was Baby Rose. That's the secret Ortiz was protecting.

FORTY-NINE

Violet sat nervously, her hands trembling on the table. Her glasses perched on her nose as she kept looking around like she was waiting for something to pounce on her.

Mackenzie regarded her fragile frame, her squeaks whenever a loud sound came from somewhere. She rubbed her throbbing knee mindlessly, trying to dissect Violet under her unwavering gaze.

That mousy little girl had lived a life too sheltered. Mackenzie had thought that Ortiz wanted to protect her from the dark world he had tasted too many times being a cop. His last act as an officer of the law was tainted. A somewhat heroic journey had ended on a bitter note, undoing everything good he had done. Perhaps, his daughter was his sanctuary, the only pristine relationship in his life.

Or perhaps he was protecting the world from her.

"Ortiz has an alibi for the night of Whitney's murder." Nick entered the observation room, his brow sporting fresh stitches. "Credit card receipts show he was at a bar during that window."

Sully paced the observation room, unable to tear his eyes off Violet. "Are you sure, Mack?"

"Did you meet Ortiz's wife when she was pregnant?" Mackenzie challenged him. "Wasn't the timing convenient that she gets pregnant again so quickly after having another miscarriage coinciding with the time Baby Rose went missing? Tell me. When was the first time you met Violet?"

"When she was two years old," Sully admitted.

He glided closer to the mirror and raised his hand, his fingers trailing over Violet's skittish face. Mackenzie saw the myriad of emotions on Sully's face. He was unable to latch onto one as they ran through him like water.

"Violet is the only person Ortiz would lie for," Nick agreed. "He's protecting her. Taking the blame for the murders."

"He doesn't know how Jennifer was killed. He said he shot her in the chest." Mackenzie looked at him knowingly.

Nick's eyes narrowed. "Becky confirmed the cause of death couldn't have been a gunshot. There was no exit wound. And no bullet in the body."

"Why would *Violet* kill them?" Sully groaned. His eyes bounced between Mackenzie and Nick. "Just look at her."

"Only she can answer that question." Nick rolled his sleeves up. "I've put in a request for Ortiz to be brought here from the hospital. We might need him to break her down."

"Agreed." She nodded.

"I can take care of this. Mack, you should rest your leg."

"No, I'll come with." She used the crutch to gain her footing.

"You should..." He paused when she glared at him. "Jesus, fine. Limp away."

Mackenzie held her head high with steely resolve and wobbled her way to the other room. When they walked in, Violet jerked at the intrusion, her chest caving in like she wanted to hide.

"Where's my dad?"

Mackenzie dropped onto a chair. "He's still in the hospital."

"Will he be okay?" she breathed, her gaze bouncing anywhere but at them. "Can I go see him?"

"Not yet." Nick leaned against the wall and crossed his ankles. "We need you to answer a few questions for us."

"Like what?"

"Like why do you think your father killed Whitney and Jennifer?"

Violet couldn't form any words. She was somewhat dumbfounded, on the edge of disassociating. "What?"

"Your father admitted to killing them and we found him holding Hazel captive," Mackenzie said, assessing her response.

A strangled sound caught in the base of her throat. She simmered with untapped energy. Her shifty eyes hopping from Mackenzie and Nick to the mirror to the white light above. Her scrawny hands kept twisting a handkerchief. "I want to talk to Dad."

"He's not available right now," Mackenzie reminded her in a stern voice.

"You and your dad are really close, aren't you?" Nick switched gears on the conversation. He pulled a chair closer to Violet, away from Mackenzie. "Especially since your mom died a long time ago."

"Yes. I don't remember her."

"I got a daughter too."

"How old is she?" She smiled.

Nick took a beat to answer. "Nine."

"What about her mother?"

"She lives with her mom."

"Oh." Violet tsked. "Fathers are more important."

Instinctively, Mackenzie's hand went to the watch she wore that belonged to Robert. There were times when she would feel his hand holding hers. She had spent less time with him than she had with her mother. But whenever she sought strength, it was from him.

"I can see how much you matter to him. He would do anything for you," Nick continued.

She nodded in jerks, swallowing. "There's no one else my father would put before me. Not even himself."

"I would also do anything for my kid. But... would you do anything for him?"

She wrung the handkerchief. "Y-yes. Of course I would. He's the reason I live and breathe. It's me and him against the world." Tears shone in her eyes.

"Why did your father take Hazel?" Mackenzie asked, trying to keep her tone soft.

But when Violet looked at Mackenzie, she withdrew and clamped up. Nick noticed that too, immediately jumping in and dragging her focus back.

"Listen, Violet. This is off the record. I have respect for your dad," he said, and Mackenzie sensed his sincerity. "The true measure of a man is how good of a parent he is. And the first job a father has is to protect his child. I would do *anything* for my daughter." He pressed a hand to his chest. "Hell, I'd kill for her if I had to. Is that what happened, Violet? Did he do everything in his power to protect you?"

Mackenzie knew what Nick was doing. He was exploiting her love for her father, trying to guilt her into a confession.

Her lips quivered, a fat tear rolled down her cheek. "P-please let me talk to Dad. I just have to talk to him *once*."

There was a sharp knock on the mirror. Nick clenched his jaw at the rude interruption. Mackenzie suppressed a sigh. They were getting closer.

"I'll get it," she told Nick. He didn't argue. It was getting obvious that Violet was only responding to Nick, seeing a father figure in him.

In the hallway, Sully met her. "Ortiz has been transported here. Do you want to take a crack at him or should I?"

"Let me. We need to check Violet's alibi for the night of the murders."

Ortiz had been placed in the small interrogation room right next door to the room where Nick was attempting to lower Violet's guard. When Mackenzie laid eyes on him, she saw the same stifled panic in him too.

She decided there and then that there was only one way to end this. They loved each other too much. "Mr. Ortiz, Violet has just confessed to killing Whitney and Jennifer."

Ortiz broke. Whatever glue was holding him together, whatever strength he had mustered in the last twenty-four hours, it all came crumbling down. Tears unleashed with full force. "No... no... no... please let me talk to her. Where is she?" He looked at the door desperately.

"She's being processed. Give it a few minutes."

"No!" He sat back, his body rattling like he was getting electrocuted. "Foolish girl. I told her I'd handle it. I told her not to talk to anyone but m-me."

"Does she know that she's Baby Rose?"

He gasped. "You don't know that."

"We can run her DNA and compare it to Barry's. Are you telling me it won't show that they are related?"

He hung his head low. "I didn't plan on it. My wife had had another miscarriage. We were broken." He hugged his chest and looked away, recalling the stinging memories. "It was a girl. We had decided to name her Violet and when... well, my wife slipped into depression. She blamed herself. I told her every day, every hour that the miscarriage wasn't her fault. But she was inconsolable. Then we were called to the Fontaine house. Grace was killed and the infant was missing. Search parties were combing the woods, looking for Baby Rose or anything. I joined them. It had been less than twenty-four hours. I still remember that moment so clearly." He closed his eyes, relishing the memory, like he was trying to relive it. "When I found my daughter in the woods…"

FIFTY

THIRTY-ONE YEARS AGO

Ortiz

Mike ventured deep into the many woods of Lakemore, his eyes scanning for anything that could lead him to the killer of Grace and Baby Rose. Perhaps the killer had dropped blood on the ground. Or Baby Rose's sock. Ancient trees reached skyward; their gnarled branches intertwined like skeletal fingers. The forest floor was carpeted with decaying leaves. The air carried a hint of dampness, the scent of earth mingling with the crispness of pine.

Veering away from the main search party, he navigated through a labyrinth of towering trunks. Sunlight filtered through the thick canopy above, casting fragmented beams on the ground. Swaying moss dangled like curtains from branches. As he pressed on, the distant murmurs of the search party faded. He stumbled upon a small meadow. The grass grew long and wild.

Suddenly, he heard a sound. A baby crying.

His senses heightened, and he followed the sound, his footsteps crunching on the dry leaves. As he approached a fallen log, he discovered a hidden hollow. Removing the foliage that concealed it, he revealed Baby Rose, nestled in a tattered blanket. Her face marked with tiny cuts that told a tale of hardship and struggle.

"Oh my God!" Mike beamed. Thrill surged through his veins as he lifted a crying Baby Rose into his arms.

But then something happened.

She stopped crying. She took steady, rhythmic breaths. Their gazes locked and Baby Rose smiled. He lost his breath, holding her tiny body. She had been left in the woods, covered in tiny cuts, but she was happy to be in his arms. Now she could sleep in peace.

Mike felt his heart swell. It could burst at the seams. He knew he could never let her go. He knew that he was meant to find her in the meadow all alone where no one could see them. Their destinies were meant to intertwine. Casting a glance around, he ran away with her.

FIFTY-ONE

"My wife was overjoyed. We left Lakemore for a small town in Pennsylvania, far away from the media frenzy and unwanted attention. I knew enough C.I.s in my line of work to get a birth certificate forged with my wife named as the biological mother. Unfortunately, she passed away a year later." He sniffed. "But when Violet was two or three years old, I brought her back. She isn't Baby Rose, Detective Price. She is Violet Ortiz. *My* daughter."

"She killed two women, Mike." Mackenzie refused to be swayed by Ortiz's story. "Two women who also have babies. She killed then just like her brother Garrett did when he was only twelve years old."

A brother and sister who had never met were possessed by the same darkness.

He was distraught. "She was trying to protect me. Whitney and Jennifer were getting closer to the truth about what Sully and I had done."

"How so?"

"Whitney told Violet that she and Jennifer had found some

evidence that Baby Rose was alive and that they suspected it was Hazel... Violet knew what I did."

"The cover-up?"

He nodded. "They wanted to look at case files. They wanted to talk to me. She... panicked. They were asking too many questions, determined to get to the truth."

"And what about Hazel? She wasn't investigating anything."

"Violet knew that Whitney had spoken to Hazel that day... she thought Hazel knew too much. She just..." He dragged his hands down his haggard face. "When I came home, I found Hazel. That's when Violet confessed everything to me. But I couldn't just let Hazel go! I didn't know how much she knew. She was blindfolded and kept saying she hadn't seen her attacker. But what if she was lying? But I also couldn't let anything happen to her. I didn't want anyone *dead*."

So Hazel stayed captive all those days, while Ortiz tried to figure out how to let Hazel go without implicating his daughter.

"Mackenzie," Ortiz whispered, his hands clasped in front of his mouth, his eyes shining with tears. "She's my *everything*. I'm so sorry for what happened. She was just trying to protect me."

Despite the sticky mass sitting heavy in her throat, heat ran up her spine. "She *killed* for *that*? To save your ass for what you did three decades ago?"

"So that we wouldn't be separated!" His voice climbed an octave. "It's me and her against the world. It always has been. She was worried the case would be reopened and charges would be brought against me. Washington doesn't have a statute of limitations for murder charges. What happens now?"

"I assume the DA will charge you as an accessory for the kidnapping of Hazel Martin and for... shooting me in the leg."

"What happens to Violet?" There was an urgency in his voice.

"How did she remove their eyes?"

"This scaling tool. We keep it in bait protection containers."

"How did camphor oil end up there?"

"We add it to keep pests away." He waved his hand dismissively. "Can she argue insanity?"

"She doesn't look insane to me."

"Do you know *why* she removed their eyes?"

"Why?"

It pained him to utter the words. "She said to me that she wanted to know what it felt like to steal their sight."

The same words her brother Garrett had said to Barry when he had killed Grace and Cecily.

FIFTY-TWO

Hours bled into each other. Condensation pressed against the window of the conference room overlooking the labyrinth of woods. Mackenzie traced her finger on the glass, drawing different shapes.

There was no hint of rain. The sky was pitch black, dotted with glittering stars. There was no wind. The trees looked static, standing like hungry monsters awaiting their next meal. The stillness was jarring. Lakemore's chaos was always on the surface. The faces here were dull and the lives mundane. While other places moved on, Lakemore stayed put. Firmly planted in the past, trying to find its glory and purpose. That hunger for an identity, that frustration with failure that built like plaque, that sweltering anger about the unfairness of how the world worked, it all manifested in the form of wind, rain, and thunder.

Tonight, Mackenzie stared at the void that stretched outward. There was no movement. There was no pulse. Just a cold chill plunging the town into a state of numbness.

"Here you go." Nick appeared with painkillers and hot chocolate.

"Thanks." She swallowed the pill. "Did you get her confession?"

"Yeah. She used a bang stick to kill Jennifer."

She shuddered. "That thing they kill sharks with."

He nodded. "I also called Barry. Thought he should know."

"Of course."

Outside the conference room, Ortiz sat in handcuffs, waiting for Violet to be brought out after they'd finished finger-printing her. His devastation was palpable on his face.

"What would you have done?" Mackenzie asked Nick. "If you discovered that Luna had done something like this, would you have protected her like Mike did?"

"Yes." Nick didn't miss a beat. "I know it's wrong. It would have killed me. And as much as I'd like to think that I would drag her ass to the police and turn her in to teach her a lesson... it's your kid."

A piercing cry erupted. Violet was brought to the area where Ortiz was sitting. They crashed into each other in a burst of tears and whimpers. Ortiz's face turned red as he squeezed a shaking Violet in his arms, no doubt reassuring her that she was not alone.

Sharp jabs of pain moved through Mackenzie as she watched their tearful union. She couldn't imagine Violet killing two women and then scooping out their eyes. But she also couldn't imagine a twelve-year-old boy doing the same to his own mother. There was a truly devious side to the pair. But Ortiz's protective upbringing away couldn't suppress that side to Violet.

Nature won over nurture.

They hugged each other and when it was time for Violet to be taken away, Ortiz refused to let go. They had to be pulled apart. A man stood around the corner with Sully. Barry Fontaine. He watched the scene unfold with his lips parted and eyes widened. Violet was escorted past Barry, but she kept screeching at the top of her lungs for the only father she knew.

Mackenzie's eyes darted to the board in the room where pictures of Whitney and Jennifer were pinned. She still remembered their gut-wrenching messages—how they wanted to bring down Tobias Mathis and The Farm to free the women and be reunited with their children.

She had seen many motives in her career. From violent psychopathy and revenge to vigilante justice and twisted obsession. But this was the first time she had witnessed love as the motive.

"I guess that's why people say that love and hate aren't that different," Mackenzie observed.

"You know what the most disappointing part is?"

"What?"

"Tobias Mathis and his Farm are still intact. They died for nothing."

NOVEMBER 16

"We have a remarkable update on the case of Hazel Martin, the missing woman whose disappearance has gripped our community. Today, the Lakemore PD made a significant breakthrough, as they not only found Hazel alive and well, but they also apprehended the individual responsible for the brutal murders of Whitney Smythe and Jennifer Peyton." Laura addressed the viewers who were glued to their screens in the early morning, including Mackenzie. "While the identity of the culprit and the motive remain unknown, this is a moment of relief as Lakemore can once again begin the process of healing. Now, let's hear what Tobias Mathis, a key figure in this investigation, had to say." The corners of her eyes creased at the mention of his name.

Tobias's face filled the screen. He had let his hair grow. It fell around his handsome face, disheveled. The last time Mackenzie saw him was the night she broke into his vault to retrieve those videos. He had stumbled out frazzled. But now he smiled at the camera serenely.

"The tragic loss of Whitney and Jennifer has left us shattered. Our family was torn apart by these violent attacks." Tobias pressed a hand to his chest. "I promise to take care of their children. In the midst of this darkness, there is a glimmer of hope as we celebrate the safe return of Hazel, a cherished member of our family. While we find solace in Hazel's wellbeing, we must also acknowledge the relentless pursuit of justice that has led us here. I have offered my unwavering support and assistance to the authorities in their investigation. I have shared everything I know to aid them in their pursuit of the truth—"

Mackenzie growled under her breath and turned off the television. Whitney and Jennifer didn't want their babies growing up on that Farm under Tobias's care. Her stomach was in knots as she thought of the strange, brainwashed life they'd live.

"How's your leg?" Nick came down the stairs. This was the third night in a row he'd spent at her place. It still blew her mind how seamlessly they'd transitioned into being together.

"Better. Swelling has gone down." Her leg was propped up on a pillow. "Tobias is selling candles made at his Farm for Whitney and Jennifer's vigil."

He made a face. "That's crass even for him."

"Hazel practically grew up on The Farm. She was thirteen when he took her in. And he has a kid with her. What do you think he's going to do to those kids being raised there in a few years?"

Nick was pouring coffee and stopped halfway. "Mack, it's eight in the morning. Can we start our day by not throwing up?"

She unlocked her phone to send Austin a message. He had

been working with Special Investigations to target Tobias. But before she could type, he called.

"Hey, Mack." His voice filtered through the background noise of traffic.

"I was just calling you. Did you find anything on Tobias?" She was hopeful to charge Tobias with a financial crime—blackmail and extortion. They were fighting for scraps when it came to causing even the slightest damage to his perverse empire.

"We did. There were transactions between Golden Gate Investments and a shell company called Oceanic Tech—which we traced to Mathis." She gestured Nick over and put her phone on speaker. "It appears that Mathis was using Oceanic Tech as a front to take advantage of tax loopholes and to procure certain materials, including ammonium nitrate and copper oxide. Guess what? These materials are also known for their potential use in the creation of explosive devices."

Mackenzie's pulse quickened. She knew that Tobias was behind the explosion that had killed Peterson, but they finally had evidence. "Did the team find remnants of that in the explosion?"

"They did. It's enough to haul him in for questioning and get a warrant to confiscate these items from The Farm for a forensic match. The explosion killed a cop. No one is blocking any warrant for this." His voice was stilted. "Listen, I'm on my way to Tacoma for some work. You got this?"

"Yes. Thanks, Austin."

"No problem." He hung up.

Static danced on Mackenzie's skin as she gathered her jacket. "You have Luna today, right?"

Nick looked apologetic. "I do, maybe I can ask Shelly—"

"No. I want to do this." Peterson's face kept permeating her thoughts like smog suffocating everything out. He was the last person remaining who hadn't been served justice.

Nick didn't argue, seeing her fierce determination. She

grabbed her Glock and left for The Farm. Throughout the ride, her mind wandered to all the possible ways they could implicate Tobias.

There was a murder charge. This pervert had killed one of their own. A hot spurt of anger flooded her veins and she floored the pedal, weaving through the streets of Lakemore. The tires splashed through the pools of water that had collected from the torrid rain, sending arcs of water on either side.

Reaching The Farm, she managed to tread slowly through the carved path. Her knee still burned in protest. She didn't want to risk exacerbating her injury. On either side of her the tall grass grew, forming a thick barricade around the women, protecting them against the world they were so afraid of. The hut where Tobias resided came into view. She knew that Tobias wouldn't easily admit to anything. He would probably put the entire blame on Caleb. But perhaps a dent to his image and operations would ignite a revolution. She pushed the door open and her breath left her body in a sharp hiss.

Tobias Mathis's bloodied body was spread on his bed.

FIFTY-THREE

Bile rose in Mackenzie's throat. Before she could get her head around the grisly scene in front of her, her training took over. Her hands moved, disconnected from her brain. She reached for her Glock, turned off the safety and pointed it at the culprit, standing behind Tobias's bleeding corpse.

Hazel Martin.

Time froze. Hazel made no attempt to run or retaliate. Her small hand still held the knife that dripped in his blood.

Plip.

Plip.

Plip.

His blood dribbled onto her bare feet. The scarlet red soaking her pale skin. Tobias was splayed on the bed. The same bed where he had engaged in intercourse with every woman at The Farm and made the rest of them watch and chant. He was naked. A bloody gash sliced his wrist. Black and deep. If Mackenzie looked closer, she could see the bone. Blood continued to ooze out of his wrist, soaking the bed sheet as his body lay limp. His eyes only half open.

"Don't move," Mackenzie managed to say despite the

macabre scene unfolding before her eyes. With the cryptic etchings on the walls, the flickering candles and unsettling aura that seemed to pulsate with a ritualistic energy, Tobias's lifeless body and the twisted pattern his blood formed looked like a fitting part of some ceremony.

"Do you know he drugged us?" Hazel's voice broke.

"What?"

"Test the food we eat and the water we drink at The Farm." Her face contorted in anger. "You'll find wild lettuce, kava, damiana... plants and herbs with psychoactive effects."

"How do you know?" Mackenzie kept the gun aimed at her.

"Whitney told me. And then when I was abducted, I was cut off from the supply here. I started to *feel* different." She started shaking, her body still quaking from the adrenaline and anger which had nowhere to go. "I was always in a haze here. I didn't feel like talking or thinking or doing. He kept us subdued, agreeable, *pliable*. And then he used our children to keep us prisoner!" Her voice echoed in the hut. She dropped to her knees, breathing raggedly, dragging her hands down her face. "This isn't right. What he's been doing to us. He would make us drink this *potion* to calm us down at night before he..." Her eyes squeezed shut as tears streamed down. "Before he gets into our beds."

Mackenzie's grip on her gun loosened but she reminded herself what had happened here. She was a cop and she had just walked in on a murder site. "Hazel, I'm so sorry for what he's done to you, to all of you. But *this*—"

"We are adult women, Detective Price. Do you have any idea how hard it is to prove manipulation? He kept us isolated from everyone else. He made us believe we couldn't survive without him, that nobody else cared about us. And he was the father of our children. Most of us didn't do anything because of our kids. We still hesitate. He would get custody. Or they would go into foster care. Tell me, what chances would former addicts have of getting immediate custody? Our kids could have spent years in the system!"

"Hazel." Mackenzie's throat was dry like sandpaper. "Drop the weapon."

The knife clanged onto the floor. Hazel burst into hysterical tears, hiding her reddening face in her hands. "I'm sorry. I ruined it. I'm going to lose Jackson now."

Mackenzie struggled to keep her own tears at bay. "I'm sorry, Hazel."

"He only has me." Her voice cracked, her desperate eyes searching Mackenzie's face for salvation. "My Jackson doesn't have anyone else. The system will fail him. It always fails them. I had no choice. Tobias would have continued forever. He would have kept building his army of slaves under the pretense of being a messiah. It wasn't right. Nothing was right."

Mackenzie found herself slipping. She was toeing the line between right and wrong. A battle ensued inside her. Logic kept trying to reassert itself. But every molecule inside her was forcing her to look away, to turn away, to back out. The line was blurring. She blinked, trying hard to see the line again.

It was her compass—sticking to the rules. She had broken them once decades ago and it had taken years for that stain to fade away from her conscience.

Hazel's crying pleas grew distant and Sully's words blared in her ears.

A time comes in the life of every officer, Mack. A time when they have to decide between following the law and doing what they feel is right. I hope that time doesn't come for you. Because if it does, it will be nearly impossible for you to ignore your gut.

THIRTY-ONE YEARS AGO

Sully

"Jake Lawson, huh?" The captain looked at the file. His thin lips around a cigarette. "How did you find him?"

"He did a plumbing job for the Fontaine family a few days ago. The man has a dangerous criminal record," Ortiz said with such conviction that Sully wondered whether Ortiz truly believed his lies.

"But Grace wasn't raped, she was just killed." The captain scowled. "That doesn't fit the guy's MO."

"It's a classic pattern of escalation, sir."

Sully stood behind Ortiz, feeling unworthy of the uniform he was in. He just wanted to disappear. But protests were growing in town. They were getting harassed and ostracized from all corners. And then there was Barry—he was painted as the face of ultimate tragedy. A man with half of his family ripped apart awaiting answers.

"All right, Ortiz. Let's get a search warrant for Lawson's property." The captain handed him the file when the phone rang. "It's probably the mayor. We better close this otherwise people are going to start getting fired."

When they left his office, Sully whispered to Ortiz, "How are we going to make this stick?"

"You leave that to me," Ortiz replied, but when he saw the hesitation in Sully's face, he shoved a file in his chest. "If this feels too hard to do then you should read about the last woman he raped in Vegas. He used a broken beer bottle."

Flames of disgust erupted inside Sully. Outside in the waiting area, he spotted Barry sitting with his son Garrett. In mere days, Barry had lost half his weight. He kept a protective arm around his son who slept with his head tucked in the crook of Barry's arm. As if Barry sensed he was being watched, he lifted his head, locking eyes with Sully.

It was that defeat in Barry's eyes that splintered something inside Sully. Sully desperately wanted to give him hope, give him *something*.

He was at a crossroads. He could either follow the law or do what he felt was right.

"Are you with me, Sully?" Ortiz's eyes bore into his with purpose.

"Yes."

THIRTEEN YEARS AGO

Nick

Nick hid in the back of the building, taking one drag after another, letting the smoke weave its magic and dull all the chaos that was brewing inside him. Perhaps his father was right. He could have just followed his footsteps and gone to law school. At least he could deal with scum from a nice office and a cushy leather chair.

He stared at the bruises on his right hand after he'd punched a suspect in self-defense.

"Nick?" Caleb joined him, wearing an expression that scared the daylights out of him.

"What's up?"

He rocked back and forth on his heels, his eyes blinking rapidly. "I fucked up, man."

Nick flicked away his cigarette and crushed it under his shoe. "What are you talking about?"

Caleb sniffed. "I… I'm sorry."

It hit Nick like a lightning rod that Caleb was using again. He pinched the bridge of his nose. "Seriously? Man, you were doing so well."

"I know. I know. I just... I don't know what happened, man." He swallowed hard and licked his lips. "That's not even the worst part."

"Then what is?" Nick asked sharply.

"You know that case Bruce is leading? The Cecily Rodriguez disappearance?"

"Yeah. Two friends went into the woods but only one came out. How is *that* related?"

"Traffic lights picked up my car driving in the vicinity within that time frame."

Nick blanched. "What were you doing there?"

"I don't know! I don't remember!" Caleb linked his fingers behind his head. "I was strung out. I can't recall a thing. But I panicked when Bruce questioned me. I said a friend borrowed my car and the lies just came out."

"What friend?"

"It's my dealer. He'll have my back..." He trailed off when Nick raised his hands in defeat. "I got scared. I'll lose my job. I might even go to *jail*."

"You should." Nick's eyes were ablaze. "What the fuck were you doing driving when you're high on drugs? You could have killed someone."

"But I didn't. I swear I didn't. Please. Help me. Give me *one* more chance."

"You said those days were behind you and you haven't used."

"I relapsed."

Nick paced back and forth, exasperated. "What have you done?"

"I panicked! Just tell Bruce that I was with you. Please. I can't afford to get into trouble. I'm *trying*."

Tension rolled off Nick's body in waves, filling the air with his harsh breaths as he listened to Caleb begging him to save his ass. Suddenly, he'd had enough. He cut him off by throwing a punch across his jaw, this time bruising his left hand.

The rain drenched his shirt. Thick locks of black hair stuck to his forehead. When Bruce's face appeared in his view, he cursed under his breath.

"Hey, Nick, was Caleb with you two nights ago?" he asked casually.

A chorus of clashing thoughts almost gave him a headache. He thought fast. Lying to Bruce about Caleb's alibi during an active investigation would be breaking the law. Caleb was moronic to drive when he was using, but he obviously didn't have anything to do with this girl's disappearance. Nick knew his partner, better than anyone else. He wasn't a bad person. He'd just had a tough life—a mother who'd killed herself and then an alcoholic father who'd beat him to a pulp. Dealing with Caleb's substance abuse was a different problem all together.

He was at a crossroads. He could either follow the rules or do what he felt was right.

"So? Was Caleb with you?"

"Yes."

PRESENT DAY

Mackenzie kept telling herself that she could figure out a way so that Jackson wouldn't end up going into the system. Perhaps a lighter sentence for Hazel, considering her ordeal. Perhaps a jury would understand... but would they? She was an adult. She hadn't been coerced into joining The Farm. Like she said, manipulation and long-term emotional abuse were hard to prove.

Hazel kept begging and pleading, her eyes swarming with desperation bordering on unhinged.

Mackenzie had reached that same juncture.

From the corner of her eye, she saw Peterson for a split second. She blinked and he was gone. Her heart shriveled up inside her chest until something finally snapped. She lowered her gun. When she did, Hazel's words died. She stared at her in shock.

"I'll take my Jackson and leave town. I promise," Hazel whispered. "Will you please let me go so that I can be with my son?"

Mackenzie returned to the station a few hours later after calling for backup. Everything had happened in a blur. Troy had arrived at the scene and asked her what had happened. She told him that when she arrived Tobias was already dead.

Truth.

He asked her if she saw anything else and she said no.

Lie.

She dragged her feet to the restroom, breathing a sigh of relief that it was empty. She studied her reflection, looking for the chink in her armor that this lie would leave. Her thoughts were too scattered. But it was a strange reality to sink in that she had indeed come full circle. She had done something questionable, even terrible *again*.

If Hazel made good on her promise, she would be far away from Lakemore now, living her life with Jackson. The other women would know true freedom with their children. This is what Whitney and Jennifer had wanted. But it had cost them their lives.

It could be a happy ending for everyone. Is this what Sully and Nick had told themselves too?

She went back to her desk and noticed the door to Sully's office was open. Nick was sitting inside. A bottle of Scotch open between them. They were in this together now. At least she wasn't alone this time. The guilt was like a monster in the darkest recesses of her brain, starved of attention. She would just have to learn how to not feed it.

Maybe the second time around she would be better prepared.

She knocked on Sully's door. "Can I join you guys?"

Nick craned his neck to look at her. "Come on in."

Sully brandished another sculpted glass and poured her a glass of the bitter liquid.

Together the three of them drank in silence with the soft sound of rain in the background.

EPILOGUE

A throng of reporters gathered outside the Lakemore PD. Cameras flashed. Antennas perched atop vans. Boom mics suspended in the air. The full force of the media had descended upon the Lakemore PD to cover the latest sensational news. Even the relentless rain couldn't keep them away. The reporters had arrived like vultures or rather vampires. Lakemore wasn't some carcass. Because a carcass ran out of meat eventually.

There was an unlimited supply of crime in Lakemore. As soon as a criminal was locked up and a crime solved, it was replenished.

Mackenzie watched them from the window, a warm cup of hot chocolate between her cold hands. Her conscience was also blackened by the same smog that plagued the streets of this town. This time she couldn't even tell herself that she was only a child.

In an odd way, she felt more connected to Lakemore. It had drilled its claws deeper into her. Their bond was unbreakable. Her heartbeat resonating with the beat of the town.

"Murphy has called a meeting," Nick said to her from across the break room.

"Murphy?"

"Yeah. Odd day."

"Maybe he's announcing his retirement."

"I wish."

As she brushed past him, she held his hand. Solid and dependable. "I don't feel alone anymore."

"Because you're not."

They still hadn't told anyone about their relationship evolving into something more. Since everything that had gone down at Tobias Mathis's, Mackenzie was quieter and contemplative. She had resigned herself to the inevitability that our worst mistakes aren't always behind us.

In the conference room, the entire Violent Crimes division was gathered. Sully was busy adding more donuts to his plate while Rivera watched him with wide eyes. Austin stood with his arms crossed and nodded at Mackenzie when she walked in. Jenna chewed gum in a corner. Troy and Finn were trying their best to look innocent and engaged.

Murphy stood, facing them, his hands behind his back. His face morphed into a permanent scowl. "I have gathered you here because I owe you an explanation."

Mackenzie's eyebrows pulled together, eager to hear what Murphy was getting at.

"There's a very good reason I was causing a hindrance. Tobias Mathis was under investigation by the FBI. They were building an active case against him. He was laundering money for some dangerous people who are part of the Chicago Outfits."

Mackenzie suppressed a groan. She reeled from that information, almost losing her balance before Nick grasped her hand and nudged her to sit down.

Murphy continued. "Because the FBI was hoping to lock away some very critical targets, I wasn't allowed to tell anyone and my mission was to ensure that the operation wasn't compromised by our investigation."

But it was. Hazel had killed Tobias in cold blood and Mackenzie had let her walk away.

"Tobias killed himself so that operation was a bust." Murphy flattened his mouth in disappointment. "But we do have a silver lining. We have a new detective joining us. Ex-FBI agent and now one of our own. Zoe." He raised his hand to the door.

All eyes drifted to the entrance where Zoe was leaning against the doorframe. A mix of confusion and shock filled the air.

Mackenzie hadn't seen Zoe like this before. She wore jeans, a black tank top and a black leather jacket. Her ankles crossed together. Her thumbs sticking in her waistband. Her dark hair in thick curls around her square-shaped face. Her serenity and demure mannerisms had vanished. Those undercurrents of confidence and wit took centerstage. She winked at Mackenzie as there was a round of applause and people lined up to congratulate Zoe.

"Did you know?" Mackenzie asked Nick, still trying to reconcile the two versions of Zoe. The one who always wore beige tunics and spoke in a soft, measured tone and the woman who stood before her, chest puffed out and shoulders pulled back. One who preferred the shadows and the other who shone bright like a star.

"No."

"Are you sure?"

He rolled his eyes. "Yes. Murphy told me nothing. If I knew, so would you."

Mackenzie glanced at him dubiously but she was already convinced. Captain Murphy might have harbored a soft spot for Nick because of his political lineage, but she knew Nick wouldn't have kept something this big from her.

"Detectives Price and Blackwood." Zoe came up to them, almost sheepish.

"Welcome to the team." Nick offered his hand. "You're really good at the undercover thing."

She smiled. "Thanks. Can't say it was easy."

He wrinkled his nose. "Good thing the bastard is dead." When Murphy called him over, he excused himself but not before lightly touching the small of Mackenzie's back.

Any mention of Tobias left Mackenzie feeling queasy. She gave Nick a slight nod before turning to Zoe. "Two years. How did you do it?"

"Wasn't my first time pretending to be someone else. I'm sorry for giving you a hard time. My bosses at the Bureau were clear that the mission was to catch the sharks back in Chicago. To them, Tobias was a low-priority target." Her voice carried a disapproving edge.

"In a small town like Lakemore he would be a big one. We were just unaware of how he was running his operation."

"No surprises there." She rocked on her heels, glancing around. "For a small town, it's shocking the things people get away with. It really is a hub of all evil." Her grin collapsed seeing Mackenzie's straight face. "Sorry. It was a joke."

Mackenzie folded her arms, her smile tight. "I'm sure it was. So why are you here? Why not go back to Chicago?"

The shadows always seemed to win in Lakemore. Despite the embers of hope burning every now and then, it took one downpour to extinguish that flame and shroud the town in doom and gloom again. And there were many, many down-pours. Perhaps that's why Mackenzie felt so protective toward it. Somewhere Lakemore was *her*.

"I'm ready for a new challenge."

"In that case, you won't be disappointed. Lakemore is more complicated than you think."

Zoe softened her stance, diffusing the tension building

between them. "I'm looking forward to working with you. And sorry about the trouble I got you in with that fabricated video. I needed you *off* duty to help break into that vault."

"Why couldn't you do it? Did you not know the code?"

"I didn't. I could have figured it out but Caleb used to watch me like a hawk and being Tobias's *manager*, I had a lot of responsibilities. It was hard for me to get away unnoticed."

She chased away the flashes of Tobias's slashed body on the bed and Hazel standing next to him with a knife dripping in his blood. "If you don't mind my asking, how did you manage to be around him for two years? Wasn't he... a pervert?"

Zoe leaned closer and lowered her voice. "The nights he *wanted* to be with me, I drugged him. Slipped him some sedatives. Not hard to come by on The Farm since he grew a lot of questionable stuff. And then the next morning, I would lie that we had a great night that he was too high to remember."

"And he believed you all those years?"

She gave her a conspiratorial smile. "I might have told him that I was infertile after the first few months of him hounding me for sex. That put a stop to his efforts. Clearly, he only thinks of women as human ovens."

"The more I find out about him the more I despise him." Mackenzie shook her head.

"Whoever killed him did us all a favor. Except for the FBI," she commented casually. But Mackenzie's heart stopped and then sunk deeper into her chest.

"W-what?"

"I spent two years with that man. He didn't kill himself." She swallowed hard before shrugging off the sorrow that had crossed her face briefly. "But who cares? Good riddance." She waved at someone behind Mackenzie. "Sergeant Sully wants me to meet my new partner—Austin Kennedy. What's he like?"

"He's great," she managed to say. Zoe floated away with an easy smile leaving Mackenzie to be the only one disturbed by the conversation. She watched Zoe interact with Sully and Austin. Her throaty laugh, her relaxed posture. A stark contrast to how rigid and contained Mackenzie was—like she was always in a straitjacket, concealing something she didn't want anyone to find out.

But Zoe didn't draw between the lines. She wasn't a stickler for the rules. She was ready to bend them to do the right thing. She found it easy to reshape the contours of morality. It was so unlike Mackenzie that it almost spurred suspicion in her. But when Zoe turned around and gave Mackenzie a reassuring smile, something clicked.

They were a team now. Mackenzie returned the smile.

"Welcome Detective Zoe Storm to the Lakemore PD," Troy said, brushing past Mackenzie. "I'm the only interesting person in the unit. We have to come up with a nickname for you."

Zoe frowned. "A nickname?"

"We've got one for Mack," Nick chimed in. "Mad Mack."

"Ah yes, I remember that from the documentary."

"I'll have to think of something. Being the only genius mind here," Troy added, feigning humility. "Your last name is a nickname itself—"

"Maverick," Mackenzie announced.

"I like it." Nick shrugged.

"Of course you do," Troy teased.

Zoe grinned. "I like it too. Fits the bill. I don't like rules."

"I'm going to have my hands full with this division," Rivera muttered, humor dancing in her eyes.

The atmosphere brimmed with renewed vigor. A boost of energy that the Lakemore PD desperately needed. It was the first time since Peterson's demise that Mackenzie had seen a spark of hope. It was a new beginning.

Zoe Storm

Zoe unleashed a relentless barrage of punches upon the heavy bag, each strike punctuated by a burst of exertion. The burn coursed through her muscles, driving her to push harder, to channel her frustration, to beat the bag until it lolled wildly in the air in protest. Beads of sweat trickled down her brow when she reached for her buzzing phone.

It was her sister.

"Z, are you coming home for Christmas? The kids miss you. They won't stop screaming about it," Gina's plea echoed through the phone, the sounds of her nephew and niece's joyous screams in the background.

"I'll try my best, G. Just have to wrap up some work here." She pressed the phone between her ear and shoulder as she removed her other boxing glove.

"Come on, Z! It's Christmas, you can't miss it!" Gina's voice carried a playful whine. "The kids have been talking about you non-stop. They're convinced you're Santa's secret agent."

Zoe chuckled, getting a cold beer from the fridge and hunting for a bottle opener. "Santa's secret agent, huh? Well, I can't let them down then, can I?"

"Most definitely not. And you owe us. You missed last Christmas."

She popped open the beer with a swift flick of the bottle opener. "I was undercover, G. You know I had no choice."

"I know." Her voice softened around the edges. "How do you do this, Z? Isn't it depressing?"

"It's interesting. Better than your boring desk job," Zoe teased. Gina was too bright and sunny to survive in the real world. She had built a bubble for herself in Vermont surrounded by like-minded people and screaming children.

"I'm sorry your undercover stint was a bust."

"Not anyone's fault the rascal killed himself." She washed

down that prickly feeling with beer. "But I'll come this time. Just don't expect me to bring *you* any gifts."

Gina laughed. "Deal! You're hopeless, just good ol' family time and some seriously delicious Christmas feasting and a *lot* of wine."

The corners of her lips tugged into a genuine smile. "That sounds perfect, Gin. I could use a bit of normalcy and holiday cheer right about now."

"Can't wait to have you home, sis. We've missed you," Gina said, before raising her voice. "Stop trying to put your sister's hand in the toaster! I gotta go, Z."

"Yeah. Bye."

Zoe still had boxes all over the new apartment she'd moved into. The furniture was yet to arrive. For dinner, she planted her butt on the floor and demolished a cold pizza while watching random YouTube videos. Outside her window, the city slept. The streets teemed with shadows. The lake her building was across from looked like a pool of thick darkness. Even the wisps of moonlight spilling from behind the clouds weren't enough to cast a light on it.

Her phone buzzed once more. A text message from her ex-boss, Simon.

S: *We'll miss you at the Bureau. I'm a call away if you need anything. Hope you find what you're looking for.*

Z: *Thanks. I'll call soon.*

Zoe took a shaky breath and opened the door to the den. It was the first room she'd set up as soon as she'd moved in. The only box she'd unpacked. She had been deep undercover for the past two years but every inch of this room was seared into her memory.

She flicked on a solitary light, illuminating a board adorned with an intricate web of pictures, papers, and red ribbons. Her gaze fixated on the entangled threads, a visual representation of her investigation. But this wasn't just some investigation—this was what the inside of her brain looked like.

She unclipped a photograph from the board. A woman with laughter in her eyes, a carefree spirit captured in a stolen moment of bliss. Memories flooded back—the wind tousling her hair, the sun's warm embrace on her face as she drove along the coast. Zoe smiled at the memory—so old but as fresh as if it was yesterday.

Alongside the photograph, a newspaper article chronicled the demise of the woman, ultimately deemed as a suicide.

"I know you didn't take your life," Zoe whispered. "You wouldn't do that to us."

The weight of the journey ahead pressed upon her shoulders. The risks were high. Her fists clenched as she took a silent vow to finish what she'd started.

Lakemore held the answers, the missing pieces that would expose the truth she was on the hunt for. She'd taken the under-cover assignment with a singular goal—to get to Lakemore. And now that the case was closed, the FBI would have wanted her back in Chicago. But she needed to stay. So she joined the Lake-more PD. It would give her access. It would give her resources. It would give her ample opportunity to shine a light into every dark corner and turn over every rock to get the answers she was looking for.

A LETTER FROM RUHI

Dear reader,

I want to say a huge thank you for choosing to read *Out of Sight*. It means the world to me. If you enjoyed the ride and wish to stay updated on my upcoming releases, do consider signing up at:

www.bookouture.com/ruhi-choudhary

Your email address will never be shared, and you can unsubscribe at any time.

Crafting Mackenzie's adventures in Lakemore has been a delightful experience. If you could spare a moment to leave a review, I'd truly appreciate it. I'd love to hear what you think, and it makes such a difference helping new readers to discover one of my books for the first time. I love hearing from my readers—you can get in touch through social media.

Thanks,

Ruhi

𝕏 x.com/RuhiSChoudhary

ACKNOWLEDGMENTS

Writing is a lonely job, but publishing is all about teamwork. My deepest gratitude goes to my editor Nina Winters—her keen eye has been instrumental in shaping this story and her enthusiasm has made this journey a lot more fun.

Big thanks to editors Mandy Kullar, Anna Paterson and Shirley Khan for their hard work, and to cover designer Chris Shamwana for the captivating cover design.

A special nod to voice actor Kate Handford for bringing a voice to the story, and my publicist, Myrto Kalavrezou, for getting the word out.

The Bookouture crew has been very gracious and supportive.

My parents for their love. Dhriti, for always being in our hearts. Akanksha Nair, for inspiring me. My partner, Aditya Pandit, for patiently listening to my countless tales. All my friends especially Rachel Drisdelle, Dafni Giannari, Scott Proulx, Kaushik Raj, and Sheida Stephens for being my cheer-leaders.

Most of all, I'm grateful to the readers. Thank you so much for taking the time! I appreciate each and every one of you and would love to hear what you thought of the book.

PUBLISHING TEAM

Turning a manuscript into a book requires the efforts of many people. The publishing team at Bookouture would like to acknowledge everyone who contributed to this publication.

Audio
Alba Proko
Sinead O'Connor
Melissa Tran

Commercial
Lauren Morrissette
Jil Thielen
Imogen Allport

Data and analysis
Mark Alder
Mohamed Bussuri

Cover design
Ghost

Editorial
Nina Winters
Sinead O'Connor

Printed in Great Britain
by Amazon